Praise for *This New Dark*:

"Chase Dearinger has penned a damn fine debut that cuts straight through to the heart of the American Mid-South. *This New Dark* is part rural crime, part psychological horror, and wholly entertaining."

—Eli Cranor, winner of the Edgar Award; author of
Ozark Dogs and *Don't Know Tough*

"Through a transmogrified Oklahoma replete with outlaw legends, dope dealers, and shapeshifters, Chase Dearinger takes readers on a heart-stopping, unput-downable journey. *This New Dark* is part Southern Gothic, part speculative horror: rich and dark and terrifying, and so exquisitely written."

—Rilla Askew, author of *The Mercy Seat* and *Fire in Beulah*

"In *This New Dark*, Chase Dearinger plunges us into the troubled town of Seven Suns, Oklahoma, exposing both the supernatural rot that has settled in its center and the more ordinary horrors of poverty, abandonment, and the rough road leading to self-acceptance. As Randy, Wyatt, and Esther battle demons inherited, imaginary, and all-too real, they must find ways to rise above their self-imposed limitations and painful pasts. Like the works of Stephen King that Randy devours, Dearinger offers up more than heinous, original monsters and generous spatters of gore (though both can be found in these pages) in order to plumb the guarded hearts, outsized ambitions, and festering hurts of an entire community. Seven Suns drew me into its dingy bars, weedy fields, and lush, dripping wild spaces, and even further into treacherous, alien realms that pulse at the edges of our understanding. With this terrifying, gritty, and impressive debut, Dearinger secures his place among the modern masters of contemporary horror."

—Katie Cortese, author of *Make Way for Her and Other Stories* and
Girl Power and Other Short-Short Stories

THIS NEW DARK

Fort Smith, Arkansas

THIS NEW DARK

A NOVEL

CHASE DEARINGER

THIS NEW DARK

Edited by Casie Dodd
Cover elements via Canva Pro license
Cover design by Casie Dodd
Title set in Neoneon by Bakoom studio
Text set in Adobe JensonPro and Garet Book by Type Forward

Belle Point Press, LLC
Fort Smith, Arkansas
bellepointpress.com
editor@bellepointpress.com

Find Belle Point Press
on Facebook, Substack,
and Instagram (@bellepointpress)

Printed in the United States of America

28 27 26 25 24   1 2 3 4 5

Library of Congress Control Number: 2023952524

ISBN: 978-1-960215-10-9

TND/BPP23

For Jenna

"*I knew that the body could be separated into its elements by external agencies, but I should have refused to believe what I saw. For there was some internal force, of which I knew nothing, that caused dissolution and change.*"

—Arthur Machen, *The Great God Pan*

FRIDAY

1

WYATT WHITECLOUD had the thing on camera. Sure, the night-vision green made things a bit fuzzy, but it was still clear as day—a cougar, a black one, just as he'd hoped. Maybe one-of-a-kind in Oklahoma. They'd all sing a different tune when they saw that he had evidence. They wouldn't just call him some crazy Indian *then*.

He'd spotted it in the wooded hills that stretched out behind his trailer six days ago and had been trying to get a shot since. It wasn't until the day before, though, that it dawned on him that the cat would probably be living much higher, something a good hunter would've considered from the beginning. It would go as high as it could get, so he moved his game cam to the top of Robbers Mountain. He'd taken the ATV before the sun was even up to retrieve the camera, and lo and behold, he'd gotten a shot on the very first night. He printed the picture and carried the still-wet paper across the trailer to the kid's room, pounded on the door. The handle was locked. In permanent marker on a piece of duct tape stuck to the door: *Fukin Knok*. He banged louder.

"You've got to see this," he said. "Hey! I said you've got to see this. I'm not crazy." He pounded on the door again, but there was no response. "Fine," he said. "I'll make sure they keep your name out when they put mine in the paper." He folded the picture and put it in his back pocket.

The powder-blue Quonset hut, which sat between his trailer and the edge of the woods, had once been a ranger station for Robbers Mountain State Park. Locals referred to it as the old state park. It had once been seven thousand acres, which stretched to the north of Wyatt's place. Broken hills and the San Bois Mountains. Hills, really, but the closest you'll come to a mountain anywhere in Oklahoma. A mile north of Wyatt's place was Robbers Mountain itself. The mountain-hill was a sandstone hump at the base of a long stretch of ridge called Green Moon. Halfway up is what gave the mountain its name: a shallow but wide-mouthed cave. It's said to have been a hideout for the James Gang and Belle Starr.

The old ranger station had been why Wyatt chose the property, moved his trailer in.

He dug his keys out of his pocket and held them up close to his face so he could see them. The light had begun to appear, but it was the sunless white light of dawn. Three stars were still bright in the north. The trees, the understory, the earth, all silver and black. The cold clawed at his face. Winter was coming on like a vicious animal. It was the coldest November on record—they were saying there might even be snow on Thanksgiving.

The primer-covered steel door of the hut had no handle, just two deadbolts—one high and one low. Inside he felt for the brass bell at the end of the beaded chain that turned on the light in the small entryway. The back of his hand brushed against the cold of it, and he pulled it until it clicked and rebounded upwards, jangled against the bare lightbulb, which buzzed to life and cast a weak yellow over the concrete floor.

He took his headlamp from a coat rack and clicked it to life. The insulation along the arched roof made the place look and feel like a padded cell. The crop—thick in its flowering—was on a night cycle, so the typical roar of the cooling system was shut off, and there wasn't a sound but the whir of oscillating fans that stood guard around the plants. The smell of cannabis was so super pungent that Wyatt was still taken aback every time he entered. He'd bred it that way, like a thick, skunky butter. The watery beam of his headlamp caught the delicate, silvery throat of an exhaust duct, which hung from a frame of two-by-fours. The light spread out across the tops of the flowering plants, their heavy colas swaying modestly in the fan-circulated air. The plants looked gray in the white light and against the blackness of the room.

Typically, in the makeshift plywood room behind the plants, he'd have a second crop under twenty-four-hour light, vegging the plants until they could handle real bulk. But it was his last crop, so he'd stopped. Medical cannabis was now legal in Oklahoma, and he was going legit with Del as soon as he came up with the rest of the money, which he would. That night. In the room now were tubs of freshly cured flower, twenty-thousand dollars' worth of it. That and one last harvest would be enough to get them started.

But still. Everything was falling apart, flying away like shingles from a roof in a tornado. Darlene was gone. And there was her kid. And Gordo didn't know anything about his new plans. Part of him wanted to just disappear.

But the *kid*. Where was his *mother*?

A couple of months before, after Darlene had been gone for a week, he'd called the sheriff's office. They'd sent out Deputy Jacktooth with his white teeth and strong jaw. The way he snapped his gum made Wyatt want to break it.

"Did you two have a fight?"

He'd yelled at her: "If you didn't want to live with a dope grower, why'd you move in with one? Seems like the thing that needs cleared out is you." She'd thrown two beer bottles at him, which exploded against the refrigerator. Foam drooled down and pooled on the floor. She slammed the door when she left.

"We didn't fight."

"Well, ninety-nine problems, right? I gotta ask." He smiled, and Wyatt imagined holding him by the teeth and prying his jaw open until he'd torn it away from the head.

"I've seen this. She'll be back."

Another week and he'd called her parents and left a message, asked if she'd stopped by. Which he knew she wouldn't do. Her parents were uptight Mennonites from up around Collinsville. They'd shunned her when she came home pregnant with the kid. Would have shunned her again if they could when they found out she didn't know who the father was. He called and left a message once a week. They never called back.

Now this is how he saw her in his dreams: gray-eyed on a cold steel cart in the basement of some county morgue. Or somewhere down in a thicket of cattails along the Arkansas River in Tulsa, dumped by some cowboy junky.

She'd walked out on him before, but not like this.

He put on an ancient pair of headphones, the black fuzz of the ears gray from sun and age. He picked a Waylon Jennings tape from a red milk crate on the floor in the corner of the room and popped it in his Walkman, which he clipped to his Wranglers at his hip. He walked the aisles, spot-checked plants. He sang along with Waylon. He believed the plants could hear him when he sang. He believed they bloomed bigger and bore more trichomes when they were treated with love.

He'd bred them to smell, to stink, to offend, and he constantly tweaked that smell. That *smell*. He didn't want people to forget they were smoking his pot—well, not *his* pot, but *somebody's* pot. Pot worth remembering. He bred only indicas—the slow-burn strand that made your limbs loose and heavy—because they had shorter flowering times, required less wattage, and, he had to admit, he loved the way they looked, so he'd bred them into something dark and fierce, turned them purple all the way down to the sugar leaves. He bred them so weird they wouldn't last a day in the actual sun. Just then he had three strands flowering— Raven Mocker and something a little lighter, Poison Sumac Kush, and his newest, what he called Bonepicker Buttered Popcorn. He sang to that one, bent over it and breathed his hot, carbon-dioxide breath on her leaves. He loved the idea that if you forced life's face against the sharpening wheel, it would mutate, bend to your will, become whatever it had to become to survive.

He pulled the picture from his back pocket and held it beneath the light of his headlamp. *This.* This was something he could hold on to, say *look at this.* It was something real. And maybe a sign that things were on the up-and-up. He was about to be a legitimate businessman, about to be rid of the kid (somehow), and about to become the man who discovered the infamous black cougar. Over the music he heard a deeper beating. He lifted one side of his headphones to hear a series of loud, angry bangs.

The kid.

Without the sun, he'd lost track of the time.

2

THE BIRDSONG hadn't yet begun when Esther Grundel pulled on her galoshes and mud-crusted denim jacket and stepped out into the cold, dark morning. She pulled the hood of the jacket up and shrugged down inside. The mountains—Winding Stair to the south and the San Bois to the north—were purple against the starless dark. Thin clouds hung low across the narrow valley. Cold air tore at her lungs.

Esther was methodical about being up before sunrise. It was a sort of discipline (joy) she reveled in. She followed the rutted road, which sloped down to the pasture some quarter mile behind the house, a hundred feet below. A black, unnamed barn cat followed at her feet, flicked its tail. "You know, cat, I have a good feeling about Mom. You should have heard us last night. Like she was getting it all back." She stopped for a moment when the fiery disc of morning emerged in the east between the mountains. Just enough to give the dark the beginnings of an orange surface, the mountains the beginnings of the shapes of trees.

At the bottom of the hill was the pasture, a quarter-section bordered by split-rail. The broken road ran parallel to the fence line to the paddock and barn. Every morning the sight of the barn broke her heart. She'd built Midnight's shed as far away from it as possible, as close to the house as she could get, so that she didn't have to go near it. The stables were full of her father: his southwestern blankets, the extra saddles, his buckets. His pitchforks and shovels and the pegboard where all his grooming tools hung, all of it collecting dust. She'd only been six when he died—some thirty years ago—but some part of Esther still felt like an open nerve.

Midnight was already waiting for her, whinnying and snorting steam by the field gate. She'd been a foal when her father died and was now the only living remains of Grundel Gables. Esther's mother had insisted that they keep the horse (memory) and then abandoned her to Esther's care. She was a grade mare. A long white blaze slid between her eyes like a fat droplet and disappeared into the black of her broad, dry nose. She shook out her mane and lowered her head into the crook of Esther's arm. Esther petted the warm fuzz of her nose, leaned in with the side of her face. "Morning, you." The cat leapt up and sat atop the gate, cleaned itself, ignored them.

She fed Midnight and checked the water, shoveled manure. She checked her hooves and was happy to find she didn't need to pick them. She hated their feet. Hated the ugliness of them. Her father had explained to her once that horses actually had three toes, but what was the same substance as a fingernail in a human had grown grotesquely enormous from one of the toes. Twisted, warped, a mindless compensation. She knew better than that, though: God had a purpose, a plan, had put every toe in the right place, saw the parade from so high he could tell where it was going before it got there.

She was kind to the horse but counted the days until it was dead.

She stopped in front of the refrigerator and regarded the chaotic white pixels of her poetry magnets. Her mother had swiped her hand across yesterday's line—*A Bird Is A Fish In The Sky*—and turned the words into a row of crooked, broken teeth. Esther slid four of them together:

Have A Blessed Day. She filled the coffee pot with precisely six cups—held the pot up, measured the level with one eye closed—and was pouring it in the back of the coffee maker when her mother, Bertie, groaned her name from the back of the house. Esther gripped the edge of the counter and closed her eyes, centered herself with an inarticulate prayer (scream). "Just a minute, Mom." She scooped coffee grounds into the filter.

Esther's name again.

"Just a *minute*, Mom." She slammed the lid of the coffee maker and turned it on.

Her hopes from the night before weren't given much of a chance. She could smell the feces before she even got to the master bedroom. She stood in the doorway and breathed through her mouth.

For a moment, all she could see was her mother, in the car, sunglasses on, singing at no one in particular. She couldn't remember what she was singing.

And then she saw what was there: Bertie at the end of her bed in nothing but her blue pajama top. She was tall and gaunt and gray. She held the pants out in front of her, the still-wet soilage across the back and the top of her hand. The quilt on her bed was pulled back to reveal a dark spot. Her face, creased and weathered, was blank (pleading).

"I was going to put on new jeans. Where did you put my jeans?" She pointed a finger at Esther.

"Oh, Mom." Esther left the doorway and came around the bed to Bertie, reached out for her pajama bottoms. Bertie tugged them away from her, and brown spattered Esther's arm. "Now, Mom."

"Might be the only pair of pants I own, for all I know."

Esther opened the bottom drawer of a tall dresser against the back wall and pointed to a drawer full of jeans. Bertie leaned over like a child at an aquarium. "Did you put those there? Where are my Wranglers?

Oh my." Her eyes went soft beneath her wiry brows. "Esther?"

"Now let me wash those for you." She relinquished the pants.

"I don't usually do this."

"I know, Mom," Esther lied. Bertie's body had begun to break down like her mind had. Like the slack was running out. Two years ago, this would have appalled her. Now it was her normal. Her mother had become the child Esther never had.

She put everything in the laundry and washed her hands and arms twice. She watched herself in a dirt-choked mirror above the handwashing sink. She kept her charcoal-black hair short except for a tall swoop of bangs across the front, which forced her to always wear her hat tilted back. Crow's feet stretched out from green eyes across dark-freckled skin. Lines had begun to appear where she both smiled and frowned.

Her mother called her name.

3

Randy Strange woke up earlier than normal and was relieved to find he was alone. Wyatt's door was open, and the room was empty. All around him a gorge of antlers and horns crowded the wood-paneled walls of the trailer. Whitetails, mountain goats, elk, Dall sheep, bighorn sheep, even a wildebeest—all twisted and gnarled, like the hands of a thousand souls reaching up from hell. He knew all the animals because he'd heard Wyatt explain them to his mother—the thought of her made Randy wince—over and over and to anyone who stepped foot inside their—*Wyatt's*—home. He was a taxidermist and had acquired them all over the years. Some of them his own trophies. A real slaughter-fest. His mother's purple windbreaker still hung from the antler of a jackalope by the front door.

But Wyatt's truck was there. So he was out in the Quonset hut, doing his taxidermy or whatever weird, perverted thing or creepy Native American ritual he did out there. It didn't seem like a man could spend that much time filling animal heads with chemicals and plucking out their eyes, replacing them with glass. The sight of the hulky steel door and its two deadbolts gave Randy a weird vibe, though, like the doorway was actually the black mouth of a tunnel leading to some dark, unknown world where creatures spoke in inarticulate clucks. He sort of liked the idea of that, if it didn't involve Wyatt. Whatever that guy did was weird. And he was stuck with him.

He sat on the couch in his underwear and socks and ate a bowl of Peanut Butter Crunch. He watched an episode of *SpongeBob* and then started another. Halfway through he lost interest and went back to his room, where he kept his set of sand-filled weights. He'd bought them, along with the padded red bench that went with them, from Wyatt for thirty-five dollars at their own garage sale. He'd worn a hole in the seat where yellow foam padding bled out. He'd arranged it so that he could face the mirror above his desk when he lifted.

He hauled two twenty-pound dumbbells up from the ground and sat them on his thighs, sucked in a quick breath, drove the weights up with his knees, and positioned both just outside his pierced ears. He did reps of overhead press until he broke into a sweat and his face turned red. He grunted and he pushed again—fifteen, sixteen—did reps until his whole body felt scraped out and nervy, and he dropped the dumbbells, which thudded onto the brown carpet surrounding the bench. He leaned forward and held his head between his forearms and let out a slow, low moan as the lactic acid flooded his arms and shoulders. When his face wasn't red anymore, he repeated the same crazed set. He stared at himself in the mirror, his long, lean limbs shaking. He breathed sharply between clenched teeth.

He put on his Wranglers and his sneakers and the cleanest dirty shirt he could find, covered it up with a flannel jacket. He took a twenty out of the top drawer of Wyatt's dresser and tucked it in his back pocket. Outside at the Quonset hut, he pounded on the door hard enough to wake the dead.

He tried to keep the cab of Wyatt's pickup filled with silence every morning. He'd been trying his hardest now for seventy-three days. Ever since his mom up and disappeared. She'd done it before—gotten pissed and spent the night with a friend—but this was different. This was months. Which meant a lot. It meant big things like he didn't have anyone, and it meant small things like not having anyone to buy him his books anymore. Which meant he had to find ways to get to the library in Seven Suns to check out new ones. He had to have something to stick between him and Wyatt, and books did just fine. (Right now it was *Salem's Lot*.) It meant he had to help Squints clean out his mom's shed just to get the money to stay in weed. It meant he didn't have a mom, something he hadn't given any thought to until one was absent. All of this was fucking up his freshman year of high school something fierce.

Wyatt finally broke the silence. He said, "Weightlifting's starting to show, buddy."

Randy lowered the book and stared ahead.

"Did I ever tell you the one about when me and Max went out and drove over mailboxes?"

"You just did."

Wyatt went quiet again.

Randy wiped his sweaty palms on his jeans and watched a lone calf at the edge of a pond burning white with the sun.

He pretended to read while Wyatt told him he was strong enough he might think about football and started in on another story about when he'd been a pole-vaulter at Bacone but quit the team, and how he'd learned all of these high-and-mighty bullshit lessons that only sports can teach you. Another thing that changed after his mom left that Randy can't stand: Wyatt's pained attempts to pretend to be interested in Randy, even though he didn't know shit about him. He looked from the calf to an endless field of wheat and thought about leaving, skipping out. On Wyatt. On Seven Suns. On Oklahoma. Maybe when he got his license and a car. Or maybe when his mom came back and took him with her somewhere. He looked at Wyatt. He looked tired, put out. Fucking football. Yeah right.

Wyatt stopped his pickup on the road at the end of Squints's driveway. "See you later?"

"Eventually."

Wyatt was driving off before Randy had even shut the door.

Squints lived with his mom in a square, white clapboard house with the porch on one corner at the front end of a couple of ratty acres nobody ever touched. A real hellscape of scrub brush and devil's weed and burrs. What Squints's mom called *Mr. Sherman's Last Great Gift*. Randy beat on the screen door and sat on a pile of junk mail in a lawn chair. The colorful pages of some of the coupon packets had blown around the yard, which was mostly just gravel and dead-yellow grass. People yelled inside, but Randy couldn't make any of it out. The deadbolt clacked and the front door opened, and Mrs. Sherman stood behind the screen smoking a cigarette. She was in sweatpants and a white tank top that said *Kansas City Is for Lovers*. She rubbed one eye with the heel of her palm and yawned.

They exchanged *mornings*. She said, "Tomorrow's Saturday. Seems like a good time for you boys to actually get to work on that shed."

"Yes, ma'am."

She smiled. "It's always good to see *you*, Randy." She creaked open the door and stood out on the porch and raised up a hand to shield herself from the sun. She moved next to him and wrapped her arm around his waist and squeezed him into her breasts, moved her hand up and down his side. "When are you going to make a man out of that boy like you are?" The door banged. *Thank god.* "What the fuck, Mom? Just leave him alone." She slammed the door on the way in, didn't say a word.

Squints wore a flat-brimmed OKC Thunder cap cocked to the side and baggy jean shorts. He wore jean shorts all year long, no matter the weather. And a tan Carhartt jacket, no matter the weather. He was short and thick, and Randy thought of him in general as an acne-faced-mouth-breather type. But he was all right. Besides, all Randy wore were white T-shirts that were growing too small and Wranglers and white sneakers from Walmart. He was starting to think he'd get along better at the high school if he had a distinctive look of his own.

Squints drove a primered '82 Firebird that his dad left behind when he packed his bags and moved to California with Daisy Blake, the tall red-headed point guard he'd coached to a district championship. Squints was proud of the car, but Randy thought it looked like shit. Only the doors had paint on them—white with blue pinstripes just above the handle. But it got them around, and it was a lot better than what Randy was going to get when he turned sixteen, which was jack shit. They listened to Dr. Dre, which Squints played through a cassette-shaped thing that connected to his Discman. Every time they hit a rut in the country roads, the CD skipped.

Randy met Squints not long after his mom pulled him out of school in Cushing (it was the *last* time, she'd told him) and moved them in with that asshole Wyatt. He mostly tried to keep his head down the first week—there were only two more until the summer break started.

He had to walk across the parking lot from the high school to the gym for his last period, and that's where he first saw Squints, in the gravel alley between the gym and the blue pole barn where 4-H met and the shop kids did their welding. He was pinned to the barn by a kid who wasn't much bigger than him. The kid's forearm was against Squints's neck; their feet scuffed in the gravel. Randy couldn't tell if the bigger guy was mad or happy or something else, but he was red in the face.

"I know how you little fucking faggots like it."

Randy stopped at the corner of the barn, faced them. Randy waited until the red-faced guy turned to him. Randy said, "How *do* you like it?"

The guy relaxed and Squints pulled himself free, sidestepped his way out of the alley. The guy was bigger than Squints, but Randy had six inches on him. He had a look of rage on his face, but upon sizing Randy up, he turned and walked down the alley the other way. It made Randy feel powerful, and he felt a sort of love for the kid he'd saved.

"I'm Squints."

"Randy."

"You're in high school?"

"Eighth grade."

"I'm a freshman. We're getting shit all of the time, yo. That kind of shit happens all the time. Welcome to Seven Suns!"

"Who said I was new?"

"Take it easy, okay? I haven't seen you around."

Squints always seemed to have weed, so Randy hung out a lot with him that summer. That's the way it was at first, anyway. Squints had introduced Randy to Gordo, whose place they hung out at a lot, where they played video games. Squints had introduced him to the abandoned sanctuary of Showbiz Video. Squints was all right. They'd gotten some acid from Gordo once and gone to Winding Stair, where they hiked the trail to the top of the mountain and tripped balls. Squints told him then, when the moon came up over the next ridge to the south, that he'd once had a vision that he would one day become a great rapper called White Tiger.

Later, after Randy's mom was gone, it became about much more than staying in weed.

He'd been half-listening to a lecture on natural selection when the office aide Jenny Hitch came with the yellow slip.

Assistant Principal Flood sat on an armless, swiveling office chair, arms crossed, and twisted back and forth in the chair with his hips, his legs tucked underneath and crossed at the ankles. Randy felt hot, so he unbuttoned his quilted flannel and crossed his arms too. On Flood's desk was a sprouting garden of manila folders, empty worksheets, checkered roll sheets, Scantrons—some empty, some full, some full of red ticks, some ungraded. Four coffee mugs, all of them white with brown, crusted tongues lapping down the sides. A picture of his fake-ass family.

Flood leaned forward and planted his elbows on the edge of his desk. He was fat and oily, and his sleeves were rolled up. There were pink spots—looked like birthmarks—on his hand, which grew in size and number until they were a solid mass that twisted around his elbows and disappeared into his rolled-up sleeves.

"Mind telling me where you were yesterday?" He straightened his tie while Randy didn't answer him. "Son, I'm speaking to you."

"Sorry. At home. I wasn't feeling good. *Well.* I wasn't feeling *well.*"

"The Sherman kid not feeling well, either?"

"None of *my* business."

"I see you two. Lone Ranger and Tonto. Not sure which one is which yet. He's every bit of your business. My business too." He sat still. Flood looked straight at him just long enough for Randy to see himself the same way Flood did: some kid that doesn't give a fuck because he's angry about something that's actually bullshit. Randy didn't like being read that way, didn't like feeling his insides written out in plain English across the surface of his body. That was one good thing about Wyatt not caring: He never tried to read him.

"Your mother. I tried contacting her yesterday about your absence—

your *absences*—but couldn't reach her. Then Miss Josey out here tells me she tried to get in touch with her for a month about your library fines."

"I returned all those books."

"What's the situation with your mother, son? Has there been some change in your family situation we need to know about?"

"She's not around right now. Not for a bit, anyway. A vacation sort of situation, you know?" He softened his face. He couldn't fuck the situation up. Fuck Wyatt, but he had to be there when she got back, not locked away at the boy's ranch or in some foster home sucking some pervert's dick.

Flood stared at him, and Randy could tell he couldn't read him anymore. "Just don't skip class again or you're out of here, mother or not."

He made his way through the sounds of the bright yellow lockers slamming and the chatter of the dumbfuck drones and found Squints by the double doors at the end of the freshman hallway.

"Fuck it, yo. Let's get the fuck out of here. Get stoned at Showbiz."

"We're reviewing for a test in Algebra II."

"What's a freak like you who gets skipped ahead in math need to study for anyway? Fuck that."

Randy watched the FFA kids stand around the water fountain in their blue jackets, sneaking pinches of Skoal, and then the football players gathered by the trophy case. One of them kneed another in the side of the leg, and they all laughed. "Fuck it," he said. "Let's go."

"Hell yeah. We have to go by Gordo's, though. I'm dry."

"It's cool," Randy said. "Wyatt gave me twenty bucks."

4

THERE ARE so many different versions of you. How many selves crowd around the warm fire of your being, rubbing their hands together, leaning over the white light? Do you ever wonder which one is actually you?

That one. That one is me.

This is my story. Blind white, everything.

I didn't have another blow job in me so I stuck the heel of my boot into Chuck Bee's knee and then his chest, opened the door of the van and spilled out onto the shoulder of the highway in the rain. My elbow landed on a shattered Corona bottle and the blood was already washing out across the shoulder of the highway when I heard the van door slam and the squeal of tires.

Not a mile down the road the clouds blazed with the red and blue of what I could only imagine was the fiery breath of a monster, an eater of cowboy-junkies. White light, fear, etc.

It was a Camaro with a Kojak light. Two of the monster's mouths opened and two bear-pigs got out, smiling. Fucking cops.

Who are you? they wanted to know.

I'm a white-hot fever. A prophet. The open nerve at the center of the earth. But I gave them a fake name and they wrote it down. I said I don't have a goddamn thing on me. I haven't done a goddamn thing.

THIS NEW DARK   21

Which was a lie of course. Something was rattling around inside of me like a change, only it wasn't an animal I was turning into. It was doom. I'd become what had been waiting on me all along. It was a bright, white thing.

One of them dragged me across the shoulder and the thorn-filled ditch and leaned me up on a barbed-wire fence.

You smell like shit. These assholes were deputy sheriffs, not HiPo— brown uniforms and Stetsons and hillbilly grins, their cheeks fat with chaw. We don't need trash like you blowing down our highway.

Amen. But they didn't like me saying that. One of them pulled his Maglite from his belt and smashed it into my ribs. I spit up blood. He laughed and handed it to the other one. He brought it down harder, crunched a hip bone. The rusted barbs dug into my back, fused to my spine. They both kicked me and my brain erupted in tiny explosions. Stay the fuck out of Seven Suns, you hear?

I smiled.

Decided that was home.

They stopped hitting me but as I looked into the luminescent light dancing above their heads, my bones kept breaking and the heat came over me and I fell forward onto all fours. I imagined a cougar. But before I could fully change—still some half man, half beast, something vile and towering and sharp-toothed—saliva slung from my fire-hungry teeth as I clamped my jaw onto the first bear-pig's throat. The throat! He was warm and I felt healthy.

The second one screamed and I caught him just in front of the head- lights. I did it before the first one died so he could watch me. He wept and begged and I pissed on him. When I was done I loaded them both up in the trunk and drove on to Seven Suns, some inexplicable creature writhing behind the wheel, slowly becoming myself again, exploding through the night toward the place where my vision had called me.

I drove so fast that the highway turned molten behind me, a clean orange line through the darkness and rain.

The wide-open mouths of wolves. Nations have come and gone and known my name in secret, but never wrote it down. I am the last. The void.

This is my story: Me bent over a brutal slush of white and red and cartilage, the glisten of stretched fat. The muted pop of bone breaking beneath flesh, the crush of my jaw. My growl. The squish of spurting vessels. My scream.

That's where I deserve for this to start.

Or maybe I deserve for it to start here: Descending into hell with my shame spilt like glowing orange lava all over my open hands.

I'm sorry about the things I've done.

Some of it, anyway.

But first you should probably know a bit of backstory that will shed a little light on the ultimate irony of me ending up in Chuck Bee's van in the first place. It's not necessarily central to the story itself, but I do think understanding the state of irony I found myself in is necessary to understand that the compounding of my fucked-ness knew no bounds, even in the most minute of details.

The first time I got baptized—the first time *he* got baptized. It was in a cow pond on property owned by a man they called Chuck Bee. The eldest elder of Good Faith Bible Baptist in Muskogee, Oklahoma, USA. I—*he*—was twelve.

Chuck had this hundred-square-foot cinderblock hut out there with a glass front door that looked like it belonged on a restaurant. There was a cot inside and he called it his *getaway*. In light of what I know

now I can only imagine what depraved things went on in that getaway. He said he'd come out on the weekends and fish the chuckleheads he kept the pond stocked with.

My man could feel their slimy flesh on his feet when he stood in the water.

Chuck Bee, of course, was the one to baptize him.

When Chuck Bee pulled him up out of the water into the cold rush of the October air, he swore he saw a bright white dove explode over the surface of the water.

Man, getting baptized is a trip. All those people around you, love all over their faces, carrying you up to the clouds with their minds and their wills and the flowing rivers of blood that they'd cried for a lifetime? There's no better high.

I've been chasing a high like that for twenty-seven centuries.

5

Wyatt went south through Seven Suns and then west through the Flats, a barbed-wire grid of pumpjacks and cattle where the hills gave way to prairie. Half a mile past CR 289 on 96th, across from a meadow full of jackrabbits, was the Baker place, a long, squat brick house set a quarter mile back from a cattle guard and a mailbox in the shape of a catfish. It was late morning, and the last piece of moon hung in a steely sky. The truck's heater blasted as the squeaky shocks hammered the ancient ruts of the dirt driveway. A cluster of Angus gathered by the drive scattered when the truck bounced by.

Wyatt had mixed feelings about Del, his farm. He was white and dimple-cheeked—had a beautiful wife, beautiful daughter. From a white person's dream. It made him hate him just a little. But they were brothers. After Wyatt's father died and his mother moved away to Muskogee to live with her mother, he'd lived with Del. Del's parents had been his parents the last two years of high school. Came to his track meets, graduation. They left the farm to Del not long ago and moved to be with family in Texas.

Everyone seemed to be moving back to family, which was one of the reasons that Wyatt had finally mustered enough courage to go talk to Darlene's parents. He drove two hours to Collinsville and knocked on their door. They were dressed plainly, in denim and cotton, and they stood in the doorway and didn't invite him in. Her mother was short, and her father was tall like her.

The sudden image of Darlene hanging her crystal wind chimes from the roof above the front porch in wind pants and big, gold hoop earrings—I need you here. I don't need you here.

There was no answer at the house, so Wyatt drove back to the pole barn by the windbreak, where he found Del leaning on a gate looking at a heifer in a stall. It was the fluke red heifer—pregnant, swollen, and still carrying at thirty-six weeks. Wyatt found the picture in his back pocket and unfolded it, elbowed Del in the ribs, shoved it in his face when he turned. "Man, you got to see this. I was *right*. Fucking *right*. I was *right*." Del turned away, ignored him.

"Lucy's not doing well. Any day now, but something doesn't feel right. Does she look right?"

Lucy's pregnant belly looked twice as large as it should. Her breathing was labored.

"I don't know, man. Maybe you ought to call Kithawk."

"I'm inoculating all afternoon."

"Congratulations. Now look at this." He put the picture into Del's hand and punched at it with his finger. "Black. Cougar." Del studied it. He studied it long enough that Wyatt knew he was taking it seriously.

He returned it. "There's no such thing as a black cougar, Wyatt. Besides, all you can see there is the back of something. Could be anything. Could be a black lab running through the woods. A bear."

"Don't talk down to me like that."

"I'm not saying you don't have something there. I'm just saying there's no such thing as a black cougar. Just ask around."

The two of them walked to the back of the barn, where they had stood and drunk and smoked and schemed as kids and stood and schemed and planned as adults.

"I'm realizing," Del said. "That we can't have the greenhouses any closer than a hundred feet from the barn. That's how far its shadow stretches at noon." They were looking at empty, open pasture, where they were very close to building four fifteen-hundred square-foot greenhouses for the purpose of growing legal medical cannabis. When Wyatt imagined the translucent houses stretching away from the shadow of the barn, he felt like a new person. A baptism of sorts.

A bird circled in the distance, far enough away that Wyatt couldn't tell if it was a hawk or a vulture—far enough he wondered where its shadow fell, what was happening in that place.

Del continued: "Jenny says he and the crew can get started as soon as we get that twenty thousand. That's still happening, right? You're still wrapping that up tonight?"

"It's just me and Gordo switching like usual."

"What time?"

"I'm thinking I might get myself a new rifle. Something that's good for short range, rapid."

"Wyatt. Are you going to take care of this tonight?"

"Yeah, of course." Wyatt held the picture up. "You want to go into town with me? I'm going to Kershaw's."

Del looked to the cold, bleak sky. "Just don't mess this up."

6

Downtown Seven Suns: The courthouse—a two-story red brick box with faux columns between tall windows—hemmed in by glass-front shops crowding in on all sides. Kershaw's Gun & Ammo, Old Tyme Pharmacy, Eaton's Diner, US Cellular, House of Beauty, the abandoned O'Reilly's, Belle's Antiques, Hospice Consignment, Planet Sun Tanning, Olim County Bank, Subway, Million Dollar Movie House. The brilliant fall-colored leaves of the two giant oaks that stood in the courthouse lawn had begun to turn brown, curl inwards like fists, and fall to the ground. They gathered broken and matted where the street met the curb.

One block south was First Baptist (safety), a beige brick, coffin-shaped building surrounded by overgrown box hedges. A white steeple bore a white cross. Esther pulled her yellow hatchback around the back and parked next to the curb by the back doors beneath a cat's cradle of power and telephone lines. For two years she'd been bringing her mother to the church's adult daycare program. She helped her out of the car.

"What are you doing today, Mom? Do you know?"

Her mother stopped and leaned on her cane.

"Mom?"

"I hate you."

"What?"

"I hate you. For making me go here. You make me go here." She pointed to the glass double doors at the back of the church, her finger trembling, her face nearly in tears.

Esther was used to it, but it still stung. "Oh, Mom." She smiled at her mother's frown. "You've been coming to this church for half a century. What's wrong with this church?" She didn't respond, just searched Esther's face for some kind of answer. A lapse in recognition. But she shook her head, and it was gone.

"There's nothing wrong with this church. I've gone here since before I married your father."

Inside she signed the clipboard and waited for Mrs. Hamilton to acknowledge her presence, but the volunteer was deep in conversation with an elderly man Esther didn't recognize. When she looked up and saw Esther, she put up a finger. The fellowship hall had a small stained-glass window up near the ceiling—a dove, the Spirit—but was mostly lit by bright overhead fluorescents. Some dozen other elderly (parents), most of them much older than her mother, sat in metal folding chairs around folding tables. One table laughed and played cards. Esther waited until Mrs. Hamilton bounced over to her, smiling and already apologizing for something with her eyes.

"Morning, Miss Esther."

"Morning."

"I was hoping to catch you so I could have a word with you about Miss Bertie."

"Oh?"

"Yes." She pressed her chin into her creased neck and brought her hands together like a prayer. "She had a bit of an incident yesterday with Mr. Haylock." She smiled and nodded toward the man she'd been speaking with.

"Oh?"

"During one of our activities yesterday—well, we had Alec Lottie here, the tribal storyteller?—and—and Mr. Haylock isn't quite clear on what happened—your mother started stomping him on the foot with the bottom of her cane. I got her to stop, but she immediately started crying. I was going to say something when you came to pick her up, but you must have slipped in and out without me seeing you. It was a bit of an ordeal. Alec Lottie didn't finish his stories."

Esther lowered her head, centered herself with prayer (scream). Her mother was sitting in a folding chair at a window, surveying the room, her cane pinched between her knees. She smiled at something outside.

"She's just not *like* that, I promise you. She hasn't been, at least. She seems to be getting angrier." With each new piece of information volunteered, she felt something spilling over the edge. Her eyes grew hot. She let the water levels settle. "I'm sorry," she said. "I'll really talk to her."

"You know we love your mother, Miss Esther."

"I do."

In the car she had to ward off one of her cold spells—her world grew icy, and she suddenly became afraid of everything in the universe all at once, an open nerve—with the breathing exercise Dr. Fraij had taught her: Inhale through her nose while counting to ten, exhale through her mouth while counting to ten, repeat.

Long ago: Each Wednesday afternoon, her mother prepared a five-cup salad—marshmallows and orange slices, coconut and pineapple, sour cream—and drove to the First Baptist Church for her women's Bible study. She dressed sharply—green polyester blouses with broad white collars, pearls, floral dresses, pleated dresses—and rubbed lavender oil in her long red hair, a smell that Esther would never forget, a smell from somewhere between the woods and the flowers that grew wild in the front yard. She descended the stairs and pulled the salad from the refrigerator, sealed the top with aluminum foil, took up her Bible and left, a ritual unlike any other the dark and sullen woman took up the rest of the week. Unlike the relentless rituals of cleaning, piano lessons with Esther, preparing meals, or ironing clothes, the holy rite of preparing for Bible study was one that she practiced with a confidence and flourish that Esther had never witnessed. It was as if each time she walked out that door, she was headed to some bright other life.

When Esther was sixteen her mother informed her without ceremony that she would begin to attend the Bible study with her, which excited Esther beyond belief. She'd finally have the opportunity to see what white light her mother stepped into each and every time she crossed the threshold of their house with her five-cup salad in the crook of her arm.

But it was just the church basement, full of women with big, tall buns and sharp-cornered glasses. They ate their afternoon victuals and gossiped bitterly and relentlessly—Lionel Kithawk was planning on marrying Maudine Perkins, who'd seen more than her fair share of the ceilings of boys' bedrooms; the Choctaws were going to build a casino and send the town to hell; the women at First Baptist in Stillwater were demanding to be deacons—and there, at the center of it all, was Esther's mother, whose social command was unlike anything Esther had ever seen. She listened intently, prodded certain women for more information about their husbands' habits and tastes, told stories about trips to Tulsa that Esther had never heard. Esther simply sat, silent, her long, thin legs awkward in the metal folding chair, the dress her mother had chosen tight around the neck.

When the gossip faded, Bibles were opened and verses were read. Discussions about their daily lives ensued, and applications of the text were brought to light. Each week they always resolved to be better wives, to care more for their families, to set better examples for their daughters. "Wait on the Lord," her mother said each week. "Wait on the Lord, and He will come."

The sight of the razor wire behind the courthouse hadn't ceased startling her each time Esther arrived in the eighteen years she'd worked for the sheriff's office. She parked beneath it and got out. She crouched by the side mirror and put on her Stetson, tilted it back. Her lips were chapped white, flaking. They got terrible when it got this cold. She found a bottle of Carmex in her jacket pocket and spread it across her lips. Brock had once told her that the stuff was addictive; it actually made them more chapped when it wore off. She hitched her leather utility belt and meticulously checked her uniform like she did every day: shoulder lapels in place, buttons and buckles.

Everything at the office was tense: A reserve deputy had shot an unarmed Cherokee named Terry Big Eagle on an unmarked county road. And the investigation that followed revealed that Sheriff Gains had approved a number of documents claiming that reserve deputies had met the minimum required training hours when they hadn't. And to pile on, Sam Frank, the reserve deputy at the center of the investigation, had previously been reported twice for excessive use of force (unforgiveable), reports that Sheriff Gains never filed. They were both under investigation. And so the state prosecutor had subpoenaed Administrative Captain Mike Jenks and every last one of his records. The Oklahoma State Bureau of Investigation was ripping the department away. On top of all of that, their two patrol deputies had gone missing.

The sheriff office's waiting room was thread-worn gray carpet and white folding chairs, a fake, dust-covered bush, wood-paneled walls, a deer mount, a rubber fish mount that danced and played the Macarena when you pressed the red button beneath it. There was a long, counter-style front desk, which was made for three assistants but only ever had one. Behind it, cardboard file boxes lined the floor against the wall, bulging, some of them stacked four high. A small man with a mustache, an unbuttoned vest, and a loosened tie moved in and out of Records. He huffed, lifted with his back. At one end of the waiting room, American and Oklahoma flags framed a door with a dimpled amber window that bore a sticker reading *Civil Services*. The pixelated shadow cast on it showed Deputy Brock Bosco with his feet up on his small desk.

He was reading one of his Louis L'Amour paperbacks beneath the heat of a bright yellow lamp. She hung her hat on an out-of-place antique coat rack shaped like a candelabra and sat down at her desk opposite Brock's. The springs under the rolling chair groaned as she leaned back. Brock held up a finger and left it there as if Esther was going to speak and he only needed a moment. When he reached the end, he dropped the finger, licked it, and turned the wavy, yellowed page, dog-eared the corner, and dropped the book on the desk.

"Had to finish the chapter. Big shoot-out at the cave—brutal stuff, you know?" Brock was barely out of high school (child) but somehow looked even younger. He was thin and knobby but smooth with what looked like baby fat all over. His skin was pale and blushed red. He didn't grow facial hair except for the beginnings of a blond mustache. He pushed himself away from the desk with his feet and rolled across the ten-foot room to Esther, put his feet up on her desk. "What's up with that guy out there?" he asked. "Is he with the state, or did some angry asshole with a box-moving problem just happen through?"

Esther pushed his feet off the desk. "Good morning to you, too." She scolded Brock a lot, acted too motherly sometimes. But he was mostly all right.

"Okay, all right. Take it easy," he said. "How's the trial going?"

She closed her eyes when she remembered, felt a warm wash of disappointment. "I sure hope it doesn't last long."

"So messed up. Would sure save some taxpayer money if some good citizens would drag him out in the middle of the night with torches and hang him from a tree on the courthouse lawn. Goddamn."

She chided him for using the Lord's name in vain and he apologized, threw up his hands. He was silent a moment, leaned back in his chair and crossed his arms across his tan uniform and thin brown tie. The gold star he wore to identify himself looked like something out of the bottom of a cereal box. She pulled a clipboard from a nail on the wall and looked through the schedule: she was in fact in court for the Miller trial that afternoon. Brock had two court documents to serve: divorce and custody. As bad as the trial was shaping up to be, part of her felt her duties as bailiff had been a great deliverance from her duties as a process server. The constant source of conflict: divorcés chasing her through wet grass with a water hose, evicted mothers throwing rocks at her cruiser windshield, the looks men gave her when they'd been served with restraining orders—the beery smell of their oily, open-shirted chests, the hate dripping down their faces like candlewax.

Brock smiled broadly. "You want to hear my theory on the latest developments?"

Esther ignored him.

"Everyone's so interested in how deep it all goes that they've stopped asking questions about *why*." He turned his head to the side and leveled an eye at her like she was a kid caught red handed in something. He said, "Which is?"

"It's *your* theory; you tell me."

"Which is?"

She waited.

"Which is Terry Big Eagle."

"And?"

"Well, why would Deputy Frank shoot him?"

"Frank said Big Eagle was drunk and hostile. He went for his taser and pulled his gun instead. They're saying he was undertrained, after all."

"But maybe there was another reason to kill him?"

"Because he was a Cherokee?"

Brock paused.

"Because Sam Frank hated Native Americans, is the only reason I see it," Esther said. .

"*Or* it's because he knew something they didn't want anyone to know about."

"So what's your big theory?"

He smiled.

And she smiled, forgot about Hooky Miller. She said, "So why are Deputies Jacktooth and Byron missing?"

"*Missing?*"

"Haven't shown in two days. One of the state agents—Martinez, I think's her name—went by their houses and they're gone."

"Seriously?"

Esther nodded, flush with the satisfaction of hearsay.

"When did you hear all this?"

"When she interviewed me."

"So we've got no patrol unit now?'

She nodded.

"You got *interviewed?*"

They both sat in the reverie that follows whispers.

7

RANDY AND SQUINTS avoided town and cruised the grid of the Flats.
The sky was vast and gray. Randy pressed the side of his face against
the window and felt the cold. They passed the Boys Ranch, a tan brick
building set back from the road, obscured by the edge of the forest like
the place was some sort of secret. The sight of it twisted Randy's stomach into knots.

Five miles north of town the prairie gave way to the San Bois Mountains,
which sat low on the horizon, where the trees still clung to their fall colors,
a canopy of bright bursts—fire and blood and sun. They crossed Olim
Creek on a red-rust truss bridge covered in dead mistletoe. The grid
twisted into winding roads: broken, sandstone country. Loblolly pines
began to tower over oaks and elms and hackberries. There were still cattle, some winter wheat, and what was left of the alfalfa, but there was
also wreckage, haunts, suspicious-looking outbuildings. Where Randy
lived—where *Wyatt* lived—where fifteen hundred and some people
lived scattered miles apart from each other in farmhouses and trailers.

A series of hand-painted signs: *Bigfoot Tours 3 Mi. Bigfoot Tours 2 Mi.
Bigfoot Tours 1 Mi.* Past a creeper-covered silo, a narrow dirt road cut
through thick woods up the rise of a hill. They passed a cherry-blossom
pink trailer with a giant Bigfoot statue in the yard. A rotting jack-o-
lantern stood watch on the porch. From a dark hole where the trailer's
corrugated skirt was peeled back like the lid on a can of potted meat, a
German Shepherd erupted, snapped its teeth, barked so mad it came
out a snarl. Just before it got to the Firebird, the slack in its chain ran out

and yanked the dog backwards. It scared Randy every time, no matter how many times he told himself it was coming.

Gordo's trailer was the last, at the top of the hill in a clearing.

"I hope to God he doesn't want us to hang out like last time," Squints said as they parked. "If he asks us to hang out, let's just say we're going back to school?"

Randy nodded.

Before they could even knock, Gordo threw open the door. "Chicos!" He came down the cinderblock steps and hugged Squints tight, gave Randy some slap-snap handshake Randy pretended to know. Gordo was cool as hell. His bare torso was covered in colorful tattoos, all of them horrific versions of Disney cartoons. Bambi stretched across Gordo's shoulder, only his eyes were red and his teeth razor sharp, foam dripping down from the corner of his mouth. One of the seven dwarves climbed up his arm on a ladder, a jagged knife between his teeth. At the top of the ladder was an open window, where a frenzied Sebastian the crab with bloodshot eyes tore away at Cinderella's flesh. Now *that* was a distinctive look.

Gordo ushered them into the trailer, which was small and warm. The kitchen was tidy and sunflower-themed—a sunflower clock, a row of matching mugs bearing sunflowers hanging from hooks beneath the cabinets, one painted on the wall next to the doorway leading to the utility room. A long bar separated it from the living room, which had dark green carpet and wood paneling and was choked by the smell of weed. A haze hung in the air, tendrils of smoke in the moment just before they vanished. At the back of the room was a tall bay window with an orange cushion seat. Behind the seat and on all the shelves lining the walls of the alcove was an impressive collection of succulents. Randy considered it one of the most beautiful things he'd ever seen—a little

piece of trapped desert sky. Thick, wide blooms of pink-edged greens
and green-edged pinks, fleshy and fat to the touch, some shaggy with
spines and others smooth and round, ending in a kiss, an altar to all
things that can live without care.

Gordo flopped down on the couch in front of a paused video game.
"So what do you little fuckheads need?" His hair was long, dark, and
slicked back, and a scar nicked his right eyebrow. He held his hands
together in front of him like a prayer.

"An eighth, yo."

"Dig, dig." Gordo went to the kitchen, ducked down behind the bar,
and returned with a foot-high jar full of dark buds, green and gray and
purple. The rumor was that Gordo dealt in some pretty big quantities
and cash but just sold a little on the side to keep people coming to his
place. "Aren't you two supposed to be in school or something?"

"Fuck that," Squints said.

Gordo popped open the seal on the glass jar and let the lid fall back
on its metal hinges. The room grew so thick with the smell of buttered
popcorn that Randy's mouth watered, an animal instinct. Randy and
Squints both stood and said, "What the fuck?"

Gordo flashed a bright white smile. "I know, right?" He held a single
bud out and Squints took it, examined it under his eye, smelled it, and
passed it to Randy.

"They call this one *Bonepicker Buttered Popcorn*." He weighed out their
pot and gave it to them. Squints pulled out two twenty-dollar bills and
handed them to Gordo. Randy handed him his twenty. Gordo looked
him up and down and gave it back to him.

Randy said, "How come they call it that?"

"Well I imagine you can understand why they call it *Buttered Popcorn*."
They all laughed. "But the *Bonepicker* part? I don't know. Some Indian

shit. You should ask your old man—"

The two words hit Randy like bullets in the chest. He balled his hands into fists. "He's not my fucking *old man*."

"Cool, whatever man. Take it easy."

"Where do you get this shit, yo?"

Gordo looked at Randy, made him feel read. "Look, I'm fixing to get fucked if you two wanna chill for a while."

Squints stuck with the plan. "Nah, we got to get back to school."

"Dig, dig. Well you ought—"

"Fuck that," Randy said. "We don't have to go back to school." Gordo smiled. Randy's foot stung, and he realized Squints was stepping on it.

"You want to do some dabs?"

Randy said, "Hell yeah." He'd never done a dab before. But he needed to feel big and free. He needed to forget that he had some place to go back to.

Squints smiled but wouldn't look at Randy.

They sat back on the couch and Gordo told them a story about his tío, who'd gone all Jesus and showed up the day before and tried to pray with him. He leaned forward and slid the bong right in front of Randy and said, "Put your mouth on it like a regular bong." He twisted the cap off of a small glass bottle and dipped what looked like a dentist's tool down inside of it and held out a small bead of brownish wax for them to see. "This shit is the real deal. When I put the wax on the bowl, you suck like you've got to suck to save your life." He held a small blowtorch to the bowl until it glowed orange, and Randy put his mouth to the pipe and Gordo put the wax on the bowl, and Randy sucked as hard as Gordo had told him to. It didn't hit hard or hot, but when he exhaled it billowed out like a cloud and he fell back on the couch, coughing.

Gordo laughed and clapped and stomped his feet on the ground and said, "Chingao!" He said, "Chingao!" But it sounded to Randy like he said it about a dozen times. He felt like he couldn't sit back up. Every muscle in his body tensed. He felt Gordo and Squints just staring at him, but he couldn't say a word. Their faces didn't tell him what they wanted. They just stared. Normally getting stoned made him feel relaxed, put a smile on his face, but now he felt cold.

"You okay, chico?" Gordo pushed a single finger into Randy's bicep, and Randy flinched. The panic began to pass. He smiled, and Gordo broke up in laughter again. He nodded at Squints. "All right, tough guy, you next." He slid the bong down to him. Randy turned and nodded and smiled, and every second that passed made him feel better, but he still didn't feel *good* like he thought he was supposed to. He was in a trailer on a hill in the middle of nowhere, but he felt like everyone could see him. Like he was floating up in the air above the trees and everyone was coming for him, pouring through the streets in their cars, clambering up the hills—Wyatt, his teachers, Vice Principal Flood. All of them. *We know what you're up to.*

And then, worst of all, he thought of his mom. Only she was the only one who *couldn't* see him. Couldn't find him. When she'd been gone only a couple weeks, Wyatt had told him that she was probably in Tulsa. He'd been nasty about it. *Probably shacked up with some asshole.* Randy tried to imagine her there. He tried to imagine Tulsa, saw downtown rise up across the Arkansas all glass and sun-glint and art deco. He imagined there was a dark heart there, a hardboiled maze of junkies and gamblers and thieves. And his mom was in there somewhere, trying to get out, crying out his name.

And there he was, stoned on Gordo's couch, trying not to be found.

And then he saw her another way: bones. A walking pile of bones. The thought made him shudder, and he returned to the conversation.

Squints said, "I'm good, yo." Gordo shrugged and picked his controller back up, restarted the game. After what felt like an eternity, Squints said, "What do you think about that shit your tío believes?"

"About Jesus and shit?"

"Yeah."

"Hell yeah I believe." He took a hand away from the controller and held it before his chest, his fingers curled up like he was holding the weight of his heart in his hand. "You've got to get Jesus into your heart."

Squints laughed. "Fuck all that. I don't think there's really a god."

"You know what?" Randy said. "My mom was a Mennonite."

Everyone grew quiet. After a while, Gordo cleared his throat. He said, "You mean like those bearded motherfuckers in carriages?"

"No. I don't know. She isn't anymore. Her parents were. But I don't think they drove a carriage. They just sort of dressed—boring." He wanted to tell them more, tell them that her parents had shunned her and that it was his fault for being born, etc., but it felt weird talking about her. He regretted bringing it up.

But before he could push her out of his mind, a vivid memory: Sitting in the waiting area at the Hair Cottage, waiting for his mother to finish her last cut of the day so she could drive him home. The bright sun cut clean lines through the blinds onto the black-and-white tiled floor. She was only a voice around the corner: *I just worry, you know?*

"It don't matter anyway, really," Gordo said. "Betty's got enough Jesus in her heart to save all our sorry asses."

And like she'd heard her name spoken, the front door swung inward, brought in Betty and a rush of cold air. She carried what looked like a hundred full Walmart bags. She was lily-white, and her hair was a heap of purple dreadlocks.

"No one get up or anything." She lugged the sacks over to the bar, where she heaved them with a grunt and dropped them on the counter.

"And what in the world are you doing with those two here?" She looked at Randy and Squints. "Why aren't you two in school?"

"It's cool," Gordo said.

"No, it is not." She dug into one of the bags and pulled out an *Us Weekly*, rolled it up as she crossed the room, hit Gordo over the head with it. He dropped the controller, and it clattered on the coffee table. He put his hands up to defend himself, but she hit him again, harder, and then again, and Randy started to laugh, first in his throat and then in his belly. "You two need to get out of here right now." Back to Gordo: "Besides, think that's going to look good when someone sees their car parked up here?" She pointed at Randy and Squints. "You two. Gone. Now."

They stood and collected their minds and left. Gordo shouted, "See you, chicos!" as Betty closed the door and they stepped out into the cold.

8

THE REASON I found myself thumbing for rides in eastern Oklahoma and in the hands and mercy and van of Chuck Bee to begin with was on account of the silver Chevy Celebrity getting stolen and me needing to get out of Tulsa *real* bad.

I was coming down pretty hard when I got back to Tulsa, so I stopped at a QuikTrip at the edge of the city and shot up all but the last bit of Tío's Dilaudid in the car and listened for those blasphemous flutes. The piping and the pounding of that hammer on that cinder block in the unlighted chambers beyond time. I had enough painkillers to kill a man. The orange sky plunged into a radioactive pink and then a purple, and then the stars shined. Headlights like glow-worms. I dry-heaved for half an hour. Like a prophecy: Nothing's coming.

It wasn't a QuikTrip at the edge of the city, I realized, but a QuikTrip at the edge of the world. I recognized the place. A red-and-black-and-white glass cathedral, the smell of grease. They kept building it higher and higher and higher and higher, all of them fat and gold-ringed and smiling and drinking gasoline right from the pump. I knew it was only a matter of time before god struck them down with the curse of babbling tongues.

The whole place breathed. I wasn't used to the opiates without the crank, and I could barely walk. The guy behind the counter had on a red smock and his name tag said *Clint*. There was some sort of red sauce smeared next to the C. My tongue swelled up when I tried to talk. I said I remember you.

What? We were underwater. And I could hear the sizzle and pop of the water hardening the lava that oozed out of the cracks in the ground. They were getting worse. Seemed like there was someone who wanted something. I said I remember you. From the updraft situation. Remember that, Clint? His eyes lit up and I jumped backwards in terror.

He said Oh yeah! Satisfied and smiling. But then a cold panic and a hardening. He said You know that man called the police? I had to give him a statement.

What did you say? What had I done? Do they know I'm here? Tell me at once! I scanned the aisles for bear-pigs but only found a shrieking forest of colored plastic.

He said I told them you were trying to save that girl.

Clint. Clint. Clint! I will always remember the face of that boy shining with the love of god.

I said Great, thanks. My elbow slipped off the counter, but I recovered nicely. I said I just need to use your bathroom. He said I had to buy something but I just walked to the back. I said Always people coming and going. Like a harbor. I said How do you wrap your head around that? I thought of the time I spent in the brig and the man I fought and broke in two, but there was the door handle to contend with, so I couldn't come to any moral conclusions.

As much as I loved him, Clint couldn't know I was there. I was, I assumed, a wanted man by that point. If it wasn't the bear-pigs, it was Tío or Elltoo's people—or some vengeful god.

So I locked the stall door and gave myself to fate.

It starts with a flicker somewhere deep down in my marrow. A flicker like that one grasshopper in the buffalo grass, that rattle that echoes across the field and makes you feel about as lonely as a man can get. Before long it's a throng of them, a whole swarm splintering my bones and invading my flesh. They get so loud that they're the only sound in the world. And then it's quiet, and the luminescence appears. A point of light. I follow that, imagine what I'm to become, and then there I am. There's some pain and some violence and some regret and some terror, but then I'm what I've become.

Into the hands of god.

My pelvic cage broke in half—a snap-pop—and I heard the gore before I saw it—a sucking like the emptying out of canned meat. The blood spattered everywhere, and some unknown organs splashed in the toilet. Torn veins trailed my heart to the tile floor. When I slipped on my heart, my head smashed against the stall wall—I could feel pieces of my skull drifting like tectonic plates. Thick black sleek feathers tore through what flesh was left. More of them and more of them and more of them.

Good lord what Clint must've seen when he rattled in there with a mop bucket and found a hundred crows, their wings slick with blood, pecking at my own gore, some microwave dare gone wrong.

I'm sorry, Clint.

It was easier than it should have been. He stepped backwards in terror and tripped on the mop bucket. It tumbled over with him, and gray water pooled on the floor.

He shouted What the fuck? And that was all he said. We took crowded flight in the small room and descended on him. One of us pecked at his eye, which broke open and poured forth the liquid of his sight. He thrashed at us and screamed, but there were too many of us. Another did the same to his other eye, blinding him, while others went at his face, his throat (the arteries!), and the soft flesh of his stomach. He suddenly sat up, the top half of his body like some sick hunk of flesh dragged across the face of a cheese grater. He rolled to his side to get up but collapsed, his hand slipping in a pool of murky water and his own blood. He hit his head on the ground and groaned.

They closed in on him then—devouring him.

The flapping of wings. The squelch of pecked flesh.

Two open doors later, and I was black seam across a black sky.

Those days: We drifted into curious shapes and seemed to know where we were going but were too afraid to say it out loud. Not me, no. Not we. Them. You. I'll drive you out into the streets, but you'll worship me anyway. You'll see who I am but be too afraid to think my name.

I grew sick of the flying thing, so I got myself straight again at the River Spirit casino, where I stole a man's suit and wallet and gambled all of his money away.

So like usual, I was out of cash. And at this point, I needed to get out of Tulsa bad.

What happened to the Celebrity, I'll never know.

Which is how I found myself in what I've previously set up as an ironic situation:

Chuck Bee is telling me that most people don't think that their jobs matter—he's a fat man with the slick red face and the hairy knuckles whose van I crawled into somewhere south of Eufaula—but that just means they're not thinking it all the way through. Take me for example. He had this hot, rotting breath. I thought maybe he'd been chewing on bones and brains. The kind of guy I could get behind. A man of real faith. It turned out he was just a shoe salesman. He pointed to the back of the van with his meaty thumb, and it was filled with yellow and purple shoeboxes. Black no-skids, all sizes.

How many lives do you think no-skid shoes have saved in kitchens all over America? How much grease and dishwater has been overcome?

I said How many lives do you think I've swallowed down into the dark chaos where grotesque shadows dance against a screen lit by the bright blue flame of my hate?

This guy's eyes swarmed all over me. Outside the windows the rain and the prairie and a legion of coyotes out there somewhere, all of them bark-bark-howl, bark-bark-howl.

And holy fuck, that's when I recognized the man's face: Chuck Bee. Chuck Fucking Bee.

He didn't recognize me, even though I asked him over and over again. He pulled the van over to the side of the road. You're a crazy one. Wild and crazy. He put his furry hand on my thigh and his warm, fleshy sweat-soaked hand poured through my jeans and spread all over my lap like a spider web.

You really don't remember me? You baptized me?

Now what does it matter who knows who?

He had me there. He unzipped his pants and pulled out his dick.

That was somewhere outside of Seven Suns.

And that's where I found the boy. That boy! That body!

Because mine is broken. Beat up. Wanted by the law all over the state. *This* body! Almost broken beyond repair. What have I done to myself, to *him*, the one who was before me.

I found the boy in downtown Seven Suns, where I show my proper face to folks. He was sneaking into an abandoned building to smoke pot. Him and his buddy. You should see these two—connected at the hip is the understatement of the century. What's most important:

I could smell his shattered soul in him, his grief and need and sorrow. And broken is just how I like them, need them.

I stalk him in town; I hunt him in the woods. He sees me as I really am downtown—a broken man, bleeding and on fire, a hopeless man in stolen clothes—and he doesn't see me as I really am as I stalk him in the woods—a sleek creature gathering intel from my station in the trees.

So sometimes I find myself in an abandoned building; sometimes I find myself in the woods. What else is new?

This is my plan for today: To shift and shift and shift all day, doing all manner of things at all manner of times to all manner of people. I'm going to take away everything the boy has one person at a time—that girl he knows, that boy, that Indian he lives with. There's not much to take.

So this should be easy.

I just have to get him to follow that one point of light.

That one point of light, which is me.

Which will be him.

9

Beyond a green steel door at the back of the sheriff's office was a courtyard of yellow grass with three picnic tables cracked and grayed by time and weather and a bell-bottomed cigarette receptacle. A cracked sidewalk led to lockup, which smelled like feces and antiseptic and whatever burned thing the inmates had been served for lunch. Captain John sat in a squeaky swivel chair behind a broad, metal desk, his Stetson pushed back on the back of his head. He read a water-damaged copy of a *Scientific American*—Inside the Neanderthal Mind.

"Come for your prize?" he asked. He coughed. As far as Esther could tell, he could be anywhere between fifty and a hundred years old. He stood, pawed at his keyring, and gestured to the hallway. Esther didn't like escorting the male prisoners. It wasn't just the whistling and jeering, the way they tore her body to pieces with their eyes and tongues, but also the hate (sin) it made boil down inside her. Once a man—some gaunt transient—had rattled the cell door on its hinges with the thrust of his hips against the steel. She hadn't been able to look away. Her mind flashed: her entering his cell, drawing the stick from her utility belt, and beating him until he twitched.

She didn't like having thoughts like that.

Down the narrow hall, lit by narrower windows near the ceiling, the prisoners watched Esther from the dorm-style cell. She knew some of them—Billy Bruner, Ernie Burkhart, Al Spencer—and recognized the faces of most of the others. She'd at least been at all of their arraignments—battery, reckless endangerment, DUIs, child neglect. She graduated with Billy, went to church with Ernie's parents. They were criminals, but no less in need of grace than Esther. She closed her eyes, made fists, and said a prayer for the group of them.

They stopped at a solitary cell just beyond. Hooky backed up to a slot in the door, where Esther cuffed him. Captain John scanned a barcode on a plastic bracelet. He pulled a wide, flat key away from his hip on an elastic cord and clanked it into the metal door. He ordered Hooky forward, who stepped out clad in an orange jumpsuit and orange Crocs. His dark hair was cut close to the scalp. The right side of his jaw was pink and swollen, his eyes sunken, dried up.

Esther said, "How are you doing today, Mr. Miller?"

Esther believed that an important part of her duty as an officer of the law—she'd never seen this quality as remarkable, either, until today—was to take the precepts of the law, particularly regarding the proceedings of a trial, as seriously and infallibly as the gospel. Which, of course, included the idea that a person was innocent until proven guilty. She'd seen the way they did it in other countries on TV, the way they kept their defendants caged in the courtroom. This involved a spiritual component as well. A putting in of faith. And so she found herself praying ceaselessly for objectivity in the short elevator trip with Hooky Miller to the second-story courtroom. She held him by his elbow. Tried to imagine the materialization of her faith passing between them, creating some equilibrium. Sometimes equilibrium meant you gave and gave and gave and waited on the Lord to tip the scales. The elevator dinged and she flinched, tightened her grip around Hooky's elbow. She opened her eyes from her chaotic prayers and found him looking down on her, smiling.

After escorting him to the defense table, she went outside of the courtroom and began to let the few spectators in—Rex Dashing, the everything-beat reporter from the *Gazette*; two silver-haired women whose names she didn't know but who came and sat through nearly every proceeding open to the public; Hooky's mother, Cat, who was already sniffling; a smattering of reporters from Tulsa, slowly circling around the carrion of spectacle and other people's suffering; and finally Hal and Bessy Berns, the grandparents of the victim. After their daughter Sarah, the mother of the victim, testified, she hadn't shown back up. But her parents had been right in the front row every day. She stopped Hal before he stepped into the courtroom. He was tall and had a thick gray mustache and wore a black Stetson. She touched him on the forearm. "For the third day in a row," she said. "Please remove your hat in the courtroom."

He shot her a hateful look and ignored the request.

The courtroom was oval-shaped, surrounded by powder-blue papered walls and white marble trim. Dark blue curtains hung high and tight around the giant windows on the sides of the room. Esther loved the way it looked, thought white marble made the justice seem more—just.

There was a squeaking noise that sounded like mice, and the courtroom grew silent. It came again, louder, and was followed by a repeated thud up high, near the ceiling. And then another series of chirpy squeaks and Esther placed it: the warble song of a barn swallow. Of more than one. They chortled again and everyone in the courtroom turned their heads this way and that, searching for the source of the birds where the wall met the high ceiling, where they must have been building their muddy nests. They hadn't been there the day before. They grew loud and wild and then waned, went silent for a period, began to sing again.

There were two soft knocks on the door behind her, and Esther stood at attention.

Esther shouted: "All rise!" And they did. It made her smile on the inside every time. "The Court of General Sessions for Oklahoma Judicial District Twenty-Seven is now in session. The Honorable Parker Bean presiding." The door opened, and Judge Bean came out and smiled at Esther. He was so skinny he looked like a scarecrow in his robes, all stiff angles. He wore wire-framed glasses on a pointed face. He climbed up to his tall-backed leather chair and turned it, sat down.

"You may be seated." The wooden benches around the court squeaked and groaned as they all sat. A single swallow screamed out. Judge Bean took off his glasses. "First of all"—he cleared his throat—"First of all, folks, I'd like to bring up the issue with the small birds that we seem to have. I've been advised they might be building nests via an air duct on the top of the building. Pest control has been contacted, but for now we don't have much of a choice but to bear it. So we won't make a fuss over their little cheeping songs, okay?" He said, "This is Bailiff Esther Grundel, and this is Court Reporter Janine Steele. Mr. Goudy, Mr. Barlow, are you ready? Good."

The summer after her father died, Esther found a barn swallow nest in the hayloft of the stables. With only her mother around, she'd taken to wandering all over their property—climbing fences, identifying tree species, exploring her father's things in the barn (the first and only summer of that), pretending to visit the many loyal regions of her kingdom, riding Midnight.

Her mother had instructed her to leave the nest alone, but as the summer came to an end and Esther's sense of adventure began to run out, she found herself climbing the rough-hewn ladder to the loft again. At the top of the ladder, her eyes level with the hay-strewn floor, the golden slants of light thick with motes, she saw the bulbous mud on the inside of the frame of the door where they lifted in the bales. She drifted like a ghost across the space to the breeze and clear light of the window and studied the mud nest, which was the size of the pitchers of sun tea her mother left out in the yard. Her mother said the swallows were a pest—she often smashed their nests with a shovel—and the thought of the swallow chick, whose cheeps sometimes filled the barn and brought it to life—made her want to warn them, to help in some way. So she stood before the nest and said a prayer.

And out of the muddy mouth a beak emerged—a flicker—and disappeared. She held her breath and stretched a finger out toward it, but stopped just short of the entrance, recoiled with a sense of fear. When the beak emerged again it wasn't a beak at all, but two sharp black pricks—the ends of antennae. Its head was nothing more than a spike of hair between two huge eyes, flat and black. It emerged further, and the faint sunlight of the loft silhouetted the radial veins of its twitchy, amber wings, spiny claws, its black-plated abdomen at the end of the long broomstick it rode on. It rubbed a claw against its mandible and took flight, hung before her face, its buzz filling up her head with panic. A wasp. She stepped back, her heart as fast as the mud dauber's wings, and then stepped again. Another wasp crawled out from the mouth and then another. Before she could turn and run, the wasps dove into the space between her hair and neck. One pushed its way around, scratched at the base of her skull, and stung her, and she stepped backwards again and again and again, shook her hair and hit the sides of her head. Her heel caught the edge of the loft, and she stepped back onto the air, nothing below her but the straw-hatched dirt floor thirty feet below. The ground punched more air out of her lungs than she'd ever even breathed in, and the inside of her eyelids exploded with orange and pink. When she woke, her mother's crying face was a blur above her.

She'd heard the whole brutal story of Hooky Miller. She'd already been posted in court for two days of the trial. The proceedings had already made her sick to her stomach even though the prosecution had done nothing yet but set up a timeline and press a few witnesses about Hooky's character, his history with crystal meth. She'd stood through some pretty horrific trials: rape, child abuse, a murder, things that were semi-common even in communities as small as Seven Suns. But the Hooky Miller trial was the worst she'd ever encountered. When Mr. Barlow stood and called Dr. Omar Fraij to the stand, Esther felt something like a locomotive barreling toward her.

Dr. Fraij unbuttoned the jacket of his blue suit and sat down in the wooden chair next to Judge Bean. A lot of people around Seven Suns weren't thrilled to take their families to some young, olive-skinned Muslim for medical care—*I don't have anything against Muslims*, they'd say, *but I just don't understand why* he *would want to be* here—but with Doc Garrison retired, he was currently the only family practitioner around. The first time she went to him about her spells, he'd told her he'd moved his family from Tulsa because he wanted to raise them somewhere there was clean, open air. He'd tried to prescribe her an antidepressant, but she refused them. That wasn't what it was about— that wasn't for her. She left with the same concerns as she'd come in with. Prayer, she decided, would suit her just fine.

Esther swore him in. He smiled nervously and straightened his tie.

Mr. Barlow stood at the wooden podium between the two counselors' tables and adjusted the black flexible microphone, then tapped it. There were two thuds, and the swallows in the walls erupted in response. Mr. Barlow waited until they'd calmed to just a few chirps and continued.

"Dr. Fraij. How are you doing today?"

Dr. Fraij leaned forward and spoke into his matching microphone. "Just fine."

"That's good to hear. Excuse me if we just get down to business." He lowered his reading glasses from his bald head and examined a legal pad. "Dr. Fraij, was Lorri Berns a patient of yours?"

"I was present at her delivery. But otherwise, no."

"But you did treat her on the first of October of this year?"

"Yes."

Mr. Barlow held the legal pad in front of him and leaned back, manually focused on the page. "At eleven-thirty p.m. or thereabouts?"

Esther balled her hands into fists and shifted her weight, leaned toward the witness, as if by the concentration of her muscles and the force of her will she could convince Dr. Fraij not to tell his story.

"That is correct. I received a call at my home from the sheriff's office at around eleven o'clock, and I dressed and went to my office to meet them."

"And who was there?"

"No one. It took about ten minutes for Mr. Miller to arrive with the child."

"Hooky Miller?"

"Yes."

Mr. Barlow pointed to Hooky Miller. "This is the gentleman?"

"Yes."

Esther wasn't supposed to show any sort of reaction, but she couldn't help looking at Hooky to read his own reaction. He simply held his head down. In the gallery, Rex wrote frantically. Hal Berns sat forward with his elbows on his knees, his giant hands clasped around his mouth and nose. When he dropped his hands, his face was red.

"And what state was Lorri in?"

"The child was unconscious."

THIS NEW DARK   55

"How long was she unconscious?"

"She remained in an unconscious state until she died at approximately three minutes past midnight."

The child. Esther had prayed for the man who'd killed her just an hour before. She reminded herself that right now he was still innocent. In the law's eyes. Deserved prayer as much as any person. She watched him, but he never lifted his gaze from the ground. It was the Berns family, though, who needed prayer. She tuned out the proceedings and centered herself to say one. *Lord, Lord.* But nothing. Something was blocked. Something inside of her, the part of her that imagined her prayers before she made them, the part of her that weighed and measured what she said and thought about others, about God, shrank back, and in its place came something hot and fierce.

"And what did Mr. Miller tell you had happened to Lorri?"

"He told me that they'd been working on getting her to take steps when she tripped and fell against the coffee table."

Hal Berns shouted *Liar!* and Judge Bean banged his gavel, and the swallows startled. "We won't be having any of that, Mr. Berns. I won't tolerate one bit of it during these proceedings. I'm going to ask you just once, and if it happens again, Captain Grundel here is going to escort you out. Do you understand?"

Mr. Berns nodded.

"And take off that hat."

He did, and the chirping faded away.

Mr. Barlow said, "And this fall happened at the accused's place of residence?"

"That's what he said, correct."

Esther was becoming increasingly distracted by the sounds of the birds. She began to feel like their cries were only in her head—as if she opened her mouth, a swallow's blue-orange head might push its way through until it had room to spread its wings and drag its long black tail feathers out of her throat.

"And did you believe Mr. Miller's story?"

"No."

"Why not?"

"Because the child's wounds were inconsistent with the accident he described."

"Can you describe those wounds?"

At this point, Hal Berns stood, sidestepped his way across the bench, and walked toward the door at the back of the courtroom. He stopped there and stood, shoved his hands in his pockets and then took them out, crossed his arms, uncrossed them, pushed back his white hair. Esther had thought the redness in his face, the blue vein in his temple that she could see from across the room had been anger, but she saw now that he'd been crying. The crying became audible, and for the first time, Hooky lifted his eyes and turned and looked at him. The birds kept on. Esther tensed, began calculating what she'd have to do to maintain order in the court. Equilibrium.

"The child's body—"

Mr. Barlow placed an open hand behind his ear and turned it toward Dr. Fraij. "I'm sorry, Dr. Fraij, can you speak up? I'm having difficulty hearing you over these birds." He chuckled, but it cut through none of the tension.

Dr. Fraij leaned into his microphone and said—and Esther braced herself for what she already knew, had read in the paper and seen in her dreams—"The child's entire body was covered in bruises and lacerations. A single bruise covered the entirety of her chest." He held a hand over his own chest, his fingers spread wide. Esther's inner voice

shrank further away, stopped looking for reasons, and she could feel
the swallow, fluttering inside of her rib cage, scratching, filling her up
with its ugly song.

"And did these wounds lead to Lorri's death?"

"Well, actually, no."

"Can you elaborate?"

"None of the wounds—individually or collectively—were enough to
take the child's life."

"And so what was the cause?"

"She died while in cardiac arrest, which was a result of the sheer trauma of the experience."

For the first time Hooky lifted his head, and his sunken, meth-scabbed
face was swollen with tears, and the swallow was a lump in Esther's
throat, and she was a step too late when Hal yelled *You sick son of a
bitch!* and charged across the courtroom at Hooky. By the time she
could get to them, Mr. Goudy had thrown back his chair and backed
away, and Hal had fallen on Hooky, buried a fist in his face. Esther ran
to them, threw a chair out of her way, and reached out and wrapped
her hand around Hal's arm. He turned back on her, his face still sharp
and cruel and raw, and swung a slow fist, which she sidestepped. Bessy
came up behind them, screaming, screaming for him, for them all, to
stop, but Esther drew her taser and fired it on Hal—who went back
to the floor in a violent spasm, his boot kicking the legs of the table—
Rex Dashing above them all, scratching and scratching in his notepad.
When she believed things were calm, Hooky shouted down at Hal, but
Esther couldn't make out what he was saying.

And then he was on top of Hal, his arms still cuffed.

The swallows screeched and scratched like a thousand mistuned vio-
lins, and the last one still inside of Esther finally found purchase and

wriggled its way up through her throat. With the taser still attached to Hal, she drew her club and struck Hooky in the leg with it, struck him again when he cried out. And when she opened her mouth to release the swallow she'd imagined, a yellow-black wasp buzzed out, and Esther struck Hooky again.

And again.

Hooky's pleas and Hal's moans and Bessy's screams and Judge Bean's *crack-crack-crack* gavel all became one deafening roar, and Esther could no longer tell if it was real or just the rush of blood behind her ears as her body surged with adrenaline, her face now hot with tears.

And again.

10

Randy and Squints cruised the country roads and then parked behind the abandoned Showbiz Video, a two-story brownstone relic that had once been a bank. It was at the edge of downtown, next to the sheltered basketball court where they sometimes had weddings and quinceañeras. It was a great place for burnouts to hang out because you could park in the back where the door that led upstairs had had the deadbolt removed. Across the street: the sale barn with its white, gambrel roof. Beyond it a half-acre labyrinth of red and white corrals, the earth turned to mud. Growling duallies idled in the washed-out, gravel parking lot, where water stood still in places, white with sky. The video store's two-story profile sat strange against everything else, like a blip or afterthought of the buildings downtown.

On the other side of the Showbiz was a Tote-A-Poke, where the asphalt parking lot shined blue and green with broken glass, and everything smelled like gasoline. They went inside and bought Mountain Dews and corn dogs with Wyatt's twenty. They sat on the curb in front of the chained-up propane tanks and ate them. Randy squirted mustard in his mouth between each bite and winced. They discussed the merits of being willing to suck another guy's dick. Squints said, "We wouldn't have to clean out the shed for weed and corn dogs. We could find us a sugar daddy." "Sure, yeah, and HIV." Squints laughed until he snorted. The jokes made

Randy uncomfortable. He couldn't finish his corn dog.

"Yo, what was your deal back at Gordo's?"

"What deal?"

"We said we weren't going to stay. We had that excuse, remember?"

Randy squirted the rest of the mustard pack onto the asphalt and smeared it around with what was left of his corn dog. "What's the big deal with hanging out with Gordo?"

"Things always get weird over there. All that shit about God and Jesus? That's fucked, yo. I just want to get some weed, you know?"

"I don't know. I think Gordo's sort of cool. We hung out with him this summer."

Squints looked thoughtful. "Well, you sort of made me look stupid when you jacked with my story like that."

Randy felt bad for him, but then said, in a mock-baby voice, "Tough-ass gangster get his feelings hurt?"

"Fuck you."

A blue minivan pulled up a few spots down, and a Mennonite woman in a denim dress and a white lace cap and sunglasses got out and went around to the sliding door. She pulled a knee-high kid in jeans and flannel out of his car seat. She lowered him to the ground and closed the door. The kid stared at Randy and then put two fingers in his mouth. Randy stared back. The boy's mother picked him up and carried him away.

As they rounded the corner behind Showbiz, the crazy preacher came out of some unnoticed shadow and stood before them, held up a hand like a traffic cop. He wore filthy khakis and a long wool coat over a gray blazer and a sweater with a reindeer on it. His nails and the creases of his knuckles were black with soot. He smoked the butts of cigarettes he found in the Tote-A-Poke parking lot and drank Olde English most of the day. Most people figured he lived in the empty first floor of the brownstone below the old video store. Some said he lived *in* the video store, but they'd never seen him there. Sometimes he'd scream obscenities at you, and sometimes he'd have the kindest word you'd ever heard, and sometimes he'd be preaching about the fiery damnation of hell. His eyes were sunken, his teeth dark. His face was recovering from being badly beaten, bruised, his bottom lip split and swollen, his right eye red and swollen shut. He limped badly but didn't seem to be in any pain.

What got Randy the most was the one good eye. The iris was black-rimmed and neon yellow like a cat. If Randy stared long enough, he swore that the pupil was just a vertical slit. It saw Randy inside of Randy, seemed to recognize him. It was a feeling familiar to Randy—that feeling of being watched, the great gaze of faces he'd never seen. The preacher smiled and winked at him.

"Now I'm not going to hurt you."

Squints said, "Yeah, we know. You better not."

"It's important that you understand I'm not going to hurt you," he said. He swayed slightly, reached out and steadied himself with the side of the building. He bent down and picked up a can of Sprite and took a long pull. You could smell the vodka in it.

"I'm not going to hurt you. But I do wonder if you have a cigarette on you for an unfortunate Christian man like myself." A crooked smile.

Squints squatted down and picked up a butt—smoked down to the yellow filter, probably one the man had already smoked—and said, "Here you go. On us." He flicked it, and it hit the preacher in the chest. When they went to pass him, he stepped in front of Randy and put an icy hand on his shoulder. Randy meant to immediately shrug it off, but when he looked into that strange, bloodshot cat eye, he froze for a moment.

"You have something," the preacher said. "Something that belongs to me."
Squints came from behind and shoved him aside. "Get the fuck out
of the way, old man."

The preacher pulled his coat tight and crossed the street. "You'll see!"
he shouted. "You'll see the face of God."

The windows in the video store were covered in dust but still let in a
strange red-yellow light. The carpet was thick with dust, and the cov-
ers of all the empty VHS boxes were covered in it. There was so much
that when you talked, the dust dampened it, robbed your voice of all
its weight.

In the back, there was a horseshoe-shaped counter with a wood-paneled front side that had a yellow dick spray-painted onto it. There was
a room behind the counter closed off by a heavy curtain, maybe purple
or blue once, now gray. It's where they'd kept the porn. They both liked
to smoke a few bowls and chill back there—Randy because he liked the
way it felt haunted and had the only window with any visibility, and
Squints because the place was ankle-deep in empty VHS boxes of smut.

The window looked out behind the building over a field of gone-to-
seed grass. At the other end of the field was a squat water tower the
same color as the sky. White plastic bags were tangled in the chain-
link fence that encircled it. Past the water tower a train chugged along.
Even from behind the window, Randy could hear the creaky groan of
its wheels. Randy loved watching trains roll by. Massive, rusted hunks
of blue and red and orange, long as hell, hauling god-knows-what. He
loved the graffiti—big crazy-crowded bubble words you couldn't read
or understand. Like someone out on the coast where the trains stood
still were sending a message into the middle of America. But they were
gone in a second. Like maybe the message wasn't for him but someone
else down the line.

They sat with their backs against the wall beneath the window and their legs spread out in front of them. Randy felt queasy, uneasy still from the dab. Squints's body was warm, and his sweet, musky smell felt familiar. He broke up some of the Bonepicker on the back of an empty *Womb Raider* box. They smoked two bowls from a small glass pipe Squints carried everywhere in his pocket. Squints smoked casually, but Randy wanted to be as stoned as possible—to get that feeling that just an hour or so before had made him feel terrified, that somewhere out there his mom was looking for him—so he ripped as hard as he could from the small pipe. He coughed and offered the last hit to Squints, who shook his head.

Squints took a long pull off his Mountain Dew and screwed the lid back on the bottle. A smile crawled across his face like he had the biggest secret in the universe. "Listen, yo. I've been too nervous to tell anybody about this yet"—his smile broadened—"check it out." He pulled off his jacket and hiked up his T-shirt sleeve.

"Holy fucking shit." It was a tattoo. It was six inches across and purple and looked like a hand with all the fingers spread out. The skin all around it was pink and puffed up, even red in places like it was still bleeding. The lines weren't clean and smooth but looked like a series of dashes and dots, like a string of beads. "Holy fucking shit."

"Right?"

"Is that a stick and poke?"

"No. Yo. You should see it—I'll show it to you. I made my own tattoo gun. My own fucking tattoo gun."

"How?" Randy suspected bullshit. It would be just like Squints to do a stick and poke and then tell you he'd done it with a tattoo gun he made himself so he'd seem cool. He said, "Where the fuck did you learn to do something like that?"

"YouTube, yo. You can learn to do *anything* on YouTube. I made it from stuff just lying around the house." He narrowed his eyes like he was thinking. "Well, not all of it. Well, technically all of it, yeah. I had to go into the garage and dig through a box of my dad's stuff to find a guitar string. But he had them. A whole box."

Randy wanted to know why his dad had guitar strings. Had he played the guitar? Sold music supplies? That seemed stupid. Randy had never met Squints's dad—only knew that he left when Squints was eight, moved to California with his teenaged sweetheart. He wanted to ask, but figured Squints didn't want to talk about his deadbeat dad any more than Randy wanted to talk about Wyatt, who wasn't even his dad. "Yeah? And?"

"And a mechanical pencil and an electric toothbrush and a bottle of fountain pen ink." Randy reached out to touch it, and Squints slapped at his hand. "Be careful—it hurts like hell." Then he looked at Randy's face and must have seen hurt or something. "Well, you can touch it. Just don't press too hard," but Randy didn't want to seem too into it, so he didn't.

"What is it?"

Squints's face turned into a horrified question of wide eyes and open mouth. "You can't fucking tell?" His face sharpened. "You can't fucking *tell*?" Like Randy was an idiot. "It's a weed leaf, yo." He'd been holding his shirt sleeve up the whole time. It wasn't quite on his bicep but on top of his bicep, almost on the outside, and Randy could tell that the location and angle were a result of him having to do it to himself.

"Oh, yeah, I can see that."

"Well, I'm not done with it, either. I got to add some stuff and touch it up—make the leaves pointier, give it veins."

"It looks purple."

"That's because it *is* purple, yo. I wanted it to look like that badass stuff that's been going around here for like forever. It's different every time, but it's sort of the same purple. Olim County shit, you know?"

"Did it hurt?"

"Fuck yeah it hurt. Hurt like hell." The tattoo looked like shit, but Randy was genuinely impressed. "You want one?"

Randy felt like he'd been asked the most important question of his life. "I don't know, man."

"That's cool, yo. It's a big commitment after all." He held up his arm and flexed his bicep and smiled—raised his eyebrows a couple of times. "Now *that's* O.G." Randy laughed. "Where would you get one if you did?"

Randy thought it over. He didn't like the idea of putting it somewhere that obscured his muscles. He also didn't like the idea of putting it in a place where there would be muscles someday. He thought about his leg. But if he got one on his leg, he could never wear shorts. Unless he wanted Wyatt either making fun of him or getting pissed at him—whatever his mood was that day. And his mom wouldn't like it. He had to think of that. She'd let him do the earrings, but a tattoo? She'd flip.

"Yeah? And?"

He pulled his shirt up and pointed to the soft spot above his pelvic bone just below where his obliques were starting to show up from the insane number of crunches he'd been doing. He didn't care about how his abs looked or anything, but he'd read on the Internet at the library that if your core is stronger that you can lift more with your upper body because it's easier to balance the weights. "Right there?"

"On your stomach?"

"Yeah."

"Damn, yo. You're starting to get sort of ripped."

For some reason it was the greatest thing anyone had ever said to him. He kept his shirt pulled up and Squints kept looking, and as long as Squints kept looking, he kept his shirt up. After a while he pulled it up more so that the whole side of his torso was showing, and neither of them said anything, but something about watching Squints watch him made Randy feel like he actually existed. He didn't stop Squints, either, when he reached out and touched his stomach, brushed the backs of his fingers against his skin. He got goosebumps, though, and dropped his shirt and slapped at Squints's hand.

Randy changed the subject: "I guess we have to actually clean that shed out, right?"

"Dig, dig, we'll start tomorrow." It was the first time Randy had heard him use the phrase—Gordo's phrase—and it felt forced and stupid. He felt sad for Squints for having to fake it like that. But he guessed any sort of style was kind of faking it. He thought about what his own style should be. He thought punk was cool and I-don't-give-a-fuck—which is what he was going for—but he didn't know anything about the music. At least Squints knew shit about hip-hop—at least he made it seem that way.

"Anything to stay away from home."

"What's up with that?"

"Man, Wyatt's a dumbfuck and always trying to get up in my shit." What he thought: Or maybe because the place feels like a waiting room. And then what he thought: Or maybe because the place doesn't exist at all. Maybe it was just something he'd imagined, something he'd dreamed up from one of his books.

"Then why do you stick around?"

"My mom's coming back."

Squints didn't say anything.

"Plus, if I run off and get caught, they'd just lock me up out at the Boys Ranch where I'd have to suck some dude's dick for my government cheese." Squints laughed and Randy felt better. Maybe he could go full-on country with his style. But Squints would want to stop hanging out.

"Look at this." Squints handed Randy an empty box with a half-nude man and the Eiffel tower on the front. "No, turn it over." Randy did. There was a man down on his knees and another one behind him. The word *pounding* came to Randy's mind. The man down on all fours looked right at Randy. His lips were parted like a kiss.

Squints said, "There's your fucking sugar daddy." They both laughed.

"I gotta piss."

"Well don't piss on me."

Randy walked through the curtain and went around to the front side of the counter, decided to piss right on the yellow dick. When he unzipped his pants, he was hard. He closed his eyes and held himself and breathed in through his nose and out through his mouth. Normally that got rid of the hard-ons. In the thick dust you could hear everything: the scrape of a shoe on the floor, the flick of a lighter, a cough. Squints was going to hear that Randy wasn't pissing and come around and find him with a hard-on in his hand, and they would never speak again.

Relief washed over him when his body and bladder began to relax, but it was cut short by the bang of the door at the bottom of the stairs. He dribbled piss on his jeans as he hurriedly zipped them up. The sound of toppling boxes came from the back room, and Randy felt a hand grip his shoulder from behind. Squints pulled him down and away, and they crouched behind the checkout counter. Silence. Randy opened his mouth to speak, laugh it off, but Squints held a shaking, white-knuckled finger up to his pursed lips.

A shuffle at the bottom of the stairs and then the creak of the first step. Randy's heart pounded. A thud against the wall. And another step, a pause. As if someone were standing at the bottom of the stairs, hesitating, trying to decide if they should come up. The preacher. Please go away.

He tapped Squints on the shoulder and when Squints turned, Randy shrugged at him. *What's going on?* Squints shrugged back.

And then the footsteps were sure. Squints shouldn't have fucked with him. Now he was here to—to do what?

The footsteps reached the top of the stairs, and he stepped into the room, the sound of his feet now a whisper in the accumulated dust. They squatted even lower behind the counter. Randy could see the man's good eye in his mind, scanning the room, hunting them.

A grunt and then something strange: the sound of mud sliding into a rain-filled ditch. The slap of the mud turned into a thumping, a pouring out, and there was the sound of another step. And more of the wet mud. And another step. And then the steps stopped, and the room filled up not with the sounds of a man moving, but of scratching and crawling and what Randy thought of as *squelching*. He slowly rose until his head was above the top of the counter. There was no one.

But when he stood up all the way and looked to the floor: rats. Maybe a hundred of them. Maybe hundreds of them. All of them crowding the open floor before the stairs, some of them making their way down, their claws scratching at the wooden steps and each other. Their chattery screams were chalky and sharp, piercing. Their fur was wet, matted with something Randy couldn't make out in the dim light. They were all furiously eating, picking up pieces of what looked like smashed fruit in their claws and chewing at it frantically. Not smashed fruit.

"What the fuck, yo? Who would dump a bunch of fucking rats off like this?"

"How are we going to get out? That stairwell is the only way out."

Squints shrugged.

Even with just the rats, Randy couldn't stop thinking about that eye, that gaze. For some reason he was convinced that if the rats found them there, they'd come for him.

Squints smiled. "We're going to have to jump. Just run down to them, jump over them—down a few steps—and then out the door."

"No fucking way."

"Fucking way."

"We can just wait?"

"It won't be long before they're *here*."

"Fuck. Okay. But fuck you."

Squints went first. He turned and gave Randy a shit-eating grin and did his best to skip across the rats to the top of the stairs. When he got to them, he reached out and gripped the handrail on both sides. He swung himself up and over the rats on the stairs, laughing.

Randy tried to skip and hop his way through the rats just as Squints did, but he hesitated and landed too soon. His heel came down onto something solid, and there was a crunch and a squeal—and when he realized he'd stepped on one's head, he reeled, fell backwards, landed on the rats beneath him, who squirmed and writhed beneath his back until he rolled over, where he found himself on more rats. They squealed and dispersed. His arm was wet—he'd landed in whatever it was that they were eating. They closed back in, and their claws pawed frantically at the flesh on the back of his hand, and an alarm so primal and buried he didn't even know it existed sounded and he shrieked like an animal, tore away from them and bolted down the stairs to the back door, which Squints held open.

Squints closed the door, laughing. "Holy fuck, yo. You should have heard you! Did you hear you?"

Randy wiped the sticky liquid on his hand across his thigh: a thick red liquid like blood.

"Sick," Squints said.

But Randy's mind wasn't on the blood. It was on the rats, which scratched furiously at the glass door, climbing on top of one another, desperate to get at them.

11

GOLD LETTERS spelled *Olim County District Judge Parker Bean* across a watery, pebbled window. Esther stalled outside the door. She followed a gold vein in the marble floor with her eyes until it disappeared into the black-green rot growing beneath a water fountain. She should have expected something like this. The Use of Force Form in her hand was damp with her sweat.

She took a breath and knocked, and a watery shape formed behind the glass and turned the brass knob. She took the form in her other hand and wiped the sweat off on her pant leg. The door opened, and Judge Bean stepped out. He looked down the hallway in both directions before motioning to Esther to come in with two fingers and a smile. He was so intense about the welcome that Esther felt like he would have dragged her in if he could.

He sat behind his desk, planted his elbows, and leaned forward. A slapdash of legal pads crowded the edge of the desk, their dark scribbles crawling over everything, off the edge of the desk and onto Esther as she sat across from him. Facing her from the corner of the desk was a cowboy on a horse, both shaped from barbed wire. For some reason she reached out and put her finger to one of the glinting barbs, which sent ice through her veins. Always trouble trundling toward her from somewhere else in the universe.

"Watch it," Judge Bean said. "They're sharper than they look."

The cold wasn't just inside her; it was outside, too. Moving through her. She'd broken four of Hooky Miller's bones. She was still shaken by the way his flesh and bone just gave out under the force of her baton. The way he'd cried out. The way she'd seen Dr. Fraij pointing to his entire chest to indicate Lorri's biggest bruise. And the way she'd thought of giving him that same bruise (trauma).

"Listen, Esther, how long have you served in my court?"

Tears began to well at the corners of her eyes. "Almost ten years, sir."

He smiled. "And in that time, has one thing ever gone wrong in that courtroom?"

She held the form up for him to see, her hand shaking, but he didn't take it. She was going to have to find a new way to support her mother. She sat it atop a short stack of trays full of dusted-over papers on the corner of the desk. She said, "I just can't believe things went the way they went today. I should have seen it coming when he got up and stood back—"

"No, no. You did the right thing. I liked it. I like that kind of initiative." He held up a fist. "Bold. *Ready to act*." He smiled. "Before you were bailiff. You worked—Process Server?"

"Yes, sir."

"So you went through deputy training?"

"Yes, sir."

He took off his glasses and rubbed the raw flesh on the bridge of his nose. The chair groaned as he leaned back. Each low creak traveled through the floor and up through her boots and into her body (soul). "You're a woman of action, Captain Grundel. Which is exactly why I'm going to ask a big favor of you."

"Sir—"

He leaned forward and planted his elbows on the edge of his desk, picked up a pen and clicked it, clicked it again. A bead of sweat formed on his temple. "Here's the situation." His smile was gone. "I'm sure you're aware of parts of this. Sheriff Gains is under investigation"—she knew that—"and as of this morning, he's been taken into custody"—she didn't know that—"on charges of fraud, conspiracy, and embezzlement."

"Embezzlement?"

He put his glasses back on. "It seems he was paying for his legal defense with money from the county's coffers. These are very serious charges. And I'm afraid they'll only lead to more allegations, more arrests."

They sat in silence. Esther had never had a strong opinion of Gains, who treated her like a schoolgirl. He was magnanimous with her but only because he believed she needed magnanimity, a quality she'd come to despise. Just another good ol' boy. She was starting to understand: All good ol' boys were bad. If you weren't bad, why convince folks you were good?

"I'm sure you're aware of the incident that brought his conduct into light?"

"Terry Big Eagle."

"Correct. And so, as you can imagine, reserve officers have been let go. And Deputies Jacktooth and Byron are still missing in action. So here's the skinny: That leaves only you, the Bosco kid, Captain John. I need John in lockup, which just leaves you and the Bosco kid—what's his name?"

"Brock."

"Brock Bosco?"

"Yes, sir."

"Hell of a name. Well, the kid can't even buy alcohol. Which just leaves you, I'm afraid. Now don't take that the wrong way."

"Me?"

"You."

Esther didn't understand (believe).

"Now as soon as I can get together a special vote to appoint a new sheriff, I will. I'm working on that—I can promise you that. I can get that done first thing Monday. Until then, though, that authority is going to go to you."

They sat in silence, save for the thick pump of her heart, which she swore could be heard all over the room. He watched her face. "Now I know you've got a lot on your plate with your mother and all, but at this point I don't have any other option. You're duly qualified for the office. Duly qualified enough, anyway."

"Wait," she said. "I don't understand. Are you doing this to me because I'm a woman of action or because I'm the only person left?"

"Well," he said. "Let's say both."

Her gaze moved back to the cowboy on the desk, the single barb at the end of the lasso, which glinted with both the white rays of daylight coming from the window behind the judge and the yellow haze of the desk lamp. The cold began to return, the terror, but this time with it: the poise of a lasso just before it is thrown. She said, "How much trouble can I get into in one weekend?"

He swore her in.

Lanette held up a fat ring with some fifty keys on it by a single key with a pink rubber end. "This one is the key to the front and back door." A blue rubber end: "This one's the office key." A green rubber end: "This one's the quartermaster's office. Sidearms are in there. I can unlock the sheriff's if—"

"I won't need anything like that," Esther said. "My taser is always more than enough." Lanette shrugged and pushed the keys into Esther's hand. "Just bring this all back to me when you're done."

When she got back to her office, Brock was reading, his feet up on the desk again. Esther sank into her chair, sighed loudly. "Good God."

"What, *you* get to use the Lord's name in vain?"

"What?"

"You just used the Lord's name in vain." He hitched his thumbs in his belt and rocked back in his chair.

"I'm Sheriff," she said, numb.

Brock's eyes widened. "No way! What? How? *Why?* Wait. You've got to deputize me. I mean, I know I'm already a deputy, technically, but—"

Esther, still numb: "I saw a wasp today." Brock waited. "A mud dauber. I opened my mouth, and it came right out."

Brock said, "Oh, geez, wow, what? Stay away from me then, wasp mouth. You would not believe how allergic I am to wasps. When I was eleven, I accidentally stepped—"

Esther walked by him and out into the hallway, where she stood and looked out the window. The sky had plunged into a dark, ruddy rust beneath long, streaking clouds. Like her father's white apron after he'd skinned and gutted a catfish.

Brock came out into the hallway. "Are you okay?"

12

EVERY DAY after school, Kitty Kershaw walked a mile down Broadway from the big gray-box school to her family's shop, Kershaw's Guns & Ammo. She didn't mind the twenty-minute walk. Couldn't wait for it, even. She finally got away from all the dirtbags. The entire eighth-grade class, really—from the bubble-gum sex talk of the popular kids to the Cro-Magnon grunts of the FFA kids to the buzz of the pigpen flies surrounding the kids who didn't talk. Tweaker parents.

It was twenty minutes by herself before she had to clock in at the shop and listen to the men of the town fire off rounds in the back-store range and wipe up their Copenhagen-drool after they were gone. Twenty minutes she didn't have to deal with the soul-crushing silence of her father. But today: as cold as it had been that year. There was a weird, warm wind, but she had to shove her fists deep into the pockets of her black pea coat as she walked in the ditch. Breathy, squeaky school buses blew by, kids of all ages yelling *Fuck you* out their windows. An elementary school boy with a wide, freckled face and red hair beetled his head out over two hands and a foggy bottom window and yelled *Nice hair, slut!* She looked away from him, held out her arm, flipped him the bird. Then she thought of Randy Strange, the ninth grader, and her anger disappeared, sublimated. Something about Randy Strange. He was tall and had earrings, and she was meeting him again. Something like a sparkler traced his name inside her rib cage. She held him in her mind the entire mile back from school.

The shop was downtown between Eaton's Diner and the new U.S. Cellular store, which used to be Sally's Consignment. Before Sally died. Man, you could find some killer costume jewelry in that place. Her mom used to take her in there sometimes and give her a ten-dollar bill. She stopped at the front door of Eaton's Diner and cupped her hands around her eyes, looked inside. Betty dropped plates down in front of two women at the bar and huffed off, wiped her forehead on her short sleeve while she scooped ice and dumped it in a plastic cup. She was busy, which made her badass. No one gave a shit about *her* hair. Kitty's was just bleached platinum, maybe a little ratty—at least since she'd started back-combing it. Betty's was purple. Again, badass. Of course.

She withdrew from the door. She'd go in later after seeing Randy Strange and sit at the counter and talk to Betty until she didn't have anything to tell.

The people she knew!

The display windows at the shop were crowded and—this had been at her mom's insistence—didn't display a single gun, because her mom thought it gave off what she called *an aggressive appearance*. On display instead: a dark oak wash basin, the rusted porcelain bowl filled with faded, plastic flowers. A life-size cardboard cutout of George W. Bush, who held two cardboard signs—*Deer Corn* and *Don't Bring It Loaded Unless You're Saving Our Lives*.

The store was a small retail space that went back thirty feet, where the rectangular faces of ammo boxes—sharp yellows, oranges, blues, whites, greens—were stacked ten feet high. Shotguns and rifles lined one whole wall. Their black barrels pointed at the ceiling like rows of jagged, point-blank teeth. They were in peak deer season, so when the storekeeper's bell plinked brassy above her, the store was full of a dozen fat, bloodthirsty, spit-mouthed sacks. They were in line for ammunition. Most of them just held court. She could smell the Copenhagen.

Her dad had an AR out on a towel on the counter, which was a glass display case that made a horseshoe around the room. Inside the cases, dirty display lights yellowed the brushed-steel barrels of the handguns. Her dad was telling Wyatt Whitecloud that an AR was what he needed if he needed to take something down fast, something he didn't want to give a chance to get away. "Eighteen-inch threaded barrel, shotgun-inspired, modular free float hand guard." Wyatt picked it up, pointed it toward a spot high on the wall and closed an eye, peered through the sights. He was tall and had a dark ponytail and was the only Native American Kitty had ever met with a (partial) mustache.

When her dad saw her, he nodded to the cash register. Kitty wove her way through the men to the back counter and stepped through an open space next to the register, where Mont Cookson was waiting on a box of Springfield .30-6s. She pulled the large green box down from the shelf on the wall, took three twenty-dollar bills, cranked open the register door, and made Mont's change without saying a word.

Herman Hollis—who was always in his camos—was telling the others what he'd heard about the forecast for the following day, news that they'd all apparently heard but listened to anyway. *Couple inches, I heard. Yep, I heard that, too. Freak thing. Freezing rain, too. What are we getting all this rain so late in November for? It's not going to come—those sons of bitches get paid to be wrong. Well they better be wrong or deer camp is going to be a bust.* Hums of thoughtful agreement.

Kitty's dad had Wyatt filling out the necessary paperwork to buy the rifle. He had Del Baker with him, who was shaking his head with the jot of Wyatt's hand. Del had wide shoulders and straw-colored hair and that sort of tan that farmers had, even in the winter. He always had blond stubble on his jaw and cleft chin. Pretty handsome, she guessed. He saw her staring at him, and she blushed. He made his way to her at the register, and she thought she might die. He pointed to her hair.

"That hair of yours is starting to look pretty—Judy would call it *interesting*." Normally this would have pissed her off, but it was Del Baker. "What's the look you're going for there?"

She pulled a strand out for him. "It's called back-combing. I've been doing it almost a month now. It's how you get dreadlocks going."

"Dreadlocks, huh?" He hitched up his jeans by the belt loops. "Well, I wish you good luck with that." He smiled. And it was a genuine smile and Kitty could feel its warmth. That was a gift she had: She could read a person's heart like a book.

Elmer Lewis, who was too old to hunt but too lonely to stay away, spoke out over a lull. "What do you need a rifle like that for, anyway, Whitecloud?"

"There's a cougar in old state park."

There was laughter.

"A *black* cougar."

More laughter. Kitty felt bad for Wyatt. She wanted to know more about the cougar, but the men didn't seem to care.

Oh, come on now. They say the same thing every year. But my brother said he saw one over near Devil's Den. Oh, he saw no such thing. There aren't any cougars around here. I heard there's not even such a thing as a black cougar anyway. It's just some stupid Indian legend. The group grew quiet.

Wyatt pulled something from his back pocket and unfolded it—a picture of some kind printed out on copy paper. He held it out to the men, who'd formed a loose circle around him. He shook it in their faces. "Is *this* funny?" he asked. He held it up in front of a number of individual faces before Elmer Lewis snatched it away. He pulled a pair of reading glasses out of his overall bib and studied the picture.

"Why you can't see a damned thing here. Just a blur." He passed it along, and then the picture moved from man to man, each of whom grunted to confirm the ambiguity of the image. As it came close to Kitty, she leaned over and saw for herself. They were right: nothing but a blur.

"Could just be a bear," Mont Cookson said.

"I've seen it," Wyatt said. His eyes were huge, and Kitty understood a little why they'd laughed at him. "It's not a normal size, either. It's big as a lion!"

They laughed.

"I'll sell him the rifle just the same," her dad said. They laughed harder.

13

T HAT NIGHT: Wyatt didn't frequent Red Door because mostly he tended not to drink. Not like his father. When he did go, it was usually to meet someone—tonight, Gordo. The place was shotgun narrow— tables, the bar, a small dance floor, a pool table. One end looked out over Fourth Street through a huge picture window boxed in by jagged sandstone blocks. The window was mostly obscured by a Confederate flag bleached pink and white by sunlight.

It was a once-in-a-while sort of meeting. Locked up in the box in the bed of his truck were sixteen neatly wrapped pounds of cannabis in barely used ruck sacks. He decided right then: This was the last time. The last remaining crop could go up in flames. That was a bit of good news, something worth celebrating.

But Darlene was swimming in his mind again, pulling him apart at the joints.

Darlene, Darlene. She was a nerve that throbbed every time a person or place brought her back—like Red Door, where Elvis Kithawk had once taken time away from his bartending duties to ask Wyatt to come pick Darlene up. When Wyatt arrived, he found her in the middle of the dance floor, where she was doing a pirouette. Instead of spinning she hopped on one foot, laughing, one hand reaching for the sky.

And the fringe vest with the big silver buckles she wore took him to them standing at the sink in the trailer just after she'd moved in, the light above blinking. They smiled at each other's reflections in the window black with night.

And then there was the kid. He'd always had to feign interest in the kid—a weird one to say the least—even when Darlene was around. But now. He'd asked about his mom a lot at first, a *lot*, as much as you'd expect from a kid when their parent went missing. Wyatt told him what the deputies had told him: she'd taken off, ditched them. The kid refused to believe it, and Wyatt inwardly respected him for that. He only asked every couple of weeks for a while, and hadn't said anything in maybe a month. Now: Sometimes the word *dead* rolled dry around the inside of Wyatt's mouth when he thought about her—was he supposed to share that with the kid?

And they'd made him a laughingstock at Kershaw's, shoved his own evidence back in his face.

Just a few drinks tonight.

The pine bar was pieced together like a bowling lane, advertisements randomly scattered beneath a thick layer of lacquer: Eastern Oklahoma NRA, Bradford Pole Barns and Garages, Tom Bragg's Shelter Insurance, Kershaw's Guns & Ammo, Oklahoma Tobacco Helpline. Behind the bar above a row of glinting liquor bottles was a shelf full of figurines, a collection of hundreds of Union and Confederate soldiers, cannons, mounted cavalry, all of them engaged in a battle unfolding on eight square feet of peat moss beneath a grimy layer of dust and smoky resin. Some owner long ago had been a Civil War buff.

Wyatt ordered a beer and then ordered another. He picked at the label with his thumbnail, rubbed the sticky residue between his fingers. The streetlight out front filtered through the flag in the front window and cast a weird pink light on the curling smoke that filled the place.

Four men played pool on the stained table beneath the window. Some faces he didn't recognize did shots at a booth beside them. At another table, three women he knew, too well—Dolly Jacktooth, Josey Cutter, and Babs Inglehart—drank fruity drinks and laughed. Darlene had worked with them all at the House of Beauty, and the sight of them having a good time broke his heart. As if they were expecting Darlene to join them anytime.

Where was Gordo?

Dolly Jacktooth caught him watching them and smiled. She held up her drink from across the room, and he did the same. He sat up straight on the stool, tipped the beer back, and drank it down, leaned forward and sat the empty on the black spill mat and waited. Elvis brought him another.

On Wyatt's thirteenth birthday, his father had simply pulled into the driveway and laid on the horn of his white-on-powder-blue truck until Wyatt's mother opened the screen door and let Wyatt out running. His parents waved to each other but didn't make eye contact.

He took Wyatt to feed Oreos to the white buffalo outside of Tulsa. On the two-hour drive, he opened the bag and ate some of them. "Wait until you see this fucker." He was tall and thick and had a pocked nose, always in a faded pearl-snap. "I mean this thing is huge. But he'll eat these things right off your hand like a baby." He held one up to indicate what thing and then ate the cookie. "It's a special thing."

He ate more Oreos. In Muskogee he pulled over at a Tote-A-Poke and bought a twelve-pack of Keystones. He put the box end up on the floor of the truck and drank one, drank two, drank three. The clearest part of it for Wyatt was the beer and the Oreos. When he was done with a beer, he'd crush the can in his hand and toss it like a hook shot into the bed of the truck, where they shimmered like minnows in the rusted blue bed.

He told Wyatt a story about a man at the Quebecor plant who'd lost a bet and had to be raised to the rafters on a forklift, a height which no one had attempted with the lift. "This guy—Benny—he laughed his head off all the way to the top, where he reached up and grabbed on to the rafter and lifted himself up, made a show of it. And while his feet were up in the air, the guy operating the forklift started to lower the lift, and Benny—remember, he'd just been laughing—cries out, really screams, screams and cries and begs, just like that. On a dime. When they got him down, he was bawling his eyes out. He took the rest of the day off and never came back to work."

When they got to the ranch, he'd eaten all of the Oreos. "Whoa, little guy, you eat all of those?" He smiled. Wyatt wanted to smile back, but he just didn't know how. They parked the truck in the small gravel parking lot that backed up to a split-rail fence. Forty yards off—at the top of a green rise in the earth—the white buffalo watched them. "Guess he's too far for Oreos, anyway. Guess you don't have to come up with a story, little man. Kind of an ugly fucker, ain't he? You know only one in ten million buffalo are like that?" It didn't look like much to Wyatt from that far off, just a gray smudge against a blue sky.

Wyatt said, "It's not a buffalo."

"What do you mean by that?"

"He's a bison. Buffalo live in Africa."

"Whatever. The point is: He's sacred."

There was a warm hand on Wyatt's arm. He turned to see who it was, but they'd already moved behind him—Dolly. She climbed up on the stool next to him and crossed her legs. She wore snakeskin boots, skintight jeans, and a denim shirt with a lasso embroidered on the collar. She wore her red hair in tight curls. She had an overpoweringly fruity smell. "How are you, Wyatt Whitecloud?"

"I do believe I'm doing all right." She picked up her drink but kept her eyes on him. The bent straw jabbed her in the nose and Wyatt laughed. "Had a few?" He winked.

She seemed like she could really occupy his mind.

The first couple whiskey-and-beer chasers burned Wyatt's throat, but the next couple went down easy. He wanted to dance. Dolly put on a set at the jukebox and sidled up next to him. The dance floor— where boots had kicked the wood-paneled floor white, constellated it with a hundred black stars of dropped, crushed cigarettes—was empty. It winked with the rainbow reflections of the CDs slowly rotating in the glass display of the jukebox. She lit up a Camel and offered it to Wyatt with a rose-red ring of lipstick on the filter. He hated smoking but took a drag.

"Sure don't see you out a lot, Wyatt."

"I guess I ought to get out more often." He smiled at her. He'd heard a thousand stories from Darlene about Dolly, whom Darlene called Trouble—Dolly dabbling in crystal, Dolly blowing Gil Byron on the side of the highway when Gil Byron pulled her over for driving dead drunk, Dolly skimming the till at work just to get her nails painted the loud purple she wore. What would Darlene think of him dancing with her?

He swallowed the thought down. Maybe tonight was the night to move on.

"You should. That's what I believe life's about, you know?" The last few words of the question slipped a little and she leaned into him, kissed him on the neck. And for a moment he was out of Olim County on an open road.

There was a loud slap at the bar and a roaring laugh—Gordo. He was at the far end of the bar, telling an animated story in the wooden glow of the light over the bar. Wyatt said, "I ought to"—Dolly took Wyatt by the chin and redirected his attention to her. "Come on now. Two-step with me, cowboy." She took him by the hand and pulled him. His head swam. The bartender turned up the volume when Dwight Yoakam came on, and the song drowned out the yelling and laughing from Gordo and his audience.

The cagey drumbeat crawled into Wyatt's skull, and the steely vibrato of the slow-picked electric guitar carried his hand up and around Dolly's back. He cupped her shoulder blade, and she rested her hand on his shoulder, gave it a squeeze. He took her hand, and they both smiled and stepped into the beat like a river—quick, quick, slow, slow—him walking her backwards. She said, "When was the last time you did the two-step?"

"Not sure, to tell you the truth. Probably last time Darlene and I did."

Her smile faded. "So a long time?" The smile returned, this time a little more forced, and Wyatt read it on her face: She was taking something away from Darlene, paying her tit-for-tat for some long-lost wrong. His protective side coiled up inside of him, but he shoved it down. Between drinks and the loneliness and the need, he couldn't afford to care. He moved her to the right, opened her like a door, turned her, stepped in the door, and there was Gordo, leaning against a crooked cocktail table at the edge of the dance floor. He smiled. Wyatt stepped through the line of dance, closed Dolly's door, turned his back to Gordo, switched roles, and let her push him back, which she did, trying her hardest to close the gap between their hips. They went around and around and he wanted to kiss her, to taste the wetness of her mouth, but before he could the song ended, and she wrapped her arms around his neck and leaned up, pressed her glossy lips against his, arched her tongue across his upper lip. She released him and laughed. "I'll get us beers." She danced as she walked, swaying her elbows along with her hips, snapping her fingers in the air.

Gordo closed in on him. He wore a greasy blue mechanic's shirt with a dark blue collar and a dark blue name tag with his name on it.

"You're not a mechanic," Wyatt said. He swayed.

"What?"

"You've got on that shirt."

"Hey, chico, looks like you got something going on tonight." Before Wyatt could respond: "Dig, dig. Well, I got to get this over with. Betty's got me on lockdown."

Before Wyatt could think, Dolly took him by the hand and pulled him toward the bathrooms at the back.

What happened in the dark green stall of the women's bathroom was unceremonious. There was no fire or drums. Just clawing at clothes and Dolly on the back of the toilet and Wyatt grunting, and then they were standing together awkwardly as she cleaned herself with a wad of toilet paper and Wyatt whimpered to himself in shame. They both zipped up their pants, and she hooked on her bra. She sat back on the top of the toilet and pulled on her shirt. She unbuttoned the breast pocket and reached inside, pulled out a crumpled joint. "Good thing that didn't get too rough." She said it like a joke, but she didn't smile. She lit the joint and then put it to her lips, puffed twice and then pulled away, picked at something on the end of her tongue and made a dry spitting sound. The stall filled up with the rich buttered-popcorn stench of his bud. She extended the joint to him, and he shook his head, held up a hand, smiled. "No ma'am, never have."

"Suit yourself." She smoked it by herself. Wyatt dug a cigarette out of her purse to mask the smell. They smoked in silence. He was unsure of what to say, to do next. He wanted another drink, something to keep the forgetting steamrolling ahead. He hated how you could feel so free one moment and then so low the next, all without leaving the same bathroom stall. When he came back out, it would be a different world now. When he climbed out of that stall, he'd find a smoky, red-lit hell darker than the place he'd escaped from—once just wobbly, now helter-skelter.

He couldn't help it: He loved Darlene.

The bright red Budweiser clock over the bar read eight-thirty, which meant eight-fifteen. Where had Gordo gone? How long had it been? Dolly had rejoined the House of Beauty table, was smiling and smoking and telling stories like she'd been when he came in. He stood from the stool and staggered a bit.

A voice behind him: "Whoa, chico, whoa. Maybe you ought to sit down." He did, and Gordo appeared in his periphery. "What's going on?" He looked around the room in a way that made Wyatt paranoid. "Where'd you go? You're wasting my time, chico." Gordo looked around the room again in the same way. "Let's get you out of here and get this done."

Outside, Wyatt leaned on Gordo, and they walked the crumbling sidewalk down the long building to the back, where Wyatt had parked his pickup beside the dumpster; Gordo had parked his Mercedes—an old hiccup diesel, nothing special—behind it. Gordo tried to help him unlock the toolbox in the back of the truck and Wyatt angered, pushed him aside, threw open the toolbox.

"Hey, whoa, take it easy, chico."

"Now just hold on there. Do not call me *chico*, chico."

The door to the bar opened, and music and voices and laughter drifted out.

"Hey, what's with the tone?"

"Nothing. Sorry." He pulled away from Gordo and stood apart from him, swayed slightly. "This is it," he said. It wasn't the time to be telling him, but he was going to do it anyway. Might as well tie another one on tonight. "By the way. This is it."

"What are you talking about, chico?"

"I said don't call me *chico*. Going straight. Legal grow op. Getting in on the Green Rush."

Gordo simply stared at him, and Wyatt could see him processing. Wyatt said, "I'm out." He said, "I'm going—"

"Aye, chinga, I heard you." He stepped closer to Wyatt.

"I don't need the risk. And I heard you've been dealing a little on the side, breaking some off for the kids and old timers and junkies."

"You're out? You know what that means for *me*? What's your *deal*? You're normally a lot cooler than this. A lot *cooler*. Let's get you home. Come on. You're just drunk." He coaxed Wyatt with his arm like you would a child. "I think you're just all fucked up over Darlene."

Wyatt's spine stiffened at her name. It wormed its way through the fissures in the gray matter of his brain. His stomach clenched. Anger bloomed at the back of his throat. He stepped closer to Gordo.

"Come on, Wyatt—don't do this shit." The blue arc lights threw sharp shadows over Gordo's face, and he looked more menacing than usual. Wyatt wavered and then Gordo's face came into focus: thinning hair, lines on his forehead, pleading eyes just short of fear. Wyatt imagined Betty waiting back at home—the house tidied, the TV on.

He punched Gordo in the face.

Gordo spit. "Fuck."

Wyatt lifted his knee and drove the heel of his boot into the outside of Gordo's knee. Something clicked. Gordo cried out and staggered backwards, tripped on a broken piece of sidewalk, fell backwards with a grunt. Wyatt went down on top of him. He clamped a hand around Gordo's neck, his fingers pink from the cold, the knuckles dry and white. He hit Gordo so hard in the cheekbone that a pain shot through all the way to his elbow. The spot immediately turned into a purple stripe. He hit him again.

Gordo pushed Wyatt off, knocked him down. Wyatt rolled over and stood, but the world rolled with him and took him back to the ground. His lungs burned, and he heaved like he had a feed sack on his chest, and before long he did—Gordo straddled him.

"You might be bigger than me, but I'm the sober one. What the fuck is this? We had a good thing going." His face was a bloody blur. "You're right about one thing: We *are* done." He brought his fist down into the middle of Wyatt's face. The cartilage in his nose splintered back into his head, exploded with yellow lights across his vision; a rainbow-lightning nerve shot through his brain, out the back of his skull.

He opened his eyes to see the Mercedes crunch through the gravel right next to him. He stared into the headlights, his shape haloed in white, the dust from the scuffle still swirling around him. Two women smoked cigarettes back toward the street. He got to his knees and vomited. He got in his truck and left the bar.

His whole head felt numb as he sped down Broadway away from town, but then it would come alive again, scream and throb with pain, blacken Wyatt's vision, only to go numb again. The road poured gray and yellow past his lights. Long, thin stretches of stratus clouds striped a fat yellow moon, a week from full.

Darlene had once built a garden out front from a tractor tire. She'd gotten the idea from the DIY channel one day in the waiting room at the tag agency. She was planting what she hoped would be bright red coral-bells. It was June. Wyatt came out with a half-full coffee mug of Dr Pepper and raised it in the air. Darlene waved and he waved back, but she was looking through him. When he turned, the kid stood in the doorway behind him.

Wyatt said, "Come back to bed." She shook her head and waved him away. He raised the mug higher. "Here's to Darlene Strange, the love of my life." He was barefoot and shirtless, nothing on but his Wranglers. The sun warmed his back. When he stepped out onto the grass, a goat-head stabbed into the soft flesh between two of his toes and he cried out, hopped on one foot, balanced the mug out in the air. She'd laughed. He'd said, "For fuck's sake, it's not funny. I got a goat-head," and she'd laughed harder.

He'd hopped through the grass all the way to the gravel washout at the front of the yard and fallen, where a burst of dirt, gray as smoke, rose and dissipated around him, flat on his back. He held the mug in the air, Dr Pepper preserved. He rolled over and held his foot in his hand, plucked out the bur. Darlene had clapped and said, "Bravo! A perfect ten!" He stood and took a bow, both of his elbows wet with blood. He went to her and offered the mug, and she took it and shook her head. He set it down on the grass, where it tipped and spilled. He sat down next to her, their backs to the tractor tire, and squeezed her thigh until she cried out. He put a hand over her mouth.

"Quiet now, you'll draw attention." He'd said, "Come back to bed." And she did.

Not far from his trailer, something dark and coiled came out of the buffalo grass to his right and crossed the road in front of him, disappeared under a barbed-wire fence and into more grass. He pushed the brake pedal to the floor and the truck screeched, fishtailed, skidded across the road until it came to a stop facing the fence line where the animal had run. The grass was a grayish salmon color in his headlights. It sat still and then danced with the wind, dipped back the other direction and then stilled again. The black silhouette of an oak stretched up and out just beyond where his headlights dissolved into the night. Ten feet beyond the fence line the grass moved when the rest was still, turned into a clean line cutting across the field, the prairie opening itself up for something and closing itself behind. It was large but moved close to the ground, effortlessly. A ghost.

His heart slowed and he put his face to the steering wheel, and the contact with his broken nose shot stabbing pains back into his head. He squeezed the wheel as his chest began to heave up and down, and he moaned, a long, low tone that grew until he shouted—inarticulate threats, prayers, words that didn't exist—and he banged his fist on the steering wheel, once, twice, his nails digging into his palms, a third time, and a fourth, faster and more violently, a fury of spit and fists.

He composed himself, and only then did he realize how quiet it had grown, how still it was. A shadow flickered at the edge of his headlights, and he shivered. He hit the wheel one last time and then laid on the horn, which blared out into the empty night, spooking a tree full of sparrows, which burst upwards in a chirpy chaos before coalescing again and darting into the night.

14

SHE WAS supposed to leave right at five so she could meet Randy Strange, but her dad made her clean the bathroom before she left. He hadn't texted anyway. Kitty went into the bathroom and pulled a caddy down from above the toilet and then a box of purple latex gloves, pulled two gloves out and slid them on her hands. She loved the way the powder felt against her dry skin but immediately hated it when her palms began to sweat and everything turned to sludge. Someone had peed all around the base of the toilet.

She cleaned the toilet and the sink and then pulled her phone from her back pocket, checked it again. No messages. 5:09 pm. She'd told him she'd meet him at 5:00. She thought about texting him but then closed the phone and put it back in her pocket. She pulled it out again. She texted *Still at work.*

Her dad pushed the flimsy particleboard door open and stood in the doorway. She saw his face in the mirror. He looked tired. Tired and like his mind was somewhere else.

"Dad—"

"Go on, get out of here."

She bounced and took off her gloves and threw them into the trash can. "Thanks, Dad." When she passed him in the bathroom doorway, he reached down and squeezed his hand on her shoulder. She looked at him and he looked back at her, but his face was expressionless. He put his hand on top of her head, and the warmth spread down through her whole body. She meant to say *I love you* or *Thank you so much* or *I'm so sorry I can't do more now that Mom's gone*, but she couldn't say anything. So she said nothing, and for a moment they were alike. She took his hand off her head and hugged him for a moment. She turned and unhooked her coat from the wall and put it on.

"Are you going to need a ride?"

"Um. Are you going to be around for a while?" She wanted to need a ride. Her back pocket buzzed to life, and she reached for her phone.

"Well, I've got to lock up customer guns in the back, and then I was thinking about—"

But she was smiling at the text, her face blue with the light of the phone. *Cool. I'm at the library.* "I don't think I need a ride. I'll try to catch one with Betty."

"She taking you to church again?"

"Um. Yeah."

"All right. I'll probably be too tired to wait up."

Randy texted *6 now.*

Where are we meeting? She looked back to her dad, thinking maybe she'd ignored him, had missed some cue, but he was already headed to the back of the shop. She watched his back until she was sure he wasn't going to turn around and then found the soft pack of Parliament Lights in his Carhartt jacket, which she snuck into her own coat pocket. Her phone buzzed again, and she pulled it out. *Meet me in the alley behind Showbiz after that. 6.*

She went to Eaton's Diner to wait. She dropped her backpack on the raised footrest below the yellow bar and sat by the cash register at the

end below the orange light of a faux stained-glass fixture. She watched
the cooks sweat and hustle over the diner's long flat-top grill. Dark
brown spots marked the bar where years of elbows and grease and
spilled coffee had worn the Formica down to the wood below. Betty
Hendrix stopped by and dropped a red basket full of tater tots in front
of her. Betty seemed to be waiting on everyone in the place—which
was full—but she stopped and smiled. "And what's going on with you,
Miss Kitty?" Her thick dreadlocks were tied into a massive ponytail at
the back of her head with a red bandana. She wore dark eyeliner and
a collared referee shirt.

"Not much."

Betty put a fist into her hip and raised an eyebrow. "That face doesn't
look like *Not Much*. Want a Dr Pepper?"

Kitty nodded and Betty disappeared. Kitty admired how Betty could
be so busy—*real* busy, sweating and blowing loose strands of her frizzy
hair out of her face with a puff from the corner of her mouth—and
still seem so cool. She smiled at everyone, and everyone smiled back.
She knew everyone's names. She was generous but badass. The more
she didn't care, the more people loved her. She gave Kitty a basket of
tater tots every time she came in. She'd taken Kitty along with her to
the Assembly of God church a few times. She was just as busy and
generous there, too. Kitty thought some of the stuff they did there was
strange, but she was beginning to like it. If Betty could fit in there, it
couldn't be that bad.

She watched her smile at a fat man in overalls, deflated orange Crocs,
and an OU ballcap and say, "And what do you think your wife would
think of that much red meat, Nash Roberts?" She scratched something
out on a green-and-white ticket, tore it out, turned, and snapped it into
the ball-bearing ticket holder at the end of a long line of tickets above

the cooks, who poured oil over hashbrown potatoes inside steel rings, smashed fistfuls of salt and chopped onions into pink balls of raw beef with their spatulas and poured French fries into baskets, where they screamed in the boiling oil. The air was blue with smoke and thick with the smell of butter.

Someone sat down in the empty seat next to Kitty. Lionel Kithawk. His green duty jacket squeaked when he sat down. Kitty knew deer season was one of the worst times of year for the game warden.

"Mr. Kithawk."

"Miss Kershaw." He tipped his hat to her.

Somewhere in the back a stack of plates shattered, and the whole diner went quiet, and then someone yelled *Hey!* and everyone clapped their hands, and Betty came out shaking her head. "Trials and tribulations. Trials and tribulations." She set a Dr Pepper down in front of Kitty and smiled at Kithawk. "What can I do you for, Lionel?"

"Double biscuits and gravy and coffee—black, like always. And maybe a kiss this time."

Something burned inside Kitty so red hot she wanted to pick up her fork and stab it into Kithawk's meaty paw. Betty just smiled, though, and winked at him. "What is up with the men in this place tonight?" She turned and yelled down the entire bar. "Do any of you men ever spend time with your wives? Imagine if they knew you were all down here clogging your arteries and suggesting adultery." Some of them laughed, and some of them grumbled. She leaned down and rested her forearms on the counter in front of Kitty. "So what's stuck in your craw, bitch?" She wriggled her nose.

"Ah, nothing. Was supposed to meet Randy after work but he put it off an hour."

Betty left and returned with a pot of coffee, filled Kithawk's mug.

"And why are you wasting your time on Randy Strange?"

"You don't like Randy?"

"Randy *Strange*? Creepy kid? Tall? With the broad shoulders?" Kitty smiled. Betty said, "He's school-skipping, deadbeat trouble."

"Maybe I just won't be there when he wants me there."

"There you go."

The tater tots were so hot that they burned her mouth. She took a swig from her drink and turned to Lionel Kithawk. "Just heard from Wyatt Whitecloud that there's a black mountain lion running loose. Is that true?"

He smiled and drank his coffee. "He *did*? Is that what Wyatt White-cloud's out telling people?" He smiled and shook his head as he drank.

"He had a picture with him."

"Game cam photo?"

"Yes."

Kithawk looked pained. He had dark, creased skin, and it seemed to redden further. He traced his gray mustache with his thumb and index finger. "I've seen photos like that a hundred times. There ain't black cougars in Oklahoma. Or Arkansas. And here's some info for you, too: Even if there was a black cat—let's say it was a cougar, which I'd like to point out hasn't been recorded in Oklahoma in ages, and it was a black cougar, which I'd like to point out are rare—you wouldn't spot them. They don't want to be spotted."

She swiveled in her chair and looked out the window. The light was fading, and something like cold went through Kitty. She felt tired. And sad. She stared at the backside of the shoe polish artwork on the front of the window, the backwards *Happy Thanksgiving* and the white silhouette of the turkey holding a knife and fork. She looked past it to Broadway, the red brick courthouse in the middle of the square. It looked empty, nearly was. The fading light gave the sky a reddish hue, and the surfaces of the cars and parking meters and the lampposts all clung to the last of the light. Everything looked awash in blood.

"I never get used to how early it gets dark," Kitty said to no one in particular.

"It's the damned Daylight Savings Time," Kithawk said. "Blame farmers like him." He pointed at the man in the orange Crocs.

"Don't look at me," the man said. "You try milking a pissed-off Holstein an hour earlier all of a sudden."

The three of them turned and looked out the windows at the coming night.

"When I was a kid," Kithawk said, "my daddy always called it *new dark*."

Kitty's phone buzzed to life. *Ready to meet.*

K.

Kitty followed the sidewalk along Broadway and then cut diagonally across the intersection toward Fifth. Old Tyme Pharmacy and its new extended hours (the new pharmacy at the Walmart now stayed open until nine) were the only light on the block, the storefront a yellow box. The dim light and shadows stretched across the sidewalk and the empty parking spaces out front. She turned down Main and followed it to the edge of downtown, turned up the alley next to the Tote-A-Poke.

Beyond the bright lights of the gas station, a single overhead safety light buzzed loudly atop a telephone pole behind the Showbiz. The yellow light hung like a halo, clouded by years of dirt. Below the light, on the ground, Randy Strange sat on a red plastic milk crate, his too-long arms and legs all sharp angles like a spider's.

"It's the man of the hour."

Randy smiled, stood, shoved his hands in his pockets. She thought

THIS NEW DARK   99

of her dad reaching into his pocket for a smoke and coming up empty, felt a pang of guilt. She dropped her bag at her feet and dug into the inside pocket of her coat, pulled out a cigarette. She was fully aware of how stupid it was to think cigarettes made you look cool—and cigarettes had been what took her mom—but cigarettes made her feel cool. She held it out, offered it to Randy, but he shook his head, looked at the ground. Part of her sank to the ground and she thought about putting it back, but instead she put it to her lips and dug a lighter from her pocket, lit up.

She held the cigarette away from her and unzipped her backpack with her free hand, pulled out a rolled-up brown paper grocery sack. "What's this one for?" She tossed it to him. He caught the package, which crinkled in his hands, and didn't waste time putting it back in his own bag.

He cracked his knuckles. "The same project."

"When do I get to hear all about this project?" She meant it as a tease, a flirtation, but it was genuine, too. If she could get him to let her in on the project—well, what would that mean?

"When I'm famous." She'd never thought she'd be attracted to someone so hick. Wranglers and T-shirts and tennis shoes that didn't even have a brand like they were from Payless or Walmart or something. He was intense, though, like placid-deep-sea intense. She'd learned he didn't like to be looked at and so would rock from foot to foot, nervously, chewing a thumbnail or acting like he was interested in some other bodily phenomenon, always looking just around you when he talked. Not that she cared about that. She took a drag from her cigarette and exhaled through her nose. The smoke burned so badly her eyes watered.

"When you're famous, you better take me with you out of here." She immediately regretted saying it. What a stupid thing to say. A stupid, girly, needy thing to say. She saw Betty rolling her eyes. She saw Betty playing the men at the bar in the diner like piano keys. "If you're lucky, I mean, I might go."

"I might be gone sooner than you think."

The rest of her that hadn't already sunk sank. "Where's mine?"

"Right, yeah. Goddamn. Sorry." He pulled a sandwich bag out of his back pocket and approached her, put it in her open hand. It was a single, giant bud. "Smell it." The plastic seal clicked when she opened it. She held her nose down and immediately withdrew it, turned her head and winced.

"Fuck it smells like—"

"Buttered popcorn?"

"*Exactly.*"

"Weird, right?"

"Real progress." She didn't smoke a lot of pot but hadn't wanted to seem too—strait-laced—so she'd accepted.

He gestured to the bag. "That right there? That there's gas. Put it in your tank, man, you'll go." He smiled. "Hey, you mind if I break off a little?"

"Sure, yeah. Oh, yeah, no problem." She handed him the bag. "Hey, guess what I heard today?"

"What?" He plucked what he wanted from the bud and handed the sack back to her. He stood there with the bud in his hand.

"Oh, here, I know." She pulled the Parliaments out. She dropped her cigarette to the ground and snuffed it out with her toe. She slid the bottom of the cellophane wrapper off, reached out and took the miniature bud from his hand, then dropped it in the cellophane. She pulled a lighter from her back pocket and melted the open end of the wrapper until it was sealed shut, handed it back to him. "Your stepdad was in today talking about how he'd seen a black mountain lion out in the woods behind your place. Lionel Kithawk says he's crazy, but—"

His face grew sharp. "He's not my stepdad."

"Who is he?"

"He's Wyatt."

"Oh."

"I should probably go."

She'd screwed it up. "Yeah, sure. Don't want to keep you."

"Mind—"

"Not telling anyone again? Sure."

He turned and walked into the dark. Alone, she pulled out another cigarette, lit up, took a drag. She dropped it to the ground and twisted it out with her foot.

She became aware of her surroundings again and felt terribly alone. The buzz of the light above her made a zapping, cracking sound and she looked up at it, stared at the glow of it, its white halo, and imagined it as a blue sun, some unwelcome star that had just appeared. There was a light brushing sound somewhere further down the alley—the sound of something moving in the grass up around the picket fence guarding the alley—but when she leveled her head to see what had caused the noise, she was blind with the blue ring of light burned into her retinas. She closed her eyes and covered them with her hands, forced them to readapt to the darkness, and there—sealed off from the world of vision—she felt a gaze all around her, felt the alleyway press in on her, watch her. She heard the brush of grass again, and then two clinks from a glass bottle. She removed her hand and opened her eyes, peered into the darkness.

"Hello?"

15

Bᴜᴛ ᴛᴏ ᴜɴᴅᴇʀsᴛᴀɴᴅ how I came to devour that poor gas station clerk and ended up in Chuck Bee's van headed toward the dark heart of Seven Suns, you've got to understand how I fell in with a man I called Tío.

Tío: salt of the earth.

I got drunk at a place called Jackrabbit Gentlemen's Club in Broken Arrow—that's where I'd gone with Elltoo's silver Celebrity—and woke up in a small room with cinderblock walls.

The hospital gown I was in didn't bode well for what was coming down the line. A fat man snored under a gray blanket on the opposite bunk.

I cried out What have we done?

He snored. The door was locked. I leaned against the cold steel of it and cried.

Why are you crying? What did you do? The man was up, sympathetic.

When they came for us and turned on the light, it was clear by the seashell wallpaper that we weren't in any kind of doomsday scenario. A drunk tank. He said he was Tío. He was of some undetermined South American heritage and fat. His blond hairpiece didn't match his jet-black hair. He'd had a girl once he loved, but he left her for a road crew gig in Dallas. That was when he was poor, though. Once they'd found oil on his crippled father's land, he was booming and even met Al Roker one night at a dinner party. He had a new life ahead of him though, one in which money would be no object. He was going to open a grocery store/deli/liquor store.

I learned all of this in the back seat of the return ride they charged us twenty-five bucks for on top of the fifty-dollar administration fee. Tío paid.

We both got out at the same spot and both tried to get into the same car. There are two silver Celebrities in this story. What fortunes! What fates!

It was his he said. He opened it with his key to prove it.

Well where is mine?

It's a mystery.

I want to love and be loved I told him.

He hugged me. He took me by the shoulders. He said Let's get fucked, brother.

The places we went in that Celebrity. Where we went, rest vanished. Where we went, we filled people's heads with screams while they slept.

Tío liked redneck cocktails, but he didn't like to mix his tweak with Oxy. Dilaudid: that was the stuff. Like a sweet hymn to Jesus, your soul laid to rest. It turned out he did have money after all, and we spent many afternoons drinking Fuzzy Navels beside his embryo-shaped pool. He'd cook the crystal down into the liquid opioid and then shoot it up. It only took a week to run out of the stuff. Maybe less.

Tío explained his business plan while we were sitting at the bar in the Waffle House on the interstate. If he got the grocery store going first, it would be simple to add on the deli once the grocery store was successful. Then you could do the same with the liquor. The sun was high and bright and filled the restaurant with a strange natural light that outshined the fluorescents above us. He said No, never mind. Let's talk about the important things. I feel too good not to solve some problems.

We're always just lying around like zombies, stoned out of our minds at home. It's good to be out.

And he was right about that. I was conscious and thinking for the first time in a while, but I wasn't coming down. Mixing an upper with a downer will do things like that to you. One planet to the next. All right, shoot.

Let's talk about this love you keep saying you want.

No. The waitress set pancakes down in front of me. The warm smell of syrup and butter filled my head. I said I'm not hungry at all. The waitress seemed to think I was talking to her. She said I'm sorry.

I almost wept.

Tío shook ketchup from the bottle onto his hash browns. He smeared it around and then wolfed it down. He said Then tell me about Jesus Christ.

Jesus, how did he know I knew about Jesus? I'd almost forgotten. My *calling*!

Everything was new then; everything shined with significance.

The worn yellow booths became humble thrones for men. From where they judged angels. The fry cook was as kind as Christ and the eggs he cracked white on the skillet kept coming out of the basket no matter how many he took.

To understand Jesus Christ, you must first understand sin.

Tell me more.

We're all sinners, see. You and me. Every last one of us.

Blood on our hands.

Exactly. And the only way you can get rid of that is through a personal relationship with Jesus Christ.

Now just how good would it feel to take Tío down to Wednesday Night Life Group fresh from the fires of confession? I'd say Look right here. Look at how the lord works even through the wretched of the earth. Was there even a Wednesday Night Life Group anymore? Where did those people go? Where do people go?

My god. Where do they all go?

Do you have a personal relationship with him?

I lied. Of course. There's nothing greater than the love of Jesus Christ. He's the fulfillment of all god's promises.

God's promises? It was more of a statement.

But I started to lose my high and didn't have the energy to tell him more.

On his couch, later, smoking cigarettes in our underwear and back on top of the world, he asked again. Tell me more about god's promises.

He promises to stand by you through everything and take you to heaven when you die. Set you free and all that. The whole package. Every last promise comes true.

His face was wet with tears. Every. Every, every last sin? Will I be free of every last fucking thing once and for all?

I jumped up and sat on the arm of the couch. For sure. Of course. That's the whole point.

Pray with me, then. Get down on your knees and pray with me. I want Jesus Christ to be my personal savior.

We prayed together, mad stoned, and he repented and cried out. We smoked cigarettes and hopped up and down around the room with our fists on our hips and yelled *Freedom* at each other and laughed. His phone rang. We stopped, and he had a short conversation and then got off.

I need you to drive to Oklahoma City, pick up a few bottles I've been waiting on. The guy's got a liquor store and you just drop in in the back.

The City? Now?

All the holy light that covered his face vanished and his eyes went dark. Do you know how much of my fucking dope you've done, brother?

I did pick up that man's drugs. But I never saw him again. The next thing I remember is poor Clint finding his way to god.

I'll draw the boy to my heart. Save him just like Tío.

Lord all this changing and changing and changing has taken a toll on this body. I need the boy's body soon. And all of this shifting for what? My plan might not exactly be working. How long would it take him to realize people were beginning to disappear? How long would it take him to discover his own empty, broken life has been stomped down to an open nerve on which I can pounce? Considering my dilapidated state, not soon enough.

So I'll approach him tonight. Nothing serious—oh, don't worry—just a *talk*.

I'm going to get him where it hurts—I'm going to take the form of his mother. At least the form of his mother in his mind.

And what is she in his mind?

Something far more horrifying than anything I would have imagined for him.

16

Randy waited in the back room of the Tote-A-Poke so he could bum a ride off Tommy Thompson when his shift was over. He was really digging *Salem's Lot*. He liked the idea of evil entering a town and slowly infecting it. And he also liked the idea of assholes getting what was coming to them.

Wyatt wasn't there when he got home, which was a relief. They always ended up ignoring each other, but it was the getting there that Randy dreaded. He wished they could just pass by and say *Hi*. Say *I don't give a fuck how you're doing, and I'm going to ignore you—enjoy your evening*. But Wyatt would pretend to give a fuck, ask him questions, tell him stories about his day. Tell Randy he ought to join the football team. And Randy would pretend to be polite, to do what he had to do to not start a fight, both going through some formal ceremony just so that Wyatt could lock himself up in the Quonset hut and Randy could lock himself in his room and lift weights, hide behind a book.

Which he did. He dug through his desk drawer through colored pencils and notebooks until he found his wooden dugout. He pulled Kitty's cellophane wrapper out of his pocket and pulled the top open like a bag of chips, dropped the bud out on the desk. He broke it apart with his fingers and dropped the pieces down into the well of the dugout, filled the pipe. He opened the window over his bed, and cold filled the room. He knelt on his pillows, smoked.

He tried to read but was too stoned to absorb anything, reading pages over and over again. So he took off his shirt and sat on the bench before the mirror, tightened his muscles and admired himself. He did reps of curls until his biceps were on fire and his forearms were too weak to hold the weights. He dropped them with a thud. He stretched his arms and leaned forward with his elbows on his knees. Breathed. His heart shook his whole torso, beat mad like a bird was accidentally stuck inside of him. He stretched his arms and picked the weights back up, did reps until he found the sweet spot he loved so much—when he felt scraped out inside, when his breath was so labored the muscles across his chest began to stretch and ignite. He sucked air between his teeth between each curl. When he could do no more, he dropped the weights and stood, let out an honest moan, leaned forward onto his desk, his biceps screaming out. He smoked another pinch out of the open window, the sweat on his face ice cold in the breeze.

A yellow moon hung low and heavy, just above the trees on the cavernous hills behind them. It would be a good night to transform, become something else.

The sliding door of his closet had come off its hinges, one of the track wheels bent out of shape, so he lifted it up and pushed it to his side. Inside there wasn't much: dirty T-shirts on the floor, dirty jeans, the heavier dumbbells he hadn't worked up to yet stacked neatly in a corner, a five-gallon bucket completely full of matchbook cars. And hanging: a few of his mother's things, which he'd taken one at a time out of Wyatt's closet. He took them down and laid them out on his bed. There was the crazy-shiny sequined purple dress she'd had cut down from her senior prom dress to go see Willie at the Hard Rock in Tulsa. She'd hidden prom from her parents—two people who existed to Randy only in his imagination as two bony, knobby, finger-pointing Puritans in breeches and buckles and floor-length dresses. There was the denim jacket with the puffy, quilted red paisley liner she wore in the winters that made her look stupid and round. Her lace-up boots with the frilly, doily-shaped fringe coming out from beneath the laces. A snakeskin belt with a silver cross for a buckle. The long, thick denim dress she'd worn when she still dressed as her mother made her. She'd told Randy once that she'd kept it because it was what she'd been wearing the night she ran away, became free. She'd kept it as a symbol at first, but then kept it because its smell and its shape reminded her of her parents. Her prayer cap— white and light as a cloud, was stuffed in the hip pocket.

He spread them out on the bed and knelt before them. He thought about what Gordo said about Betty having enough Jesus in her heart for everyone. His mother had been someone who prayed, and he hoped that her prayers were enough for them all—enough, at least, that they'd send her back. He stood and returned them one at a time to the closet—all but the denim dress, the boots, and the jacket. He took off all his clothes except for his socks and stood before his mirror. Over the course of the last year—especially in the last few months, a thick black patch of hair had grown in around his penis, stretched its way up and encircled his belly button. Hair had begun filling in his chest, too—first a tawny fuzz, then coarse and dark.

He searched through the dirty clothes at the bottom of the closet until he found a yellow-and-white striped beach towel, shook it out and covered the mirror with it, so only two strips of shadowed silver showed on both sides. He unbuttoned the denim dress down the front and stepped into it, buttoned it back up. The weight of it on his shoulders did something to him—a metallic coating gathered around his tongue, and he became aroused. He put on the lacy boots. He found his backpack and dumped its contents on the bed, measured the weight of Kitty's grocery sack in his hand, tore it open. He pulled out the long, black wig and pulled it on over his head, straightened the elastic, pushed the sides behind his ears. He took the prayer cap from the hip pocket and perched it on the back of his head, tied the strings loosely beneath his chin.

He stood before the mirror and removed the beach towel, let it fall under its own weight with a whoosh to the floor. And in the mirror: someone else. He ran his hands down his chest to his hips and turned his head side to side, examined her. He put on the puffy jacket, dug through his desk drawer for a black pen light, and made his way out through the window into the night.

The sky was blue-gray against the inky ridge of red pine that lined the hills. Randy made his way along the banks of Olim Creek with ease. He never took the ATV trail but climbed through the underbrush of woods to Robbers Mountain. He knew where not to step: rockslides, thorny brambles, muddy drainage, sheer drops.

The air was near freezing; it emboldened him, drove him to move quickly, run whenever the underbrush opened up. A sheen of sweat broke out over him, and he grew colder. He didn't understand why, but for some reason every bit of him throbbed when he wore the dress, felt the oily denim up against his skin. He followed the creek east in the light of the moon and made his way to the cave.

With his mom gone, this was exactly how he liked it—no Wyatt, no Randy. It was just her, the woods. She was the last person on Earth.

He stayed just far enough from the edge of the slate creek bed that his boots didn't slosh and suck in the wet sand. He walked carefully over the roots of the oaks along the shore, which had broken free from the soil and stabbed themselves, thirsty, into the creek's silty moisture.

As he approached the foot of the hill, the sandy creek bed gave way to sandstone gravel, mint green and black with lichen, silver in the moonlight. That sandstone gravel grew into larger rocks, large enough that he had to climb on top of them to move past them. Where the runoff from the cave made its way to the creek, boulders the size of compact cars fanned out from the base of a silvery, hundred-foot sandstone bluff. The acidic runoff from the top of the mountain had carved the bluff in half, reduced the face of it to rubble pouring out of the hill's maw.

Randy found himself doing several things out in the woods—collecting things (quartz, wildflowers), stargazing, masturbating—anything to remove his mind from the tilt-a-whirl of life below. He found himself stalking around the mountain, imagining a hunt for Bigfoot. There was a kind of freedom in a childlike state of imagination, where real possibility could exist. He understood that he was too old for that now, but still.

What he did most often, though, was sit at the mouth of the cave and strategize how he would leave. If he would leave.

He jumped across a drain of water onto another rock, balanced himself, did the same to another, from where, lucky for him, the state park crew had painted a subtle red arrow, which pointed to a set of natural stairs that climbed up the incline of the ravine to the cave mouth. He kept a hand on the rock wall to steady himself against the wet steps. When he was far enough into the throat of the hill, the traces of light lost their power, and there was nothing but the trickle of water—the long blare of a horn in the distance, the howl of a dog that followed, and then nothing but the water. He pulled the pen light from the hip pocket, clicked it on, bobbled the ping-pong of light against the walls of rock around him until he was bored, then trained the light on his path.

At the top of the bluff, the mouth of the cave was a tall, black triangle, just big enough for a few people to camp in. It would have been nothing if there hadn't been stories of the James Gang hiding out after stealing horses. From the edge of the bluff, he could see the San Bois roll lazily away to the east and west, heavy lines of moppy wilderness. A mackerel sky scrambled the moon. He could see his breath. He held his shoulders.

If he didn't have a car when he skipped town, the woods would be the way he'd go. If he went south, he'd be spotted in Seven Suns. And despite what all the songs and novels said, going west was a bad idea, too. Nothing but prairie and county roads, where people could see you from as far as the Dakotas. He'd go north and east. When he was clear of the whole county (however he got that far, he still didn't know—that was something he was still working on), he could go wherever he wanted. He didn't want to go someplace like Tulsa or OKC. He wanted to go farther. Little Rock or Kansas City, some kind of city. He wasn't sure what he'd do when he got there.

But what if he was gone when his mom came back?

Overhead there was a rustle, and the shadow of a screech owl fluttered across his face like black lace. He turned to take it all in. The overlook had a view of his whole world: the woods, the trailer, the highway—the growl of a dually cut across the space between them, briefly brought him back to the real world—the slow-burning lights of Seven Suns, tucked away in the wooded valley. From a distance, the Quonset hut looked like a turtle making its way from the forest toward the highway. He closed his eyes and imagined it slowly stretching across the road, only to be smashed to pieces by the dually. Maybe then he'd know what exactly was in there. Sometimes he wondered if it had something to do with his mom.

His shadow appeared at his feet, and he turned, heart pounding, to look for the source of the light. Something bright in the back of the cave coalesced into a single point, a luminescence. A firefly. Yellow, red, blue. It moved toward him slowly and directly as if attached to some taut line that ran into the heart of the cave. He stepped backwards, and the point stopped. He closed his eyes and opened them, but the light was still there. He closed them and opened them again, and the light was before his face. And these three visions:

His mother: In the yellow blinking lights of the funnel cake stand at the carnival in the Cushing High School parking lot. The smell of the fried cakes, the sound of screams from the tilt-a-whirl behind them growing louder each time they passed. She was laughing, and powdered sugar covered the front of her black Def Leppard T-shirt. "You're such an asshole, Randy."

His mother: Pulling him from the icy water of the Illinois River, her black hair wet, matted against the side of her face. The sharp burn of cold air in his lungs, the high sharp wind. The sun and the moon were both out, both bleak and high in the gray sky. And then in the car with the heater rattling and wheezing, the way she kept herself from crying, her hands at ten and two.

His mother: Digging, shoveling, the rich smell of soil, the sound of her crystal chimes in the hot wind, which spun the weather vane on top of the trailer endlessly. When she'd started the flower bed, the afternoon had been bright, but now the sky was green and bruised. She shaded her eyes with her hand and looked up at the sky. And Wyatt, looking on from the window at the front door.

And the light was gone.

A deep tearing sound—almost a crunch—came up from the ground within the cave. A scratching, something pushing the dirt back and forth. A copperhead. And a copperhead would strike. The scraping dirt moved closer, and every wet crawling thing he'd ever imagined wound cold up his dress, and he let out a choked scream. The scratching stopped, and he waited.

Its shadow was first, some jagged puppet nightmare against the white rock in the moonlight. Then he saw it—or *them*: human bones, digging their way out of the mud. A shadowed skull and two arms, which flattened themselves against the ground while it heaved its spine and rib cage out of the silt and clay. Red mud clung to the ribs, dripped off like sludge. The bones unearthed their legs next, one at a time, and stood on its hands and knees, looked at him. Its face was expressionless, a fluttering of hollows and shadows that only changed with the light. When it moved it sounded like wooden wind chimes. It cocked its head and regarded him—still expressionless—crawled toward him. He scrambled for the top step of the path back down to the bottom and jumped several rocks down, assured by adrenaline and his animal mind.

From behind him someone said, *Wait.* It said, *Wait. Wait. Wait.*

Instinct took over, and he made it down the tumbledown of rocks at the mouth of the cave without stopping or falling once. He just bounced from one rock to the next like it had been choreographed. At the bottom he stepped into the creek, and the cold water sucked down the top of his boot and filled it, an icy rush. The other did the same, and his feet were heavy as he covered the mile between the cave and the trailer, running where the moonlight allowed it, groping when the dark closed in. At his window, he bent with his hands on his knees, gasped. His feet were numb from the creek water. He stood and put his hands on top of his head, leaned back, gulped down more cold air. The crunch of gravel and yellow headlights caught the tops of the trees above him. Fuck.

He jumped, caught the windowsill with his fingertips, fell back down. Wyatt sang, shouted, sobbed—he couldn't tell which. He jumped up again, grabbed the windowsill, and pulled himself up, hiked up his leg as he heard the front door open and slam and the singing and crying come inside.

The first thing that came off was the wig, which he tossed into the corner of the closet. He pulled the prayer cap off and stuffed it back in the pocket. He was pulling the dress up over his head when Wyatt banged on the door.

"Randy *Strange!*"

Randy found the T-shirt he'd been wearing, and the banging got louder.

"Randy Strange, come out—come out!"

"Fuck off!"

Wyatt banged so loud that the door shook on its hinges. "Randy *Strange!*"

He found a pair of jeans and didn't realize the boots were still on until he tried to put his foot in one leg of the pants and it wouldn't fit. He got on his knees before his closet and searched through every last item until he found a pair of gym shorts. He slipped them on over the boots and stood in front of the mirror, inhaled and exhaled once, crossed the room, threw open the door, and yelled, "What the fuck do you want?"

Wyatt's face looked like a deflated football, some alien sunset—all purples and yellows, something Randy could only call green. Both of his eyes were nearly swollen shut, wrinkled, blue-black. He swayed, one hand on the top of the doorway to balance himself.

"What the fuck is your problem?" He blew past Wyatt into the hallway, hoping to keep him out of his room. It was just what he should have expected after such brief, sweet escape—to come back to things worse than he'd left them. The walls of the trailer felt like they were closing in on him—expanding, closing in, a sort of breathing. Wyatt turned and faced away from the room, and relief washed over Randy, but he remembered the boots and realized he was standing in them in the yellow light of the hallway, fully exposed. He hoped Wyatt's swollen eyes were swollen enough.

"What the fuck happened to you?" He said it with as much disgust behind it as he could muster. Wyatt removed his hand from the door-frame, and when he did, he stumbled, sidestepped into Randy and put his arm around him. He laughed—more of a spitting, exclamatory breath—and patted Randy on the head.

"Randy Strange!" If Randy had to hear his name one more time. Wyatt stumbled back up the hallway to the living room and fell face first into the yellow, corduroy couch. He screamed—from the pain, Randy guessed—but it was muffled by the cushion. He rolled back over. The rubber band holding his ponytail together was almost to the end of his hair, which fell around his face. He pushed it back. "Randy Fucking Strange! So glad to see you. So glad to have a little buddy to come home to. Even if he is a little prick." He laughed.

"What the fuck, Wyatt?"

Wyatt unbuttoned the top of his pants. He kicked off his boots. "So good to see you." He pulled his pants down past his ass, tried to get them the rest of the way off just by kicking. He rolled off the couch, but this time didn't hit his face. "Fuck. Fuck."

Randy got down and hooked his arms up under Wyatt's armpits and raised him back up on the couch. "What is fucking *wrong* with you?" He was tired of waiting and waiting and waiting; he just wanted something to actually happen in his life—just actually *happen*—for some blood to spill or *something*, so he reached back, let everything inside of him push its way through his body and into his arm, and he sank his fist into Wyatt's stomach so hard he heard beer slosh around, and he thought he could feel Wyatt's spine on the back of his knuckles. He said, "Fuck." He got ready to run or jump or whatever the hell he had to do, but when he stepped back he hit the coffee table and fell backwards. Randy's head thumped something fierce against the floor. He felt dizzy and couldn't breathe, and his ears rang. The ringing subsided, and all he could hear was Wyatt laughing.

Randy said, "Fuck you Fuck you fuck you *fuck you!*" He said what he knew Wyatt would hate most: "Fuck you, you drunk Indian." It was a dumbfuck thing to say, because the sound of the phrase pulled every sober string in Wyatt's body taut, and he sat up and bent over the coffee table, grabbed Randy by the wrist. He got down in the space between the couch and the coffee table and with a single swipe cleared off an ashtray and magazines and Coke cans that Randy hadn't taken with him. He planted his elbow on the table, and Randy knew right away Wyatt was going to make him arm wrestle. Which was a thing he did. Which was a thing he did that Randy hated. He struggled against Wyatt's grip, but it was so tight that Randy could feel his hand losing its sensation.

"Let's have a go, buddy."

The horns and the antlers on the walls crowded around them in the dim yellow light.

Randy couldn't make out the expression on Wyatt's face because of all the swelling. It reminded him of a skeleton. He said, pissed: "Sure, yeah," knelt down opposite him, and made his face as mean as he'd ever tried to make it in his life. Maybe he was big enough to actually beat him.

Wyatt must have sensed the thought: "Hell yeah, there you go, buddy—get pissed off." He put his free hand on top of their interlocked hands and swayed and burped and winced at the burp and said, "Ready?" "Fuck you." And they went at it. Randy squared up his shoulder and concentrated on his hand, put his whole arm into it. And he held Wyatt there, dead center. Wyatt grunted and narrowed his face, and the creases that made must have sent a shock through the swollen tissue, because he cried out. Randy's arm started to go. But he kept putting it all out there, opened his mouth and let out a growl that turned into a yell, and his shoulder and arm turned to rubber and then gave out. Wyatt slammed the back of his hand on the table. Normally he'd smile and laugh and say, "Now what do you think of that?" but this time he did nothing.

Randy locked himself in his room and did push-ups until he felt scraped out inside. He smoked a pinch out the window and went to bed but didn't sleep. At some point he thought he heard a knock on the door—this one slow and quiet—*Randy?*—this time a question. But all Randy thought was *Go the fuck away.*

And like Wyatt had read his mind, he did.

17

Earlier: The sun was down, but the sky still glowed rust red when Esther picked her mother up from the Baptist church. She was apparently the last one; Mrs. Hamilton brought Bertie out to the car herself and helped her get in.

"Mrs. Grundel had a wonderful day," she said. She helped her with her seat belt. "Even ate the fruit cup at lunch. Didn't you?".

Her mother looked at her, mouth wide, her lips pulled back in a smile, and made a circular nod that was part agreement and part question.

"That's good to hear," Esther said. "We'll see you on Monday." She got away as quickly as she could. "Guess what, Mom?" But her mother wouldn't speak to her the whole ride home.

She hung her Stetson on the coat rack and kicked off her boots in the mudroom. Bertie hung her cane from the same coat rack. Esther's feet hurt. She could feel the bags under her eyes. She untucked her shirt, took her bra off through her sleeve.

Her mother said, "You know, sweetie. Listen. I really appreciate you giving me these rides. I know I probably don't say it enough, but thank you. I'm starting to think I wouldn't know what to do without you."

Her mother (real mother). Before Esther could think or speak, she hugged her. "Oh Mom." A good night. They were becoming rarer and rarer. And she was beginning to wonder, each time, if it would be the last good night. She hugged her again. "We're going to have a good night," she said. "I recorded *Dancing with the Stars*." She helped her to her recliner in front of the TV and switched it on.

In the kitchen, she put a frozen lasagna in the microwave. She'd had to unhook the stove when her mother left bacon on the range and nearly burned the house down with a grease fire. She felt almost giddy with the prospect of telling her mother all about what had happened that day. Every single detail. She closed the freezer door and read that morning's poem: *Have a Blessed Day*. She searched through the chaos of words cluttered above them like a cloud, found the word *Scare*, and slid it beneath the *Blessed*. Her hand hovered there until the microwave dinged.

She'd never really known anything but living with her mother. Since her father had slipped in the bathtub and split his head open on the faucet when she was six, it had been the two of them. She hadn't dated in high school. She'd seen some men through the years—there was Lionel Kithawk, of course, but that had ended badly. She was at a loss for how to explain it, but she just wasn't that interested in men. Her mother had needed her.

While the lasagna cooled, she stood at the sink and watched the darkness outside. Winding Stair was a dark smudge in the dark night, barely visible. All around them, all around the county, some ten thousand people were getting ready for bed, having dinner, leaving for late shifts, feeding their children, filling their cars up with gas, and she was somehow responsible for all of them. The cold and a great weight came over her and then immediately left. No, not responsible. There were the state police. Her eyes focused on the window, and the hills disappeared. There was nothing but blackness and the reflection of the dancers on the TV behind her.

In the reflection: Something passed in front of the TV screen behind her. She froze and was unable to turn around. Quietly: "Mom?" Louder: "Mom?" Nothing. She breathed and tried to keep the cold spell at bay, but it flooded her all at once. She couldn't bring herself to turn around or to look back into that reflection. Because she just knew that whatever it was that troubled her mind was standing there. She could sense it like any rational animal could. She felt him—her, *it*—in the arched doorway behind her. She squeezed her eyes shut and gripped the counter, her back frozen beneath its gaze. There, in the doorway—she could see it in her mind—every shadow in the house gathered, grew a vacant face, and watched her. She breathed in through her nose, out through her mouth. It came closer, spread across the floors and walls of the kitchen. Then there was a sound—a bristle, like animal hair. The cold licked across the back of her legs.

There was a thud on the counter and the black barn cat meowed, and Esther let out a choked gasp, rattled the dishes in the sink when she jumped. The cat flicked its tail and licked one of its incisors. She gripped the counter again and leaned over the sink, tightened her eyes. She prayed for peace until she was centered again. "How did you get in?" She took it to the back door and put it out. "Am I going to have some things to tell you in the morning," she told it, and it ran beneath the house.

Her cell phone buzzed to life, and she jumped before answering it, bewildered.

"This the sheriff's department?"

Everything sank inside her as she remembered she'd had calls forwarded to her phone. "Yes, it is. Sheriff—Grundel speaking."

"This is Bill Kershaw, and—"

"Oh, hi, Bill."

"I'm not sure if I'm worrying too much, but my daughter, Kitty?"

"Yes."

"Well, she never came home tonight. I've tried her cell phone—the only damn reason I even got her the thing—but it goes straight to voicemail."

She looked at the time—7:47. "You sure she's not just out messing around? It is a Friday night after all."

"Well, she told me she'd be with Betty Hendrix. But I called down to Eaton's Diner, and Betty said she came by the diner but left. Said she was supposed to be seeing a boy named Randy Strange."

A boy. "Now Bill, I don't know how to tell you this, but if she's with a boy, that sounds like something that might be between you and his parents."

He was silent a moment. "Okay, well, that's a good point. Doesn't seem much like Kitty." More silence. "Guess maybe I don't know much about Kitty though, these days."

"Teenagers."

"I'll wait up for her, thank you. Supposed to be out hunting early tomorrow, though. Guess I'll call back."

"You do that." She hung up the phone. Thank you, Lord. Thank you, Lord.

Inside she divided the lasagna onto two plates and got forks from the drawer, but when she came into the living room, her mother was snoring softly in her recliner in the blue glow of the TV.

SATURDAY

1

Del Baker picked up his boots and carried them. His socked feet whispered against the carpet. He pulled the bedroom door shut slowly, stopped just short of the click of the handle, left the hall light off, and crept to Meg's door, where he gripped the handle hard and turned it slowly. He cracked the door—grew still for a moment at a slight creak—and looked in on her. Dead still in the green glow of her fish tank, the bubble and hum of its pump. In the kitchen, he filled the back of the Mr. Coffee with fresh water, dumped grounds in the filter, and turned on the machine, which crackled and steamed, dripped.

And then Meg was in the hall in the trapezoid of faint, liquid green coming from her half-opened door.

"Is it time for Nana Baker's?"

"What do you think, dummy?" He went to her, squatted down on the balls of his feet, his elbows on his knee. She had his and her mother's straw hair, would be tall like him.

"It's too dark to go to Nana Baker's." He didn't want to excite her so she couldn't go back to sleep, but he couldn't resist the way she rubbed at the corner of her half-opened eye, so he grabbed and pulled her toward her, kissed her on the top of the head. "Stole that one." He said, "It's way too early for Nana Baker's. Go get back in bed." The way she ran and jumped in bed was a dead giveaway she wasn't going back to sleep. He

125

watched her until she pulled the blanket up over her head. He closed her door back to just a crack.

It was quiet as death when he pulled his Carhartt jacket on, zipped it up, and stepped down from the kitchen to the back patio into the biting cold of the morning air. His thermos of coffee steamed. He closed the sliding glass door behind him. A nearly full moon hung high and hard in the still-black sky, twilight threatening. He blew into his hands, rubbed them together.

Behind the house, where the neatly mowed grass turned to a brush-hogged field, his gun dog Roxy—a black-and-tan mutt—went wild in her twenty-foot run, each bark a smudge of steam, her body coming out of its seams. He crossed the yard and lowered his hand into the pen, which she sniffed and then licked furiously. "Well hello, beautiful." He patted the top of her head and scratched the backside of her ears.

When he opened her gate, she bee-lined for the bed of his truck. She put her front paws on the side and barked at nothing. Del took his time getting to the truck then opened the driver's-side door and waited on her. He nodded inside at the cab. "Go on." Roxy stood frozen, unsure of what to do. "Now go on." She jumped down and piled into the cab, her tail thumping against the worn bench seat.

He drove his fence line, casually checked the wire, and looked for signs of damage. He found his Angus—what he was sure was all sixty-eight head—huddled together in the northeast quarter-section, where he'd planted the winter wheat. The bright green grass looked alien under the black cattle and the brightening slate sky. A halo of steam from their bodies and nostrils clung tightly above them. Lucy—the fluke red heifer, pregnant when he'd never seen the bull take to her—stood apart from them. She was black in that moment, though, in shadow. He forgot her sometimes, forgot she was carrying. How had she gotten out?

He backed the truck up and turned it around, parked with Lucy in his headlights. She looked up into the light once, craned her neck, and then went back to grazing, her belly low and painful-looking. She was docile—Del climbed down from the truck and fished Roxy's rope from behind the seat. He approached Lucy in the thin white of the headlights and patted her on the shoulder. He looped the leash through its own clip and gently lassoed her with it. Lucy snorted. He walked her like that—like a dog on a leash—toward the back of the quarter-section to the pole barn. He dropped the leash and pulled open one of the red, clapboard doors, moved her inside. He used a pitchfork to bed a sprawling corner stall with six inches of straw hay and turned on three of the overhead heaters, dumped alfalfa in the trough. He stood at the rough wooden gate and watched her.

Outside, the peeking sun was turning the frost into dew into fog. Like every day, he went out behind the barn and took inventory of the wreckage behind the barn: the piles of cinder blocks, the stacks of rebar, the grass grown up around the polycarbonate. Wyatt had insisted they put it together piecemeal, wouldn't consider a loan or simply waiting. He'd wanted to build it himself as it came. But he'd drifted away from that after Darlene never came back. That's what Wyatt had always sort of done—drifted. He'd drifted into the Bakers' lives when they were in high school, welcomed but uninvited. He'd drifted in and out of college, out of his track scholarship. Drifted in and out of his landscaping business and then his taxidermy business. The pot seemed to be the thing that interested him the most, seemed like something he was going to stick with.

Still, it was a risk.

Still, he was his friend.

He had a full day of inoculating to do but instead went back inside. He knew he shouldn't let a hunting dog in the house, but he felt like spoiling Roxy. At the sliding glass doors at the back of the house, she just stood at the bottom of the steps. Her tongue hung out of the corner of her mouth. Del stood inside the open door, his hand on the handle. "Come on." She looked at him. In a serious tone: "Roxy, come." She sprang to obedience, came into the warmth of the house with her tail wagging. In the bedroom, Del kicked off his boots and took off his layers. Roxy jumped into the bed, and he followed her. Her tail knocked against Judy's back, who rolled over like she'd been woken by an intruder.

"Goddammit, Del." Roxy inched forward slowly, overeager, a paw at a time, and then licked at Judy's face. "Goddammit." She rolled over, sat up in bed. He heard her groping for the lamp in the dark, and then the room clicked to life with yellow. Her hair was a rat's nest. "What do you think you're doing?"

"Coming back to bed." He smiled. "My, you look lovely."

She sat up further. "Get out of here. And take this thing with you."

Del pushed Roxy away and curled up into Judy's warmth, kissed her on the back of the neck. He wrapped one arm under her and the other over her shoulder. "I love you."

She reached out and clicked the light dark again. "Yeah, yeah. Bringing that filthy thing in here."

He said, "I love you," and he put the sharp of his chin into the soft of her neck—right where she hated it. She tried to twist away, but he squeezed tighter. He said, "I love you, I love you." He dug deeper with his chin. She pulled the pillow out from under her head and swung it backwards at him, missing. "I love you."

She let out a yelp and laughed. "Fuck you." Roxy lunged onto them both, licked Judy in the face. "All right," she said. "You win."

2

Like every morning, Esther prayed. She opened the drawer on her nightstand and pulled out a diary with a blue ticking cover. She knelt at the bed and opened the book to where the blue silk marker was, examined her inventory of prayers, both personal and for the women in her Wednesday night group. In the mornings she lifted people up—*I lift up Mom: Give her mind peace and fill her remaining days with purpose and Your love. I lift up Ina and Jack: Lay your healing hand on their relationship; bring Jack back to the family, to Your grace; heal his addiction. I lift up Thelma: Be present in Phil's surgery; restore his health and fill Thelma with peace. I lift up the Driscoll family and their new twins: Let them grow up to be godly girls.* She said *Amen* and opened her eyes, closed the book, and returned it to the table.

In the bathroom, she took one of the antidepressants Dr. Fraij had prescribed her on her second visit. She popped one in her mouth with a flat hand, swallowed it without water.

And also: *Lord, please let Kitty Kershaw have come home last night.*

Out the kitchen window, the still-dark earth rolled away from the house toward the paddock and barn. Midnight was nowhere to be seen, probably hiding from the cold in the shed.

The stars died and morning came. Bertie stirred in the hallway and then rattled at the coffee machine, readied a fresh pot in the mote-heavy morning light. She smiled at Esther and joined her at the window, sought out what Esther watched.

Bertie said, "Big plans today?" but before Esther could answer: "I thought I'd go down to see Midnight. Think I'm too old to ride?" She laughed, and it felt like they'd both somehow stepped backwards thirty years, which saddened Esther.

"Not really. But I'm sort of on call today. The whole weekend, actually."

Bertie was still smiling (too long). "On call, you say?"

Esther told her about Gains and Sallisaw and Terry Big Eagle and the fraud and embezzlement and the disappeared deputies. "So guess who's filling in the sheriff shoes for the weekend?"

Bertie smiled and clapped and laughed like a kid. She laughed until she snorted. "Well I'll be," she said. "Well I'll be. Did you know how strange of a world it is?"

"Come on, Mom." She felt like a teenager. "It's just the weekend. All I have to do is keep the town from burning down for two days."

When the coffee was finished, she pulled two mugs down from brass hooks above the window and filled them. They were out of half and half, so she took it black like her mother did. They sat at the table in the crisscrossed light of the bay window. The coffee was too hot—burned and numbed the tip of her tongue—but her body and mind came to life.

"Weekend justice," Bertie said. She laughed again. She pointed at Esther, and Esther noticed her hand shook; the image of a nursing home bubbled up in her mind, and she pushed it away. Right now, she had her mother for a moment. The past stretched before them.

"Listen, Mom. I heard at the church yesterday that you attacked a man? With your cane?"

Bertie looked down at her lap like a child. "He called that Indian a nigger."

"He what?"

"You lock me up in that church all day. Stick me with those pee-pants."
Her head shook, but her gaze was steady on Esther.

And that was that. "Listen," Esther said. "Mom. You cannot be acting
like that when you're at church—you can't be acting like that anywhere.
What were you thinking?"

Bertie drank the rest of her coffee and stood, returned to the counter.
She picked up the coffee pot and raised it in the air like a toast. "Going
wild today."

"Mom."

Bertie moved the coffee pot to her mouth and stopped short, looked
at it. She turned and held it up to the light of the window, inspected
it. "What am I supposed to do with this?" When she turned to Esther,
she looked as if she might cry. Esther went to her, and the tone of her
voice returned to that of a mother and not a daughter. "Put that down,
Mom." She took it from her and poured a small amount in her cup,
hoping the visual of the action would set her mind straight again. But
Bertie simply shook her head, turned away. Esther poured the coffee
down the drain. That moment (all these moments). She wished she
could tie them off with a knot.

She remembered Midnight, but before she left for the pasture, she
left a new line on the refrigerator: *When Days Are Full of New.* She
wasn't sure what it meant, but it sounded optimistic.

As she neared the pasture, her phone buzzed in her pocket.

A familiar voice: "Is this the sheriff's office?"

"Esther Grundel. Yes. What can I do for you?"

"Bill Kershaw here again, Kitty never came home last night."

The impending winter blasted through the crooks and crevices of her
clothes; wet wings struggled to unfold from her throat.

3

WYATT WOKE UP on the couch with a full bladder demanding attention and a five-ton haul of regret telling him he'd better never get up. When he did sit up, the air chilled the saliva that had pooled around his face. His blood dumped from his head to the rest of his body, which pricked with pins and needles. He went back to the bathroom, but before he could get his jeans unzipped to piss, what was left of the booze swirled somewhere inside of him, his head felt fuzzy, and he opened up the toilet lid and vomited. The muscles across his chest felt torn apart. He pissed and flushed and lowered his head into the small square sink, drank from the calcium-crusted faucet. He winced with each gulp. What he found in the mirror compounded things. The bridge of his nose was in the shape of an *S*, the bottom lids of his eyes were purple goblets of blood, the bruises on his cheeks were somewhere between yellow and green, and the white of his right eye was blood red.

One fucking punch.

Why had he gotten into a fight? Drinking, fighting, things he never did. Well, things he'd done plenty of in his time. But not much since Darlene came around. His thoughts moved backwards from the fight—Gordo doing what? Dolly, Dolly, *Dolly*. Shots, beers. And a dark spot before that he could make no sense of. The word *Dolly* heaved up inside of him, and he thought he might vomit again. He'd crossed some line.

Once he'd crossed that line, the fight made sense. No, not sense—it didn't make sense. But it had purpose. He'd wanted to turn the night's fuckups into a singularity, one so heavy he'd have no choice but to cut himself loose from it, to drift away. Sometimes he thought if you were going to go in, you might as well go whole hog.

He swayed over the sink, a hand over his mouth, water dripping from the twisted bridge of his nose. He got close to the mirror and examined it. He stood and shook out his arms, bounced at the knees, breathed loudly through his teeth, pinched the bridge of his nose between both hands, breathed again. He snapped it back into place. Pain shot through his head like a starburst of razorblades. He yelled and yelled again, and when yelling wasn't enough, he kicked the toilet seat—again and again and again. The plastic lid snapped in half and then off, but he kept at it, broke the seat. He kicked at the porcelain then, hell-bent on shattering that too, but it wouldn't budge.

"What the fuck are you doing?" Randy stood in the doorway with a tired face.

Wyatt gave up on the toilet and leaned back on the sink, checked his nose, which was straight but bleeding profusely. He *really* didn't want to fight with the kid right now, and his guilt from the night before was compounded by the memory of the fight they'd already had—the shot the kid took. He probably deserved it, to be honest. The arm wrestling was something his dad used to do to him, and he hated it. Just another thing to jettison. He said, "I guess you saw this last night," and pointed to his face. "You cooled off?"

"Who did it?"

"No one you know."

"I got to get to Squints later so we can get that job done. Can I get a ride?"

"Later. I got something I got to do."

In his bedroom, Wyatt plugged his dead cell phone into the charger at his dresser. The top was covered with loose change, his wallet and keys, random receipts, a stack of mail. A stack of *Darlene*'s mail. He'd been saving it—all of it junk mail except for one bill that had come from the urgent care clinic. Pre-approved credit card applications, flyers from local politicians, postcards from churches, some not marked at all. He sometimes saved the ones addressed to *Resident*, too, liked to imagine they were referring to Darlene.

He tried his best to keep the room closed off from the kid, because it was full of reminders. He wanted to protect the kid from them but somehow couldn't let go of them himself. Darlene's half of the room was still the same mess that she'd left the last day she lived there. Her nightstand was an entire ecosystem—tea-ringed mugs, used tissues, her crystal salt lamp, rings, the tarot cards she was learning to read, a dictionary. She'd once declared that she was going to broaden her vocabulary by reading a new word each night. She'd moved the dictionary to her nightstand, but that was as far as she got.

The floor by her bed was covered in dirty clothes and clean clothes she'd tried on in front of the closet mirror before tossing them to the floor. There were her skintight jeans—the belt still in them—and snakeskins that she wore when they went out dancing. He couldn't move any of it.

The new rifle was up on the top shelf of the closet next to the one possession of Darlene's that bothered him the most—her suitcase. He pulled the heavy black gun case down and put it on the bed, opened it. He already had buyer's remorse—it was just too much *gun*. He'd guessed he might need it since it was a fast animal that he didn't want to get away, but he hadn't even stopped and thought about the fact that

he didn't even know if he was going to kill it. Why would he kill it? To
have the trophy, to show people he wasn't crazy? What if some teenager came across it while out in the woods? He put the magazine in the
rifle, which he hoisted onto his back with a strap.

He needed to check the crop but was too excited to get out there. He
had to deal with Gordo though, the prospect of which filled him with
dread. His battery still wasn't charged, so he stood and made the call
at the dresser. He made and unmade a fist and bobbed at the knees
before pressing *call*. He almost hung up after the first ring, but Gordo
picked up immediately.

"You got a lot of nerve calling, *chico*."

"Listen, Gordo, I know I fucked up—"

"You fucked my face up at least."

"You should see mine."

There was silence on the other end of the line. Then, "What the fuck
ever. No chit-chat. We aren't friends."

"I got to tell you, that's about as drunk as I've been in I don't know
how long, and you didn't even do anything when I got—"

"It don't matter. If it were up to me, I wouldn't do shit for you, but I'm
already all set up with my boy in Tulsa."

Relief washed over Wyatt, and he relaxed a tight fist that he didn't
even know he'd been making. "I can make it right now."

"Tonight. Same time, same place."

The cold air tore at his face as he stepped into the woods behind his
home and headed for the old park road, two ruts that had become his
ATV trail. He went on foot, though, to avoid making a sound. He carried a fold-up aluminum tree stand on his back and a coil of rope. He
held his rifle steady, alert to the fact that the cougar could be anywhere.

He'd frequented the park as a kid, could still feel the heat of camp-fires and the parties that gathered around them. He hunted there now, with concessions from the game warden, Lionel Kithawk, who he'd run track with in high school. Since there was no one else hunting, there was always plenty of game.

At the bottom of the mountains, the deciduous trees held fast. Bare, a graveyard of pink-brown leaves rose around their trunks. Every year mean weather came and went—brutal winds, drought, twisters, ice, and slick-stone hail—but the trees persisted. After half a mile scattered green joined them, the stubbier shortleaf pine. The news that the business with Gordo was back on the table despite his fuckups and the prospect of tracking the cat—of a hunt in general—lifted his spirits. When you hunted, no real trouble could follow you past the edge of the woods.

Much of Robbers Mountain was boulders and rocks, lichen-covered sandstone. Below the cave—which might have held a robber—the water coming out of its mouth had eroded the soil and laid bare its sandstone guts in the form of a forty-foot bluff, which itself had crumpled after a million years and a thousand forked streams. If you knew the place well enough, it was easy enough to get to the cave. During the Depression, when the Conservation Corps had built the place up, workers had painted certain rocks with slashes of red. If you stepped from red rock to red rock, you could make it to the cave.

His theory was that the cat was living in the cave—which is why, when he got close to the top of the insane, red-paint staircase, he veered away from the cave itself so that his feet were on flat, nettled ground. Higher up was the tree where he'd put the camera, got his definitive proof. At the bottom, he uncoiled the rope and heaved a heavy-knotted end up at the branches, where it found purchase in the crook of a thick fork fifteen feet up. He fed slack until the knot was back to the ground, then tied it off around the trunk of the tree with two half hitches.

He hung his rifle from the chair on his back. He reached up and gripped the rope, pulled himself up with little effort, clapped his boots on it and moved himself up again. At the base of the oak's crown, he gripped a thick branch and pulled himself up—and up to another, faced the trunk of the tree and swung a leg over it, straddled it. He pulled his rifle up over the aluminum legs of the stand and rested it across a forked branch above him. He pulled the climber from his back and opened it up, strapped it to the tree, swung himself around and sat in it, buckled himself in, immediately relaxed, then brought the rifle back down and rested it in his lap. He could see the creek and the base of the hill and the cave and the whole east side of Robbers Mountain—everything was quiet. He smiled.

Now that his life was nearly fucked up beyond all measure, he took to finding solutions. He would fix things with Gordo tonight. He'd be ready to go straight with Del. He'd clean out his room and put Darlene behind him. And the kid—he thought long and hard about this one— the kid he would hand over to the state. And just like that: a new life.

Years of hunting and the wisdom he'd gathered couldn't protect Wyatt from a lousy night of drinking, so sitting in the tree stand, high above the ground, he fell asleep, his rifle in his lap and his chin to his chest. He had an inscrutable dream—he moved across the top of a dark ocean, the sky empty, everything black and slick like oil. Something moved beneath him, waving and writhing, smooth and unsure, endless.

He woke to the sounds of rustling leaves and scratching and the vibrations of the tree at his back. He stretched his arms and groaned. When he looked out at the woods—what time was it?—something cold moved over him. His rifle. Gone from his lap. When he looked for it on the ground, he found the source of the rustling and scratching. Something large, something black as midnight circled the tree, wound itself around the trunk. Standing over his rifle.

It stopped and stood on its hind legs, wrapped its front legs around the trunk of the tree and then slapped its massive paws against the bark and scratched. A growl—a low and long snarl, a warning—rose up to him, and a long, thick tail whipped out from behind it.

The black cougar. The black cougar that didn't exist. His mind jumped from irrational scenario to scenario—something escaped from the zoo in Tulsa, something escaped from a traveling circus truck, something released as a joke—none of them made sense, but they were all more likely than what he feared the most. That it had simply always lived there, right in his back yard.

And his rifle on the ground.

The animal stopped, put its front paws on the tree again, and then stepped forward until its belly was flat against the trunk. It snarled again, and he remembered a cougar could climb a tree—had been the one to *invent* climbing trees—and he unbuckled himself and stood on the branch, ready to jump or climb higher, however the dice rolled. He looked up into the branches above him as if there were some sort of exit there, as if he could just save himself by climbing higher and higher until he was gone.

But the lion stayed at the bottom, sank its claws into the bark of the tree and ripped away at the sappy flesh with such force Wyatt could feel it in the tree. It dropped back down and lowered its head, flattened its ears, stabbed its shoulder blades toward the sky. It growled again, and Wyatt trembled so much he lost his balance on the branch and had to reach out and grab another to keep from tumbling down. The cat rolled over, twisted and grinded its back into the earth and leaves, shook its tail. It righted itself and pissed a hard, wide stream with a hiss. It slunk off, wove through the trees toward the top of the hill, then disappeared behind a sandstone boulder.

4

I was so intent on saving Tío on account of the events that unfolded during my time with a man named Elltoo. It was that insanity that landed me in the Jackrabbit Gentlemen's Club and into the arms of Tío to begin with.

After the returns on my born-again trip began to diminish—that's another story—and my truck was stolen at the QuikTrip at the edge of the city, I made it to Elltoo's on foot. My boy in Dallas had set me up with the guy. He was tall as hell and had a sort of caved-in chest. He was about as country-ass redneck as you could get. Lived in a double-wide at the back of a trailer park where you had to call ahead to get in or know the six-digit pin. The place was right off the interstate on the west side of the Arkansas River between an oil refinery and an ocean of bright orange storage units. I had no car and no cash and needed both. So every night—tweaked out of my mind—I'd ride out with Elltoo, and we'd steal window A/C units and cart them back one at a time in the trunk of his silver Celebrity. He sold them on Craigslist.

I told him once, I said Man, you've got to do something about that kid. That kid. It's a fucked-up situation. Can he even read? He just stands around hammering things. Which was true. There was a kid, of course—that's what this particular story is all about.

How could he read? he said. He's three. He bled when he said that.
This guy was ground so fine by tweak that the scabs on his face were
growing beyond my typical threshold for depravity. That should tell
you a lot.

What can I say about Elltoo?

His hands—long twisted-root fingers—were always trembling. He
always cleaned under his fingernails with a toothpick, but only ever
with one hand, so his left hand was always clean and his right dirty.
His eyes reminded me of the bright bulbous nightmares you stick in
Mr. Potato Head's face.

In the master bedroom we stacked the six A/C units we'd pulled that
night on top of the three rows of unsold units. With all the foreclosures
in North Tulsa, business was booming, but that didn't mean everything
was going great. He was always holding, sometimes dealing a little. Real
fucking filthy, stepped-on-chicken-scratch shit. Just brown. But dirty
tweak is better than staring into the eyes of doom.

His girlfriend—I think she was Cherokee—smoked cigarettes on
the bed in the white glow of some four-a.m. infomercial nightmare. He
yammered threats at her and slapped the wood-paneled wall. He always
did that. The walls all around the trailer were pocked with his rage.

They started shouting in Spanish, which always confused me, so
I sat on the couch in the living room next to Elltoo's third source of
income—an unidentified old gray woman with a social security check.
I fired up a bowl and got a nasty twitch. Just couldn't stop the goddamn bobbing—in both my legs and my head. My tongue was so dry
it scraped across my teeth.

The pulse of dreams, the towers of ancient cities, the charnel choirs of
gods who don't exist, who do exist, beyond the edges of space. Roman
candles. You get the drift.

And for fuck's sake: the throbbing primal clank-clank-clank-clank that took hold of my body.

A hammer. The kid—Elltoo's boy—in the corner of the living room banging a hammer on a cinder block: clank-clank. Nothing lazy about it either. He put his whole back into it and punctuated the horrible beat with an occasional grunt. Pieces had broken off from the edges.

And I saw right through the belly of the madness.

What do you got going on, partner?

He stopped and looked at me. The cheek under his blue right eye was black and purple and pulsing. He didn't say anything.

What's your name? We never talk. You never talk.

Daddy says he hates quiet. He never wants quiet.

More drunk than tweaked in the tall grass beyond Elltoo's back yard: I felt the grasshoppers in my bones and watched the bright luminescence dance through the sky and come for me. I watched the red sludge of my face pool on the ground. Something smooth, and my scalp slapped as it landed on the gore.

And then: a bobcat. A great secret. Stalking the prairie since it descended from a crevasse in a continent-sized glacier that spread across the heartbreaking bed of what had once been a great Cambrian sea.

I climbed trees and watched through the windows. Watched them pace and smoke cigarettes and hit their pipes. I watched the boy. The old woman got up twice a day and sliced up hot dogs and melted cheese over them in the microwave. Or opened a can of Vienna sausages. That's what the boy ate. He was too young for school, but he did nothing all day. He hammered or watched TV with the old woman. One night he wandered out back when no one was looking, and I let him find me in the grass. I purred as loudly as possible and nudged him under the chin until he laughed.

What the fuck are you doing? It was Elltoo. The back door creaked and his boots banged down the wooden steps. I backed away and flattened my ears. Something gripped my heart—some black, bilious tumor. The fear in that boy's eyes! That need! But before I could snatch him and drag him away—to some kind of freedom, scattered about in the hills—Elltoo's open hand came down so fast and hard on the side of the boy's head that he crumpled down in the grass unconscious without a whisper.

I tried for Elltoo's throat. I wanted to see and hear the squirt and squelch and gurgle. He fell back from the shock of the sight of me, and I pounced on his chest. The wind went out of him with my weight, but before I could close my jaw and tear out his arteries, he rolled over on me.

A bobcat is not a mankiller. I was crushed under his weight, all four of my legs scrambling. But then the thought of dying—crushed beneath Ell-fucking-too, his hands encircling my throat—opened the great eye of the god of blasphemy and untold worlds within me and I clawed at his face with everything I had. One of my claws hooked the corner of his mouth and I tore out his cheek. That scream! It filled my bones with ice. He was on his back, and I had my breath, and he rolled around the grass like a swarm of wasps were after him, and that's when I went to work.

I tore out his throat and lapped at the spurting blood.

I'd killed two men.

I'd killed ten thousand.

But I'd saved the boy, who breathed shallow in the grass.

I saved no one.

You will follow me past the corpses of dead worlds to your death.

And that's how I ended up with the first Celebrity.

The boy still isn't broken enough. I'm going to rip out that Indian's throat, too.

5

Esther sat Bertie down in her recliner and gave her the remote. She squatted down next to her, rested on the arm of the chair. "Mom. I'm going to have to go somewhere now, okay?" Bertie nodded, flippantly clicked on the TV. "Mom. Please stay right here until I get back, okay? I'm going to put the phone right here next to you. Answer it if it rings. Okay? Mom?"

"Okay. Go. Don't be a rat. I'm fine."

It made Esther sick to leave her. The last time she did, she came home to an empty house with both the freezer and refrigerator standing wide open. After searching every room frantically, she moved outside, unsure of whether to look up and down the street or in the pasture. She'd found her sitting on the ground all the way out by the barn. "I got tired," she'd said. "So I sat down."

Esther leaned over and kissed Bertie on the forehead. "It's not the rat, Mom. It's Esther."

"I know that."

She moved the phone, put on her utility belt, and locked the door behind her.

The whole world was pale except for the deep green pines on the humped horizon on the other side of Seven Suns. Her breath hung before her. She'd be quick about it. Fix the situation and get back to her mother. She drove north.

Bill Kershaw had sounded rushed and exhausted. "I drove half the night looking for her—downtown, the roads out to the house, the school—sat parked, just waiting. But she's not anywhere. She's nowhere. And you told me to wait—to *wait*—until morning, and now it's morning and my daughter is gone. And—"

"Bill," she said. "Calm down. Calm down." She said, "We'll figure this out. I'll call the state police." It was a sensible course of action that simply came to her. She was certain (wasn't) that was what she was supposed to do.

"Well, okay. That sounds promising. What are you going to do?"

"Like I said, Bill, I think calling the state police is the best option."

"I know, but what are *you* going to do?" The cold rushed over her. She said nothing. "Esther? What are you going to do?"

Call the state police. "I'll look, of course."

"What are you going to do?"

"You said she was supposed to be with Betty Hendrix last?"

"Yes. I called. I called. I called over there, no one answered—drove up there, the place was dark."

She'd called the number that Judge Bean had given her and told a captain what was happening. They'd send someone, he said, but they typically waited twenty-four hours. Had she told him that? Had he considered that she might have run away? Did she ask him about that? About friends that might have run away with her?

Her first bit of investigative work was to get Betty Hendrix's address, which she got from Hal at Eaton's.

County Road 289 went up a hill through scattered trailers. Not a neighborhood, really, but a timid collection of recluses. The sun was thin and weak, and the heater barely blew warm. A checkmark of geese floated by overhead. All Esther knew about Betty Hendrix was that she was different than the other weirdos, which was starting to crop up amongst the kids: weird hair, piercings, city kids trapped in a small town. She understood some rebellion, but no one was stopping them anymore; they seemed to be slowly taking over the town. Betty, though, had a kindness about her, even if it was just because she didn't charge Esther for coffee when she was in uniform. There was the fact, though, too, that she went to the Assembly of God church (tongues) and often used the Lord's name in vain.

She stood before the thin metal door of the trailer for a moment and collected herself before she knocked. She pulled her bottle of Carmex from her jacket pocket and quickly smeared some on her lips, smacked. She had no idea what she was doing. She had a vague idea that she should be exuding some kind of confidence but wasn't sure where to draw it from. The less confident she was, the more concerned Betty would be. Her job wasn't to spread worry or panic. Her job was to express optimism and gather facts.

She had to go back and down a step for the door to open. A man with an open shirt exposing a tattoo-covered chest (look away) leaned out with a smile that immediately vanished when his eyes fell on her. His face looked like a bunch of purple grapes, but there was still a moment of horrific recognition before he slammed the door in Esther's face, something that had happened to her a thousand times while working Civil Service. She knocked again. "Sheriff." There was shuffling and what sounded like angry whispers. She knocked again. This time Betty answered the door, her thick purple dreadlocks pulled back in a ponytail. She wore a black cardigan over a silky, floral slip. Esther couldn't help but notice how beautiful she was; it made her feel nervous, out of place.

"Don't worry about Gordo," she said, smiling. "He's just rude. Sorry. Acts a little crazy sometimes." The way she watched the space behind Esther, like she was on the lookout for something, made Esther want to turn around and look. Betty lingered in the half-open door. She wore a kind, false face. "What are you doing out here, Esther?"

"I've got a couple of questions to ask, if you don't mind—about Kitty Kershaw?"

Betty's false smile melted into an authentic look of panic before returning into a faint, half-hearted smile. "Sorry," she said. "Come on in. I'm making tea." She stepped back from the doorway.

Esther wiped her boots on the rug outside and entered cautiously, ducked her head even though the door frame stood a foot above her. The living room was bare except for a couch and a TV. A bay window in the rear of the house was surrounded by succulents and other houseplants, spiny cacti; the whole thing disgusted her for some reason. Maybe it was the way everything grew toward the sun, but all out of order, haphazardly reaching toward the window in a permanent state of screaming.

The man came through a door, which he shut behind him, pulling on the handle until there was an audible click. He stood nervously in the middle of the living room, his arms crossed, knees bobbing. She tried to make eye contact with him; he was shifty and wouldn't hold her gaze. She bore down on him with her stare and, she had to admit, felt a certain thrill. He dropped his arms, and she could see him attempting to compose himself—deep breaths, clenched fists, like he'd been caught red-handed doing some heinous crime he would never confess to (maybe he knows about Kitty).

"What's with the face?" she asked, still high on her inexplicable author ity. She drew a circle with her finger around her own.

"Oh, that? Ha, you know. Just a bit of a mix-up. Too much to drink, you know? My mouth. Sure, ha. Well"—he looked to Betty, who looked to Esther, whose quick thrill had dissolved into confusion again. Was this a part of it? Had it started? What was she supposed to be paying attention to? Whatever was going on, he was hiding something.

"Don't worry," Esther said. "I'm just here to ask your wife?—"

"Gordo, get out of here," Betty said. He lingered in the living room. "Now." She turned to Esther and smiled. "I'm having ginger tea. You like honey?" She led Esther to a bright yellow kitchen, where Esther took off her Stetson and put it on the table, sat. Betty poured the tea into a red mug that read *Joy To The Eggnog*. She added honey and stirred it with a wooden spoon, gave it to Esther. She sat across from her, held her own mug by both hands.

"It's a funny thing," Esther said, unsure of where to start (already started). "Funny thing." She held the mug up to her lips and recoiled at the scalding heat. "I'm actually acting sheriff this weekend." She made an open-mouthed smile.

Betty said, "They indicted Sheriff Gains."

"You know?"

"I hear everything at the diner. I'm surprised I didn't hear about you."

Esther stirred her tea, blew at the steam. "Do you know Kitty Kershaw?"

Betty stiffened, and her smile disappeared.

"Why?" Betty said. "Is something the matter? Is she okay? Did she *do* something?" Her face relaxed at the thought. "She *did* something. What has she gotten herself into?" She put her elbows on the table and leaned over her tea toward Esther, who noticed, for the first time, that the orange, stained-glass light fixture hanging over them was the same that she had in her own dining room. "Esther?"

"Again, I'm here about Kitty Kershaw." She knew that. "Kitty's father says she was with you at church last night. She never came home after that." Should she have said that? Should she have added that last part?

Betty looked panicked. "What? No. No, she didn't go to church with me. *I* didn't go to church last night at all."

"So you didn't see her last night?"

"Well, I did."

The information, even as limited as it was, began to overwhelm Esther. She checked each pocket—slowly, so it didn't come across as panicky—and found her notepad and pen in her front coat pocket. She opened it and wrote *She saw her* at the top of a blank page. She said, "When and where was that?"

"I don't know. Five? She came into Eaton's. Is she okay?"

5pm eatons. "Did she say anything about where she was going?"

Betty's eyes widened. "She said she was going to meet Randy Strange."

The second piece of information clicked into place, and Esther felt that thrill of confidence again. She leaned forward. "Randy Strange?"

Betty nodded.

"What kind of name is that?"

"Oh god. Kitty could see bullshit a mile away, but she wasn't seeing straight with Randy Strange. Did he do something? Where is she? You don't know *anything*?"

"Well, you're the first person I've talked to," Esther said. She leaned back in her chair and crossed her arms. "We don't even know if she's run away or not"—(good)—"I'm just following up on—"

"She wouldn't run away. Never."

"Now who is this Randy Strange? What do you know about him?"

Betty said nothing.

Esther took a sip from her tea, which was sharp with ginger and hot with pepper. Made her wince. She set down the mug and slid it away from her, found Betty staring across the kitchen and living room at the door where Gordo had slipped away. "That have black pepper in it?"

"Randy's just some kid. Goes to the high school. Lanky, has gold earrings. That's about all I know. That and Kitty acted like he'd hung the moon." Her eyes scanned out the window, clearly combing her memory. "I think he lives with Wyatt Whitecloud."

Another click. Esther smiled and then swallowed it down. *Randy Whitcloud.* "He related to the boy?"

"I don't think so."

"Listen," Esther said, growing worried at the growing worry on Betty's face. "These kinds of things happen now and then, and it turns out to be nothing."

"That girl," Betty said. "I put her in God's hands."

Esther reached across the table toward Betty's hands but stopped short. She said, "My mom? I put her in God's hands a long time ago. Sometimes it's all you've got. Is there anything else you can think to tell me? Anything else I ought to follow up on?"

"No." And like that she was overcome with tears, shoulder sobs, a near wail. "No." Esther stood, looked to the door, but couldn't bring herself to pull away from Betty. "No. Nothing. And now I'm never going to sleep again." She sobbed again. Esther moved toward her and stood over her. Betty was a pile of dreads beneath her. She didn't know what to make of it, wasn't sure what Betty was making of it. So she put her hand on Betty's back. Betty looked up at her and smiled. "I'll be okay," she said. "Sometimes I just get a little overwhelmed. Sometimes the Spirit just takes me places, you know?"

Esther relaxed. She wrote her number down in her notebook and gave it to Betty. "Call me if you think of anything or hear anything, okay?"

Betty took the sheet and wiped her eyes with the back of her hand. "Okay, right. We're on it, right?" She gave Esther her number. "Call me as soon as you find her."

Esther put the notepad in her pocket. She picked up her hat and put it on. "I'll look into this Randy Strange character."

But before she could, her phone rang with a strange number, and the calls officially started coming in. The first one was at 9:12, a domestic disturbance at 321 Washington, called in by a neighbor. The call turned out to concern Fred Jackson—the preacher at Zion Baptist, the black church—and his wife Fern. The two had been dancing in their kitchen after having a little too much Boone's Farm, and Fred had fallen backwards and gotten stuck between the washing machine and the kitchen counter. The neighbors had heard Fern screaming and made the call. Esther helped Fern pull him out with a heave and promised them both, upon their request, that she wouldn't mention the Boone's Farm. She was still filling out the report in the car when the next call came—9:58— and she had to leave again. An elderly man at 1819 12th Street had a raccoon in his pickup. He'd caged the thing in his back yard and left it in his truck. The animal had gotten out, and the old man was afraid. Esther told him he should have called the game warden, but the man had, had been told he was too busy chasing drunk hunters. All Esther had done was open the truck door and let the animal out. The man wanted to know if she was going to go to the trouble of resetting the trap. 10:14: Allison Ketchum, a woman in her Wednesday night church group who lived at 217 Choctaw Drive, called and reported seeing a naked man in a cowboy hat stalking the neighborhood. Esther drove the streets for half an hour and then finally gave up. She filed reports for the raccoon and the naked man and decided to just take a stack of blank reports with her in the car.

6

WYATT WAS so excited when he got home that he knocked Darlene's crystal wind chimes off the eaves of the trailer when he threw open the storm door and stumbled inside. The kid was on the couch eating cereal from a plastic cup in his underwear.

"You're not going to believe this." The kid wouldn't care. "Up on Robbers Mountain. The black cougar. *The* black cougar, the one I've been telling *everyone* about? I saw it with my own two eyes." He stood in front of the TV, blocking the kid's view. "I was scared shitless the whole way back it was going to come after me." He saw the image of his new rifle on the leaves below him. "I *could've* killed it—had it dead in my sights, finger on the trigger."

"Wait," Randy said. "Are you serious?"

"Yes. I let it be, though. *Him.* I think it's a him. Seems very territorial. I let him live. He's too great of a sight."

"Seriously?"

"It's a natural wonder, of course."

"No, seriously—you *saw* it. Like you *saw*-saw it?"

"Just twenty feet below me."

"You're full of shit."

"You know what? I don't give a fuck." But he did, and he was surprised to find that it stung.

The kid smiled at him, and the cat's bulging snarl bloomed in his mind. There was a knock at the door and Wyatt jumped, threw his hands up in the air. The kid laughed at him. "Get out of here," Wyatt said. "You don't have any pants on." Randy went to his room and shut the door. There was another knock, and Wyatt opened the door to a brown deputy uniform on a tall woman. She was thin and birdlike and puffy; jet-black bangs poured out from under her Stetson. He thought he recognized her from somewhere. High school? She smiled at him. He felt what his face looked like, and there was a flash of Gordo and a flash of Dolly and a flash of the Red Door and a flash of the Quonset hut and the rich-smelling colas of his harvest, a flash of the black cougar grinding against his tree, and he almost threw up in his mouth. "Hello," he said. He coughed into his hand, which he wiped on his jeans. "What can I do you for?"

"You're Wyatt Whitecloud, right? I didn't place the name, but seeing you now, I'm remembering." She half flinched when she said it, and Wyatt looked around as if to see what she was flinching at. Behind her was some kind of yellow hatchback that didn't look particularly official.

"Am."

"I'm Esther Grundel."

Grundel, that was it. A couple of years behind him, color guard, organized the big prayer chain. "Esther, yeah, of course. Yeah, I remember you." She stood, smiling. They lingered like that there in the doorway for a moment until Wyatt realized her silence was an insinuation that he should invite her in. "Oh. Will you come on in?" He did an inventory in his mind of every legal thing he owned and every illegal thing he owned and where all of those things were as he guided her to the couch.

When she turned, her eyes widened at the horns and antlers around them. She sat. "It's the funniest thing, see." She picked at the fibers on the cushion, and her nervousness began to writhe all over him. "I've found myself acting as the sheriff this weekend." She smiled and pointed to her own badge, gave him a slight, crazy-right smile. "And I'm out looking." She stopped. She held her hands together like a prayer under her chin.

Sheriff?

"Okay," she said. "Let me start again. I'm investigating the whereabouts of an individual that may have come in contact with a Randy"—she pulled out a notebook and opened it—"Strange? That's his name?"

"Yes, that's his name."

"He lives here?"

This was about the *kid*. Was she here to take him? News about Darlene.

"Randy lives here, yes."

"Are you his father?" She put pen to notepad.

"No." His mind raced. "I'm watching him for a friend."

She scribbled something. He craned to see what it was, but he couldn't read her chicken-scratch handwriting.

"Can I speak with Randy?"

"Can I ask what this is about?"

"I told you—he was seen with someone, and I need to ask him about that?"

"Who?"

"Can I please speak with Randy?" She stood, and Wyatt stepped back. He motioned her back down to the couch. "Hey kid," he shouted. "Get out here." No response. "Hey *kid*—"

They waited, awkwardly. Esther said, "Sure is cold out there, isn't it?"

"Sure is," Wyatt said. "Supposed to be a big storm brewing, though—freezing rain. Better stock up, right?"

She smiled. The bedroom door opened and the kid came out, and relief washed over Wyatt.

The kid: "What."

"You got a visitor. Seems you've been up to something. Come on in and have a seat." He came and stood behind the couch, and Grundel had to twist around to see him. "Come around and have a *seat*, man. Be polite. She's got some questions."

"That's okay," Grundel said cheerfully. She stood and turned to the kid. "Where were you, Randy? I mean, last night after six p.m.?"

"Home."

"Can you verify that, Mr. Whitecloud?"

"What was that?"

"Can you *verify* that, Mr. Whitecloud?"

"What, Randy being home?"

"Yes."

"Uh, sure. Yeah. We were here all night."

The kid said, "Who are you?"

"This is the *sheriff*," Wyatt said, smiled.

Grundel said, "How do you know Kitty Kershaw?"

What had he covered the kid for? *Why* had he covered for the kid?

"School."

He was being sketchy. He knew the kid snuck out at night and traipsed through the woods in his mother's clothes. The first time he'd seen a picture of it on his game cam, his heart had almost stopped—it was Darlene, right there in the woods—but there was another picture with the boy's face in plain sight. It was weird, Wyatt had to admit, but it meant nothing to him, neither added to nor subtracted from the way he saw the kid. But he somehow understood that if the kid found out Wyatt had seen, he would hate Wyatt more than he already did. The point was that the kid had secrets. Wyatt could tell he was nervous—he was making direct eye contact with Grundel when he answered her questions, something he never did.

"Did you see Kitty last night, Randy?"

"No."

"So you didn't meet her?"

"Well."

"What? *Well* as in you did meet her?"

"But it was before six. I don't know when. But earlier."

"When she was working?" She wrote voraciously in her notebook.

"No. After. But before later, when you're saying. I was home—ask Wyatt."

"Right. What did she say to you when you saw her? Anything? Anything out of the ordinary? Why were you meeting her?"

"She said she was going home. I didn't meet her, I guess. I sort of just bumped into her downtown."

"Okay," she said.

As she moved toward the door, the kid came around the end of the couch, and Wyatt saw Grundel see it at the same time he did—something red like blood was smeared across one of the thighs of the kid's jeans.

Grundel stopped in her tracks. "Now what's that all about?"

The mood in the room darkened.

"Oh," the kid said. "There was some sort of dog food, or catfish heads or something at the Showbiz." He paused, looked regretful. "There were rats. Someone dumped off a boxful of rats and fed them or something. I slipped in it."

"What?" Wyatt said. "You *what?*"

"You didn't know about this?" Grundel asked. "It just looks a little like blood."

"Why are you worried about *blood?*" Wyatt asked. "Is she dead or something?"

"No, no, no. Nothing like that. No, no. Not at all. Just got to ask questions, you know. You said that happened at the Showbiz? What were you doing there?"

"All right," Wyatt said. He stepped toward the door. "Sounds like we can't help anymore." He motioned toward the door politely.

"Sure thing," she told them. She smiled and waved as she left. Outside she stopped and wrote something in her notepad, tore it out, handed it to him. "Call if you think of anything, okay?"

Wyatt and the kid nodded and closed the door on her. He wanted to know where the kid had been, what his connection to Kitty Kershaw was, what he'd been doing at the old video store. He had so many questions but decided then and there not to care. Not at this point. The kid would be gone soon, and when the kid was gone the questions would be gone. He pried open the blinds by the front door and watched the Grundel lady. She just sat in the car, staring forward. Weird lady.

"I need a ride to Squints's," the kid said. "I mean I guess if I start walking now, I'll be there by midnight?"

"Doesn't that boy have a car? Can he pick you up? I've got big stuff here, kid." But he felt guilty about the night before. "Okay," he said. "But put a different pair of pants on. We'll burn those later. You know, about last night—"

"Yeah," Randy said. "I'm sorry. I really fucked you up."

7

RANDY DECIDED that all black was what he was going to go for. But to his surprise, a pair of black jeans were the only thing he owned. While Wyatt was in the bathroom, he pilfered his closet and found a black pearl snap. It was a stupid outfit, he knew—it didn't look Goth at all. As soon as he got paid for cleaning out the shed, he'd go to the consignment shop by the sale barn, pick out a few things. He wondered where he could find a wallet with a chain on it. That would be a good find.

Wyatt opened the door without knocking and caught Randy looking at himself in the mirror.

"The *sign*," Randy said.

Wyatt looked him up and down, and Randy suddenly felt seen, found out. It was the same way that Principal Flood made him feel. "What's with the getup?" Wyatt asked.

"No getup."

"That my shirt? Looks like my shirt."

"Can you just give me that ride to Squints's?"

Randy couldn't believe that Wyatt had covered for him, and to be honest, it felt like it might point toward more trouble than what the sheriff lady might have caused. He was safe, though, for now. Most of the ride to Squints, Wyatt was on the phone with his pal Del, raving about the cougar. So much raving—*crazy*, almost—that Randy realized that there probably wasn't a cougar. Which also didn't bode well.

"Fuck the inoculating—just get your ass over there," Wyatt said before hanging up the phone. He dropped it on the bench between them and gave Randy a side-glance. "What did I cover for you back there? Were you at home?"—but before Randy could answer—"And what were you doing around that video store downtown?"

"Nothing, man. Jesus. Take it easy. Was that really the sheriff?"

"No. I don't know."

"Didn't she say she was?"

"Yes. What did I cover you for?"

"Fucking nothing. I know that Kitty girl, okay? We hooked up last night and made out a little, after she got off work."

"You don't have a girlfriend. I can tell you that. What's going on?"

"That's it. She's not my girlfriend. We just hook up sometimes."

Wyatt pulled the truck over by the Shermans' mailbox. He gripped the wheel. "Listen," he said. "This isn't a good time to fuck up, okay? I need you to keep your shit together. You understand?"

"What are you talking about?"

"Just keep your shit together, okay?" .

"What's with all the black, yo?"

"What's the fucking problem? So I decided to wear black today."

They sat out back of the shed in the weed-choked gravel and shared half a joint that Squints had found in his ashtray. It was different than the kind they'd been smoking. Not as good, but the change in strand got them as high as they'd been in a while. He told Squints about the black cougar and Wyatt's face and the arm wrestling. He told him that he almost won.

"Yeah, I bet," Squints said. Randy couldn't tell whether he was being sarcastic or not. "That black mountain lion thing is crazy, yo. Wyatt is one fucking crazy Indian."

"Don't be fucked up, man." He felt bad for saying it. "And—the cops came by this morning. Freaked me the fuck out."

"What? And you're just telling me *now*?"

"Well, it wasn't a big deal, really. I mean it *was*, but not really. They found out I saw Kitty last night—"

"You saw Kitty last night?"

"I was the last one to see her last night." He heard himself say it out loud. "Oh no," he said. "This shit *is* a big deal. She saw the shit on my pants."

"What shit? What were you doing with Kitty?"

"I sold her some weed."

"Wait, you have some money?"

"What? No. Are you listening?"

"What happened to Kitty?"

"I don't know. I tried to call her, but it went to voicemail."

"You guys call each other? Why are you hanging out with Kitty so much, yo?"

"And she saw the shit—the cop—she saw it. Why did I put those *on*? I'm *fucked*." He could tell Squints didn't understand but didn't want to mention that he'd told her about Showbiz, too.

"Well, did you do something?"

"No."

"Then fuck it. It's kind of badass if you think about it."

The knocking of the wooden wind chimes on the front porch travelled across the yard to them, and Randy felt a chill. The image of the skeleton arose in his mind. He tried to shove it down. Had that been his mother? Had that been real? It obviously wasn't real. He'd nearly forgotten about it, after all.

They stood in front of the shed and assessed the situation, which was bleak.

"Goddamn, yo."

"I bet we can knock it out in an hour or two if we really go at it."

"Bullshit, no fucking way."

It was some long-dead farmer's tool shed—gray, weather-beaten wood boards for sides and a corrugated steel roof. At some point it had been turned into a graveyard for busted furniture, rusted tools, rusted nails, and rusted appliances. A real tetanus hellscape. Squints's mom wanted it to be a garage.

Squints said, "This is going to take all day."

They put on leather gloves and moved everything to the dumpster Squints's mom had rented. It was cold, but all the movement and work eventually warmed them up. Squints's sweat steamed from his shoulders and head. They pulled out a set of eight school desks—one of which had a nest of black widows in it—and found matching chairs stacked up behind those. They moved a broken-down bed frame with a rusted brass headboard. Randy went through four shelves of tools, one at a time, and checked to see if they were salvageable. He threw them all away. There were two busted lawnmowers, a piece of a tractor that Randy recognized but couldn't name, a pink Formica table with two legs. They worked and choked on the dust they kicked up. But fuck it felt good. They were doing something—actually accomplishing something—and not just being fuckups. They worked for hours until the whole place was clear except for an avocado refrigerator on its side in the back and a massive wall-unit air conditioner sitting on the arms of a backless rocking chair.

They stood with the A/C unit between them. They stood and breathed and stalled, not wanting to move the hulk of steel and copper piping but wanting to be done with the job.

Squints said, "Okay. I guess we ought to get this fucker done with." He wiped his forehead with the bottom of his T-shirt.

They were about to pick the beast up when Squints's mom came around the corner of the house. Randy could tell by the way she had to stop and lean against a tree that she was drunk. No: drunk as hell. She came toward the shed trailing cigarette smoke from the limp hand in front of her face. She stopped midway and reached down and pulled off her shoes one at a time. She'd been wearing high heels. She stepped carefully through the gravel. "How you boys doing?"

Randy said, "Fine."

"What's with all the black, Randy?"

Squints said, "He just likes black, Mom, so whatever."

She wore gray sweatpants, a black sports bra, and a pink bathrobe that hung open. She held her high heels in one hand, smoked with the other, and smelled like vodka. "Jesus, Randy. You're getting big." She dropped her shoes, which clattered on the gravel, and leaned on Randy's shoulder. "You're getting strong, aren't you?" She slid her hand up his rolled-up shirt sleeve and squeezed his bicep. "Yes you are." Randy didn't like her touching him. But he had to admit it was nice that people were starting to notice the weightlifting. She blew smoke in his face. "Oh my god, I'm so sorry—that was an accident."

"Sure, yeah."

"I came out to bring you boys some water. But look at me! I forgot it." Her hand was still up Randy's sleeve, had made its way up to his shoulder, which she squeezed.

Squints said, "Leave him alone, Mom."

She turned to face him. "Son—" and she started to say something, but it came out in a long slur. She cut herself off. "Son, are you going to finish this or stand there like a do-nothing?"

Squints nodded at Randy. Randy decided he'd better follow his lead because Squints's mom was seriously freaking him out. Wyatt was a huge pain in the ass, but at least he wasn't mean like that. Just down-right fucking mean. For the most part. And he also wasn't Randy's flesh and blood. So they got underneath the unit and lifted, and just when it was off the rocking chair, Squints said *Holy fuck holy fuck holy fuck set it back down* and Randy said *No don't be a pussy, it's already up* and Squints said *Holy fuck holy fuck fuck fuck the edge is cutting into my hand* and Randy said *We already got it up!* and Squints's mom said *Yeah, son, don't be a pussy, get it up,* and Squints dropped his end and fell back-wards. The unit crashed down and broke the arms of the rocking chair, tumbled face-first into the ground. Dark liquid pooled out into the dirt.

His mom gave a *just-what-I-thought* snort, and Randy felt sick. Half of her cigarette was just ash. It broke and fell down the front of her bathrobe. She looked Randy up and down. "Go on, hot stuff: show him." She pointed at Randy and then the A/C unit with her burned-out cigarette. Randy just stood there. "Go on."

He looked at Squints for some kind of information: a signal, a look, an anything. But he just sat on the ground with his knees up and his head down.

She pointed at the steel box again. "Just show him how a fucking man does things." She reached into her bathrobe pocket and, when she found nothing, reached into the other, pulling out a cigarette, which was broken in the middle. She tore the end off and felt in her pocket again, brought out a lighter and cupped her hand over the end of the cigarette, lit up. "Go on now." She pointed at the unit. "Show him how a man does things."

A lump was forming at the back of Randy's throat. She leaned in and put her cheek on his shoulder, blew out a cloud of smoke that caught in the wind and blew right back into their faces. Randy's eyes watered, and the lump grew so thick he couldn't breathe. She ran her hand down to his rear end, squeezed.

The cherry of her cigarette found the back of his hand, and when he winced, his shoulder knocked her chin, and he could hear her teeth clack together. He pushed her away and she stumbled, stepped on the end of her loose bathrobe belt, and went backwards. Her arms churned, and she crumpled to the ground and cried out.

Squints cried *Mom* and went to her, tried to help her up, but when he reached down, she balled her hand into a fist, raised it up, and brought it down on his arm, right where his tattoo was. "Goddamn you," she cried. He held his arm in his hand. Randy could tell that Squints was about to start crying but doing everything he could not to.

Randy said, "Mrs. Sherman." He stepped toward her.

"Stay away from me." She slapped at the air. "Goddamn you. Goddamn you both." She stood and examined her elbow, where blood had begun to soak through the pink fleece.

Randy squatted down, put his hands under both sides of the A/C unit, and lifted. His back and his arms and his legs caught fire, but he stood, held it at his hips. He wished he'd picked it up a minute earlier, thought about what it would have looked like to drop it on her head. He lugged it the twenty feet to the dumpster, heaved it up over his head with a shout, and dropped it down inside, where it crashed against the side and then shattered on a stack of windowpanes. It hurt Randy's back so bad that he cried out. When he turned back to the shed, Squints watched him alone.

He put his Carhartt jacket back on, and the two of them went to the backside of the shed, sat on the ground, and leaned against it—their legs spread out in front of them, their shoulders leaning into each other.

It was too cold to hang outside, but cold was better than Squints's mom. Randy didn't know what to say, but he knew he should say something. And it might as well at least sound like something he felt.

"Your mom's fucking shit up."

"Yeah, what else is new?"

In the long silence that followed, Randy considered making Squints a part of his master plan. "Why don't we split town together? You've got a car. Ditch your mom. I got no one to ditch. We can get out of here."

Bones, bones.

"No way," he said. "Someone's got to take care of her."

They smoked a bowl and then another. Randy pulled hard on the pipe, and the cherry crackled and glowed orange. He tamped it down with the edge of the lighter, passed it to Squints.

"Yo, you're pretty fucking strong."

"Thanks, I guess. It feels good to actually do something, you know?" But he regretted saying it because it sounded stupid and probably ruined the moment. Squints didn't say anything. Randy could feel him getting closer, could feel his shoulder turning against his. He could hear his breath, which grew hot and fuzzy on Randy's neck. Randy didn't look at him—it was cool, they'd done all that work together and were tired and sort of like one person—and Squints kissed him on the cheek. Something got going in Randy's blood like a pumpjack gone mad. He turned to Squints, who kissed him on the mouth with wet lips. Randy pushed him away but didn't say anything.

They sat next to each other in silence. The sky was so big and gray it broke Randy's heart. A contrail from a jet pointed down toward Tulsa. Squints stood, picked up a piece of gravel. He ran after the jet and threw the rock at it. Randy followed it with his eyes until it winked out in the sun.

8

BUT BEFORE Esther could get to the old video store to check out Randy Strange's story, she got a call from Elvis Kithawk at the Red Door. "You got to get out here right now," he said. "There's a brawl going on in the parking lot." Silence. "Who is this?"

"Sheriff Grundel."

Silence. "Esther?"

"The sheriff—that's what matters. It's barely noon, Elvis. You've already got fights going on?"

"*Grundel?*"

She hung up.

She sat in the car and looked out over Wyatt Whitecloud's view—the wooded descent to the foot of Green Moon, the blue ridge and gray sky. In these very mountains, outlaws and moonshiners had hidden, tucked away in the caves and crannies of the hills. That was how Wyatt Whitecloud had felt to her: shifty, guilty. Pummeled face. And that suspicious-looking Quonset hut.

She weighed her options.

Surely, if she took her time, the brawl would be over when she got there. Even that word, *brawl*: violence (animal).

She gripped her taser. Maybe she shouldn't walk into a violent situation unarmed; there were side arms in the quartermaster's closet. She knew how to operate all of them, but the thought of the weight of one on her utility belt made her heart beat faster than the prospect of walking into a fight without a gun. Besides, she wasn't really the sheriff. She was just what they were floating over the weekend.

The coldness in her spine abated when there was no fight in the Red Door parking lot when she arrived. Inside, the smoke made her eyes water. She hoped she didn't look like she was crying. Elvis Kithawk, who had a gnarled, blooming red nose (alcoholic), greeted her at the end of the bar by the door. "You're too late. They're both gone. Where you been, anyway?"

"Who was it?"

"Rob Dale Ray. And that preacher freak you see around town sometimes. You know the one?"

She did. His face and neck were covered in scabs. He was no preacher. She pulled out her notebook. *Rob del Ray, preacher. Elvis kithawk, red door.*

"They've been gone almost an hour." He leaned forward. "Maybe we need a bit more police presence around here," Elvis said. "Had one last night, too. Gordo Ramirez and Wyatt Whitecloud."

Click. She pulled her notepad out. She said, "Disney cartoons all over him?"

"That's the one."

Gordo whitcloud fight red door Fri—"What time?"

"I don't know, ten? Eleven?" *10?11?* "Why'd they send *you* of all people?"

"Because I'm the one"—but she didn't know how to finish the sentence. Esther Grundel: the only one they got left. "It's Sheriff Grundel, now." She pointed to the five-pointed star on her jacket, which she'd gone out of her way to pick up from the quartermaster's office (missed fight).

He laughed. He threw a towel over his shoulder, snapped his gum, and yelled down to the end of the bar. "Hey Ernie! We got Esther Grundel here. *Sheriff* Esther Grundel."

Ernie's eyes widened. He said, "What the fuck?" He said, "What the actual fuck—you serious?" He got down off his stool and made his way down the length of the bar. Esther had just seen him in lockup the day before. One of the ones she'd prayed for. As she should. Due process. The man had served his time. She made a mental note to start praying for the well-being of men and women who left lockup. Surely it was hard for them to function. Surely it had already been hard, and that's why they were there.

"Ernie."

He got close to her with his small-pocked face and his stubble and his long, thinning hair and the smell of cigarettes. "Sheriff Grundel." For a moment he seemed to tremble, to shake with anger or hate. He turned to Elvis and laughed. He hung his mouth open in mock surprise. He looked back to Elvis, but Elvis wasn't laughing. "You gonna arrest somebody?" A flicker of cold and she realized that her hand was on her hip, just above her taser. Elvis took the towel off his shoulder, swung it over the other shoulder.

"Ernie," he said. "I don't know if you want to go talking to her like that."

"Like what?"

"I guess you didn't hear about what happened yesterday?"

In the small space between the ceiling and a bright red Budweiser clock high up on the wall: a nest, its face a hundred mindless holes. Something was clicking down in those daubed tunnels, she knew it. She said, "You got a wasp nest up there." Elvis turned and looked, shrugged.

"What happened yesterday?" Ernie asked.

"Your bailiff-sheriff over here whooped a whole courtroom, sent Hooky Miller to the hospital."

"Hooky's in the hospital?"

Esther shed herself and leaned into it. She stepped toward Ernie and rested the heel of her hand on her taser, pressed down hard enough that it squeaked just a bit in its holster. "And what about you, Mr. Burkhart? You got anything to say about this so-called brawl?"

Ernie hesitated a moment and then shrank away. She took another step toward him. "How about it, Mr. Burkhart? You think consorting with fellows like this"—and she flipped open her notebook even though she knew who they were—"this Rob Dale Ray and this stranger is going to end up settling well with the terms of your probation?" She didn't know the terms of his probation, wasn't sure if there was even a probation officer around anymore.

"No, ma'am—I've got nothing to say." And that ugly, mean look came back. He tried to lean in, but she wouldn't allow it. "We stick to our own around here."

"Mighty fine of Mr. Kithawk here calling me in so y'all can stick to your own." Ernie shot Elvis a look and Elvis snapped his gum, threw up his hands in a joke surrender.

In the car she threw the notepad on the passenger seat and nearly hyperventilated. She coughed from the burn of smoke on her lungs and wished she could scrape the taste of the place off her tongue. She wanted to cry. She took slow, measured breaths to keep herself level. She could feel every fear in the world sitting in the seat right behind her.

When she called her mother, Bertie was cogent and safe and eager for Esther to return. When she called Brock, he agreed to help her out.

Measures of peace.

9

THE BEAUTIFUL and strange events that led me to meet Elltoo:

But first, the last thing I remember about my daddy:

He said Take this. And then I don't want you coming around here again. He gave me a thousand bucks and a truck. I'd disgraced him, I guessed, but the concept didn't register with me. What did I actually do to him? What do we actually do to anyone?

Jesus it's too much to think on.

Things weren't that bad then—Down in Dallas I'd been loaded a lot, messed with a little tweak but nothing major. Not right then. Then I was mostly into booze and coke. It's funny what a couple of drinks will get you into.

But then my daddy died. So I drove back up to Muskogee (oh the insanity of that trip—but that's another story).

But I couldn't bring myself to go to the funeral.

The liquor and the coke weren't doing it for me anymore.

I might've gotten into speed then or the general thrills of a life of crime, but I knew what I needed was the Holy Ghost.

And wouldn't you know it, Good Faith Bible Baptist was still at it, dunking the newest addition to Christ's Beautiful White Bride in Chuck Bee's cow pond.

They said We're sorry about your father. They said He was a real pil-
lar in the community. I nodded and listened. This was at a Wednesday
Night Life Group. I'd moved into my daddy's house. I was lining up
my attack. Just like tweak or any high, I already knew that the Prodigal
Son trip had diminishing returns.

I sank down in a red loveseat surrounded by shining, beautiful, loving
folks. I didn't say much and acted skeptical. Good lord I could smell
their silent prayers for my soul. A salty smell, like tears. Warm, warm,
warm, man. *Cozy.*

Did they know who I was? Could they feel it? Could they see the
kaleidoscope of hate and love, the bottomless bondage, the oppressor in
the field, the biting cosmic despair that shakes the stars and the planets?

What they saw was some dumb hick teetering on the edge of junky.

Later their low-lit faces were slick with tears and I kneeled, their
moist palms and sweater sleeves gathered around my head, and I wept
and told them about the drugs and the booze and the manslaughter
and the disappointment I murdered my father with and I cried and
cried and cried. Etc.

Those people and their boundless hearts! Their hopes for the good
of the world in my hands. I made it work awhile anyway. I glowed.
I looked to the skylight above me and imagined my sins a black smoke
twisting up like a double helix from my chest. I said I accept the New
Life. I said I want New Life.

But the golden glow was fading, and my animal mind started calculating and told me what I had to do to stay alive.

So I found a little tweak and found a connection in Tulsa named
Elltoo through my boy in Dallas.

Weird weather when I got to Tulsa. It was warm and the sky was dark with heavy clouds bearing the neon orange of sunset on their backs. I stopped at a QuikTrip at the edge of town for cigarettes and tried to prime myself for a series of doomed questions of which the calculations necessary to answer would destroy your mind.

Clear reflection in the wet blacktop.

And what happened next.

I watched the overcooked hot dogs spin on the warmer up by the counter.

The clerk said You wanna buy something?

What?

But the lights dimmed—just a dip, but enough that the cash register and cooler and soda fountains restarted themselves and the glass across the front of the store shook in its frame but didn't break.

The clerk: What in the hell is this?

Listen, I've seen this before.

What is it? Nothing else was happening, but for some reason we were shouting. I read his name tag, smooth and white. Listen, *Clint*, things are about to get weird. Just be still, man.

They call the thing an updraft.

The clouds grew into a thick gray wall. The sky turned green. It was one of those times when it's the middle of the day, but the sun's been swallowed up. Not night, though. Like a third time of day. When you look up at the sky and even though you know you've looked up into that sky before—blue and blazing with sunlight or black and full of stars—then, with the clouds blackening just above you, suffocating the earth, you have no idea what lies beyond, and for a moment you feel safe in the womb of terror.

Clint said There weren't tornado sirens. He was down from his cash register, standing at the door with his hand pressed on the glass, holding out against all that gray weirdness.

Not a tornado. Just watch. I was eating one of the hot dogs and couldn't stop smiling.

A telephone pole went down first; then two fifty-barrel steel trash cans in the parking lot shot forty feet up in the air and blew across the highway like newspapers. There was a minivan under the canopy that rocked mad. And outside of it a towheaded girl yanked on the door handle. Then the rain came. Horizontal rain, drops fat as cotton bolls, splashing across the glass front of the station, the world upside down.

In a moment like that, you feel small again. Everything stands out to you as nothing but a possibility, a roll of the dice, the universe.

And in eight minutes, it was over. Man, you live in a moment like that—a moment like *that*—and I tell you what: You'll never wish for another kind of moment the rest of your life, believe me.

What in Christ's name are you doing? This middle-aged man with a bald spot but long hair in the back blocked the entrance to the store. I was outside, with the girl in my arms. One arm draped around my neck and her head on my shoulder. Sunlight marbled through the dark clouds. I handed her to him. A chance to set it right. But she started crying, and he pulled her away from me so quickly she fell to the ground. He was crying, too, when he scooped her up and ran back to the minivan.

I went inside and bought cigarettes and tried to make conversation with Clint. Did you see that? What was that all about? Good lord.

I think you walking through the rain and picking up that little girl made the guy a little uneasy.

I looked down at myself and saw that I was soaking wet for the first time.

Did you know her?

I didn't get a close enough look.

I am the cataclysm of your mind. The beauty of fiendish dreams. The fury of electric thought.

I was supposed to hook up with a man named Elltoo in North Tulsa, but when I went back outside my truck was gone.

10

Wyatt filled a milk jug with water—his only hope at curing his hangover—and took it with him out to the Quonset hut. He believed what the kid had said to the Grundel woman, but something about it stuck in his craw. He'd just seen Kitty the day before.

People disappearing.

The grow was a whisper at night but a roar during the day. Each of the seventeen lights—burning hot and bright—were cooled by high-powered eight-inch fans. The purple-green sea that greeted him calmed him for a moment. They meant solitude, repetition, a world unto himself. Beyond the halo of light around them was nothing but darkness. He inspected the plants and sang to them. He sweat under the heat of the lights and drank from his jug. He took a sample of runoff back to his particleboard room and tested the pH level.

He and Del were going to grow differently than Wyatt did in the Quonset. They'd decided on hydroponics. Del had been against it because of the initial costs and all the maintenance and supervision it required, but Wyatt had convinced him. After all, Wyatt would be the one doing the maintenance and supervision. It meant regulating pH and nutrients with more ease, greater yield and strength. The horticultural perfectionist in him couldn't resist the idea of cleaner, more potent pot. There were more variables involved, but that just meant there were more variables for Wyatt to tweak to perfection.

Darlene would have loved the idea of he and Del working together, doing something above board. She'd grown tired of him being a criminal—a view he didn't have of himself—and wanted him doing something responsible, especially with the kid around. *Especially with Randy around.* He wished she could tell him what that meant. Dolly rose up in his mind like a bubble of air, and his body tensed. He'd done nothing wrong but felt sick. He squeezed his eyes tightly, pinched the bridge of his nose, and bobbed his knees until the feeling passed. He looked out over his plants and felt the sudden urge to just destroy it all—to kick each table over and tear the lights from above, smash them on the ground—but he was too tired, too hungover.

Those thoughts were gone, though, at the sound of Del's shocks bouncing over the trailer's uneven drive.

A hunt would clear his mind.

"Hell, Wyatt, what happened to your face?"

"Well."

"I mean, look at that face." Del pulled a canvas gun case from the cab and swung it over his shoulder.

"Yeah," Wyatt said, unsure of what information he wanted to spill and in what order. "I got into it a bit last night at the Red Door." He avoided eye contact with Del, instead took a step toward Del's truck so he could look at the dog, Roxy, in her cage.

"Who was it?"

"Gordo."

"Gordo?"

Wyatt kept his eyes on Roxy, who was whining, running tight circles, desperate to get out. "Well," he said. He looked Del in the eye. "I got drunk and fought with Gordo, yeah."

Del turned and looked at Roxy, too. "You got *drunk?*" He leaned into the back of the truck and opened the dog cage, whose hinges screeched so loudly a blue jay scared from a nearby tree. Roxy bounded out of the bed and beelined for Wyatt, who patted her on the head.

"And now I have to try and make the switch again tonight."

Del said nothing. He looked well rested, and Wyatt resented him for a moment. He put his hands on his hips and shook his head. "What in Sam Hill were you doing?"

"I was drunk, that's it. Gordo started—*condescending*, you know? If you knew him, you'd understand. If anything, he's had this coming a long time. He's always begging for a fight. But don't *worry*. I've got it covered. We're meeting tonight. So don't get all worked up."

"Worked up? You—Worked up?"

"I said I'd take care of it."

"And now this business with the cougar"—he gestured at the woods—"I don't know, bud. I don't know. Did you call Kithawk about this?"

"He laughed me off the phone. Told me not to go looking for it. He sounded a little pissed, actually."

They both put their gun cases on Del's open tailgate. Wyatt unlatched his and pulled out his new rifle. The image of it lying on the ground beneath him that morning flashed, and he was embarrassed at what Del would think. He checked the chamber and then clicked the magazine in place. He thought about chambering a round and didn't.

Del said, "I still think that's pointless, but I've got to admit it's a tough-looking gun." Roxy ran to the near distance, looked back at them. What was left of her tail shook feverishly. "Whoa," Del said, and she stilled.

"You know how I feel about bringing a dog on a hunt, Del. I give you shit about it being a pain in the ass, but this is different—we're talking about a real predator. Roxy's likely to get eaten up before she does any good."

Del visibly stiffened. He fed .35s into the side of his rifle, a short, cherry-wood-stocked lever action, each cartridge glinting white with sun before disappearing with a click. "Maybe she'll tree the thing," he said. He held out his rifle, cradled it with a hand at each end. "See how short that is? See how many rounds the chamber holds?"

"I never heard a man brag about his little dick before."

"It's about *impact*. Technique. It's about listening to the quiet and waiting for the animal and using your mind instead of chasing them through the woods splashing lead everywhere in hopes you'll take it down. This weighs less than seven pounds. It's about *portability*."

Wyatt considered regretting asking Del over.

They took the ATV trail by foot. Wyatt strapped his aluminum tree stand to his back, and they both carried their rifles. Ahead of them, beyond the rocky hill, the dark back of Green Moon Ridge cut a clean line against the cold, bleak sky, serrated by blackjack and pine.

"I'm supposed to be inoculating all afternoon. And that's because I was supposed to be inoculating *yesterday* afternoon. You better be serious about this. And why are we walking?"

"We're not going to find it if we announce our presence with the ATV coughing up exhaust for a mile."

Roxy ran ahead of them, her tail wagging mad, and sprinted away, disappeared behind a boulder.

"Don't you worry she'll just run off some day?"

"She'll be back. If she runs off, I don't want her anyway."

There was a cold wind, and Wyatt regretted not bringing another layer, a shell of some kind. "Do you believe what they're saying about the storm?"

"Hell, I don't know who to believe any more. But it's a reason to get going. That and the sun setting. The last thing I want to do is hunt some mystery cougar out in the dark."

"Listen, I didn't tell you—Have you heard anything about Esther Grundel being *Sheriff*?"

"What? Who?"

"Her dad ran that horse place. We were in school with her for a year."

"I don't remember her."

"Well, I guess that takes all the shock out of the story."

"What happened to Gains?"

"Gone somehow. She was asking questions about Kitty Kershaw—she ran away is what it sounds like, and get this, the *kid* was making out with her. So the new sheriff came asking questions."

"Randy?"

"Right?"

"So you've got the law snooping around here now?"

"Well—she wasn't exactly snooping around. Just asking a few questions about Kitty. She was driving a little yellow hatchback, for Christ's sake."

"Hell, Wyatt, it don't matter. You can't have the law crawling around. We're *this* close"—he held out his fingers in the air as if to measure an inch—"and that *kid* is going to fuck things up for us?" He looked thoughtful. "That is if *you* don't go and fuck things up first." He didn't use the word *fuck* very much.

Eventually they made it to the picnic area, the broken-down remains of one of the old state park amenities. Now it was only a rotting table and a steel-drum fire pit rusted through with holes. He remembered eating boiled eggs and fry bread with his family when he was ten and the park was still open, and he was hit with the excruciating pang of loss that sometimes accompanies the memories of the most unremarkable of things. The picnic area overlooked Olim Creek—gurgling and white-capped—a tumbled-down rock footbridge—and Robbers Mountain beyond.

Del said, as if picking up his train of thought immediately from where he'd stopped speaking last—"Deciding not to do that last crop, running around the woods chasing some rumor, getting drunk, getting in fights." He paused as if to consider what he was going to say next. "Months now—You haven't been the same since Darlene left."

Wyatt tensed at her name. "Now hold up," he said. "You don't know—"

"I'll tell you what I do know," Del said. His Boy Scout face had grown flat and mean. "You got a chance here to get yourself straight, to do some straight business with a friend and make good money. Why don't you start acting like it?"

"I'll tell you what *I* know," Wyatt said. He stepped toward Del and pointed a finger at his chest. "You already *got* a straight thing going. You need *me* to get this up and running. This is something *I'm* doing for *you*." He felt the impulse to shove him, to get his nose broken for a second day in a row.

"Calm down, Wyatt. Just calm down. I'm just saying—You ought to get rid of the kid and get moving on with your life. Stop living the day she walked out over and over again." There was a bark in the distance and then a louder bark, and then Roxy bounded back across the creek and fell at Wyatt's feet, rolled over.

"Damn dog." She stared up at him, and her short tail thumped against his boot. He relented and squatted, scratched her stomach. She righted herself, and he rubbed one of her ears. He slapped her flank. "She's in good shape," Wyatt said, glad to have something to get them off the subject of his life. He looked in every direction and looked at the sun. "I'll go east and you go west. We'll meet back here before dark."

"We're splitting up?"

"Yes. I think I've decided I'd like to hunt alone."

Wyatt crossed the creek and followed the base of the hill to the east before beginning his ascent to his tree. Del was right about the kid. He needed to quit putting it off and do something. Randy was a pain in the ass, but recently it had gotten even more complicated. He remembered the arm wrestling from the night before and winced. His father had been drunk when he did it, too, and Wyatt felt a great wave of shame. He'd apologized, which was more than his father had ever done, but it didn't feel like enough. He needed to keep those sorts of feelings out of his life. He was relieved that he'd decided to call the state. And he could do it on Monday. He *would* do it on Monday. It was probably as simple as calling human services. Maybe he could just drop him off with Esther Grundel and tell her the kid was her problem.

The sun was high over the ridge—which felt like the northern rim of the world—and provided as much warmth as it would the whole day, which wasn't much. There was enough that he took off his gloves and stocking cap and shoved them in one of the pockets of his hunting vest. They had maybe two, three hours of quality light. Del had drained some of his enthusiasm for the cougar, but as soon as he was alone, the anticipation and fear began to reabsorb him. He cut through the switchbacks by climbing up one of the rocky, sometime-runoffs that made their way down to Olim Creek. Most of them were fed by the water that rushed through the boulders of the ravine coming down from the cave.

The cougar's cave.

A cold wind came from the southeast and he listened, hoped it would carry a growl or a scent, something. But it passed and the air stilled, and there was only the sweet trill of a single sparrow. And then the throaty caw of a crow—three, four, five caws, like someone banging on your door. The crow was grappled to the top of a tall pine, the branch bowing under its weight. It watched him.

Along his way he stopped at a twisted blackjack. Mistletoe as thick as a garden hose had wrapped itself tightly around the base, grown so thick that the trunk of the tree had grown back around it, joined in the weave. Two long gashes slanted down and around the trunk. Splintered bark. The cuts were so deep they were wet and tacky to his touch. The sharp smell of sap filled his nostrils. The scratches were high—eye level. He scanned the trees around him and saw another set a few yards up the hill. He moved to those. Just as deep. He stepped back and found his boots on open ground, the brown leaves and the clunky gray-green gravel that filled the hills scratched away down to black soil and red clay. He crouched down and found the scratches there, too. A foot long, half as deep. But filled with liquid. He dipped two fingers into muddied slashes and held them under his nose. Acrid, pungent, still warm. Piss.

He grew still, then stood and slowly raised the stock of his rifle against his shoulder, turned a quiet three-sixty—watched the woods, felt them watching him. When he saw nothing, he scanned the trees around him for more scars but found none. He lowered the rifle and forced a quiet laugh, a reassurance. He stood still and felt for the wind. You couldn't count on the wind much to read the weather when you were in hilly country—topography was all that mattered, the way the wind swept through valleys and made hairpin turns around windbreaks, created little local weathers—but you sure as hell could tell where your scent was going. Quiet.

A bobwhite. A bobwhite again.

The gravelly ground accumulated into larger rocks. And with the larger rocks came faults and rifts, crooks and crannies, a thousand places for a cat to hide. He shouldered the rifle completely and observed everything around him down the barrel through the sight, stepped carefully from rock to rock, colored every corner with the muzzle of his gun. The sound of the creek behind him faded away as he moved up the slow grade toward the cave.

The bobwhite again, this time closer.

And then the crashing of leaves below him, a clacking against the rocks, some of which tumbled, and two beautiful bucks appeared from behind a thicket of blackjacks, frantic, crashing down the hill. He froze. The deer hunter's heart in him raced, but when he saw the blaze of black fur between them, it stilled. He moved his finger to the trigger, waited for the shot. The deer turned blindly and ran right for him, a measure of their fear, and when they reached a ten-foot boulder, they veered hard to the right, one buck opening up a lead, the cat between them. With the shape and colors of the ground so uneven, the shot was difficult, but Wyatt steadied himself and with the sight just ahead of the animal he fired. His ear rang with the deafening crack of the bullet through the sounds of the forest.

The hidden covey of bobwhites half flushed beyond, returned to the ground.

There was a small spray of blood somewhere around the front buck's flank—no, his back leg—and it stumbled, cried out a mad, guttural honk. The cat slid across the ground behind it, threw up a shower of leaves, the momentum of its graceful bounding interred into nothing more than another one of the rocks surrounding it. The injured buck righted itself, tore off jack-legged with the other. Wyatt swelled with adrenaline and something like joy, and he hopscotched from rock to rock up the hill, the muscles in his legs burning. Without meaning to, he let out a whoop. He ran right through choked, thorny bramble, which tore at the back of his hands, toward the dark blood on the back of the rock behind which it had come to a rest. When he made it there, when he stood up on that rock, and looked down at his trophy, something dropped open in Wyatt like the trap door of a gallows, and something heavy as a human body dropped through, snapped taut alongside his vertebrae. It was Roxy.

Lightheaded, the ground felt crooked beneath him. He got on his knees before her and found her still breathing, panting quick and shallow, a muffled whine with each breath. The bullet had gone through her flank and exited at the opposite shoulder, opened her up, left a trail of pink behind her. He put his hand on her head, petted her, and she looked at him, straining to see him from the corners of her eyes, unable to lift her head. He petted her until her chest grew still.

A sharp pain pinched his chest, and he bowed his head and let out a single, quiet sob, which flushed the once-scared covey of bobwhites, a flurry of cream and chestnut, their silvery flap like a deck of cards splashed across a room. They flew up, together, then moved apart from one another, each flying to the singular place in the gray-white sky they believed was safe.

11

THE LAST-GASP BEAUTY of the fall colors had begun to die away. Del wished he'd put on another layer. It was the time when the coming winter leeched the earth of its warmth, its personality. It was a gift, he thought, to get the chance to see something teetering at the edge of life.

He was stuck somewhere between happy to be on such a strange, spontaneous hunt and pissed at Wyatt for ruining a perfectly good workday. At Wyatt for the teetering he was doing of his own. He should have known something like this would happen. He'd been so concerned with him not following through that he'd never stopped to consider that he'd just completely self-sabotage. But also: Wyatt the friend.

Just one night of drinking.

A strong wind came from the southwest and rattled the dried-up leaves in the trees all around him, scattered some across the forest. The quiet that followed brought his attention to the weird green atmosphere that came before weird weather. It felt like it was too late in the year for this type of storm. A sharp, cold wind came from the opposite direction, and there was something like a crack east, further up the mountain. A broken limb. But Roxy turned back in that direction, froze. He didn't realize she'd stopped until he was ten yards away.

"Here, girl." He coaxed her with a whistle, but she was frozen, her black-and-tan back just beneath the surface of a stand of buffalo grass.

"Here, girl," again, then louder, "Roxy, come." When she didn't respond to his call—the call they'd spent a hundred hours training her for—he angered. "Goddammit, Roxy." He went to her. Even with him at her side she stayed frozen, crouched, her eyes on something in the distance. She growled, fierce, bore her teeth, and just before Del could get his fingers hooked into her collar, her whole body erupted forward and she went flying, a blaze of fur and teeth and muscle through the grass and into the trees. Just what in the hell had gotten into everyone around here?

She'd come back. If she didn't, he didn't want her anyway. But his own rule hurt his heart. He continued to the west, following a wash of rocks that looked like a natural runoff. A crow cawed somewhere in the distance.

Goddamn Darlene. This was mostly her fault. She was the one that had him all haywire. Del had been the one who made Wyatt call the sheriff's office a second time and made Pete Jacktooth come back out. Del had sat at the kitchen table and listened to Pete just tell Wyatt again that Darlene had left, plain and simple. Del had said, "Now hold on, now Pete," but Pete had stopped him. Pete said, "I've been a deputy for a decade and a half, and I can't count the number of times I've seen this." Did she take anything with her? Not her suitcase. An overnight bag? He wasn't sure. Did she take her car? Well, yes, of course. Did she leave of her own free will? Well, yes. Sounds like she left, then, don't it? When Wyatt turned angry and told him to get the hell out of his house, Pete softened a bit and told Wyatt he'd keep an eye out for her car.

That weekend Wyatt started looking. Went to Cushing looking for her every weekend, all the way through September, tried calling her stuck-up parents again and again. He called police and sheriff departments in the surrounding counties. He stopped looking when he got to the last thing on Pete's list: hospitals.

Del didn't have the heart to tell Wyatt, but he figured Pete was right.

After another hour there was another crack, but this one was clearly the sound of a rifle. He figured it was Wyatt, a mile and a half southeast of him, somewhere up on the mountain.

The cougar? A warning shot? Would he kill the thing?

No, it was a deer, he figured. Wyatt had stumbled across a buck and hadn't been able to resist.

Still, it could be that he'd found what they'd come looking for, and the prospect of the cat being real registered with him for the first time. What a weird stretch of woods. How long had it been there? Was it the only one? How had no one seen it? He veered back through the woods toward the ATV trail—he had to see for himself.

He followed the trail north toward the mountain. The darkness of a storm was coming, and again Del was disappointed in his failed prediction. The atmosphere continued to shift. Again, that greenish color. The air pressure vanished, and for a moment it felt like there was no sound but his own breath, the moistness of his mouth. But then—what sounded like the scream of a woman. He felt exposed. And there it was, ten feet up in a blackjack some fifty feet on the other side of the trail: a black cat.

Just as Wyatt had described it. Massive, tawny, sleek. Almost as big as a panther. A lion. A cat of indiscernible darkness. A stretch of wispy cirrus streaked across the green sky behind the cat, brought the limbs of the tree to life, made them appendages, the shadows of appendages, all of them reaching out from the cat's body. It stretched its neck out and screamed at him. Jagged and angry. Like it was amid some great pain or sorrow. Its body coiled. All four paws pressed into one singular place to explode toward him.

If he took a shot and missed, it would be the end. Every blood vessel in his body was icy with adrenaline, and he did the one thing that would seem least feasible in the situation to an outside observer: He dropped his rifle and ran.

He blazed out from the path and ran southwest—away from the cat and toward the highway. And as he calculated the distance, he understood that there was no way that he'd outrun an animal like that. If he climbed, it would follow; if he hid, it would sniff him out. But the highway—just the thought of that meager sign of human life—made him run harder, lactic acid engorging his legs. But his foot caught on the branch of a dead tree, and he fell forward. He put his hand out in front of him to catch himself and a jagged, broken branch drove in and through the hand, parting the hundreds of bones like someone peeking out between two curtains.

He rolled on his back to right himself and stand, but a heavy weight came down on him and pushed the air from his lungs, the cat's spitting hot breath rattling like a diesel engine on his neck. Its free paw came down, and its claws went through his clothes and skin, burning hot. He felt split open, his skin on fire. He couldn't move his legs. It sliced through him again. It lifted the paw pinning him down and he was able to prop himself up on his elbow, but he only fell backwards, the grit of the forest floor filling up the places where his flesh had been torn away. With air in his lungs again he screamed. A paw came down on his face. The dampened pop of his cracked cheekbone exploded through his head and the claw that sank into his eye hit a nerve that shook his whole body. The cat screamed in his face—its breath hot and rotten.

And for a moment Del was still, and he thought he heard something inside the cat, a person, somewhere down the cat's raw throat. Someone not screaming with anger but with pain. And as he felt the hardness of its teeth on his face and the pressure of its jaw clamping down, he

screamed one last time, screamed down its throat in hopes that someone, something inside would hear him.

And the cat ripped off his face.

12

Squints had a TV in his bedroom, which was badass. It was raining outside, and the drops made a flat slapping noise on the windows in the corner of the room, and it felt cozy inside for a change, which was nice. They'd come in when it started to rain, and Randy had been relieved that Mrs. Sherman was passed out on the couch. He hadn't meant to push her down. When he saw her on the couch with her pants pulled down enough that you could see half of her bare ass and the clear glass ashtray overturned on the brown sculpted carpet, he actually sort of felt sorry for her.

Squints's room had an entire wall filled with a collage of posters that looked like they'd been ordered out of the *I Own a Generic Poster* catalog. *Fight Club, Fear and Loathing in Las Vegas, The Boondock Saints, Scarface,* Wu Tang Clan, Cypress Hill, *three* with Eminem, Bob Marley smoking a joint. His dirty clothes were usually ankle-deep all over the room. Randy couldn't judge that—his clothes were almost always dirty—it was just that Randy didn't own enough to pile that deep. He wondered what Squints's dad did that let them live like they did. Squints had told Randy that he sent him money every month. Wyatt had a decent-seeming job—even if it was weird—and they lived like shit.

Squints was lying on his bed watching football. It was Bedlam—OU vs. OSU—and Squints thought it was a pretty big deal. Squints was always saying that when he graduated, he was going to go to OU. Randy gave him shit about it, told him there was no way his flunky ass was getting into any college. Which was probably true. But Randy thought that if he joked about it, it would feel like it wasn't. When a commercial came on, Squints rolled over and propped his head up on his hand. "Yo, I'm sorry about that shit with my mom earlier."

"It's cool. I mean. Parents are pretty fucked up sometimes."

"Yeah, I guess."

In his mind, Randy made his way through the woods of the old state park. At night, as always, without a trail. The whole world in the cone of a flashlight. There was a fog, and the rocks he climbed over were wet to the touch. He was unsure of where he was, and, as if someone else were invading his own vision—the sound of wooden wind chimes. Or something like them. You needed something to keep you oriented in the woods, he decided. A reference point. To be tied to something that wouldn't move.

He turned to Squints. He said, "How about that tattoo? You think I could get one? Like, now?"

Squints grinned. He heaved himself up with a grunt and sat at the edge of the bed with his fists punched into the mattress. "You sure about that? I mean you can't puss out or anything halfway, or it will look like total shit, yo. You've got to be committed. And it's got to be something that'll mean something to you the rest of your life, like part of your destiny or some shit."

"Yeah, I'm sure."

"Fuck yeah." He walked over his clothes to the closet, where he stepped up on an overturned plastic crate and stretched his arm up to the top shelf and felt around in the corner. He pulled out a red-and-black Nike shoebox and set it down on the bed, opened it. It was just the white handle of an electric toothbrush with what looked like a needle on the end of it.

Randy said, "Let me look at that." When he did, a shudder went through him—it wasn't a needle, but the thinnest guitar string he'd ever seen.

"You cut it at an angle. What do you want? Still want it on your stomach?"

"Nah, I want it to be more prominent, where I can see it when I'm lifting."

"That's pretty hardcore."

Randy liked hearing that. It had been a day of bad news, but he'd also been dealt his fair share of compliments, which wasn't typical. He pulled off his shirt and went to the mirror hanging on the closet door. He pointed to his chest—the right side; "Right there. I want a skull right there."

The first time the guitar string punctured his skin, he let out a throaty cry.

"Don't move or it will fuck it up. I told you it would hurt like hell." He dipped it back in the ink—which was purple, but Randy didn't care, he sort of liked the idea of them both having purple ink on them forever, even if it was sort of weird—and stuck him again. This time he pressed down on the button and let the thing really pump, and it hurt like hell, but Randy just bit his lip and laid his head back on the bed and stared at the ceiling, where Squints had a poster of a red Firebird parked in front of a bunch of palm trees. It hurt, but it also felt good. He liked having someone pay so much attention to him. Like there was a spotlight on his body. Like it was all Squints cared about in the world.

It reminded him of a feeling he used to get when he was in Cushing and in the sixth grade—this was before he started to fuck everything up—and he'd go once a week to help third graders with their spelling and their cursive. Sometimes he'd demonstrate the cursive for them. The four kids in his group would bunch in all around him and sometimes even put their hands on his shoulders and lean against him. There was something about the way they all got in close and didn't think twice about touching him or being near him, how they were so interested in what he was doing. He didn't know what it was, but it gave him goosebumps. He liked it so much that sometimes he'd draw the cursive words as slowly as possible so he could make the moment last longer.

He felt like that with Squints now. He liked the way he leaned his palm on his chest and the way he sometimes took a towel he dipped in water and wiped away the excess ink. He closed his eyes and listened to the buzz of the electric toothbrush handle and the rain and the thunder that was getting louder and louder and the sound of the game on the TV and Squints's heavy mouth breathing, which was warm on his chest. He figured someday if he was ever happy, it would feel something like that.

He wondered what his mom would think about him having a tattoo. If she came back—and he found himself thinking that way for the first time—if instead of when—he'd basically be a different person. He was taller. According to everyone else, he was getting to be pretty ripped. He'd have a tattoo. Would she be pissed, or would she be sad, or would she be amazed? When he started getting pretty heavy into weed—it was the seventh grade, near the end of the year, when he started hanging out with this eighth-grade girl named LaShawnda whose dad sold the stuff—he brought up to his mom that he wanted to get his ears pierced. No way, not ever, and she wanted to know why. He said he didn't know, but it was because LaShawnda said he'd look handsome in them. He'd bring it up every couple of weeks and she'd get mad at him. Finally, she screamed at him about it and said if she ever saw him with pierced ears, she'd rip them right out.

He figured it wasn't just about the earrings, though. Or the fact that she knew he was smoking a lot of pot even though she never said anything. He'd smell like it when he came home, and since they shared the same space in that little hotel room, there wasn't any way around it. It probably also wasn't about the fact that he'd started getting in trouble at school for dumb shit. He wrote *Cunt* in chalk on Miss Clayborn's chalkboard one day at lunch. He pointed the sharp end of a compass at a kid in art class once when he called Randy a faggot. When they had recess in the gym one day because it was raining so hard, he threw a basketball at a sixth-grade girl's face so hard that she cried. They called his mom about all of it. She told him she didn't know what she was supposed to do. She told him she needed him to help her and meet her halfway, whatever that meant. None of that was what made her the maddest, though, at least not the way he saw it.

He figured it was because he'd ruined her life in general. She'd gotten pregnant with him when she was sixteen, which fucked her up right out of the gates—she couldn't finish high school, and her parents shunned her and kicked her out of the house (well, she ran away before they could). She'd had to live in a women's shelter in Stillwater until she had him. So she didn't exactly have a lot of prospects from the get-go. Pretty soon, though, she met a roughneck named Wells who treated her all right and moved them in with him in his trailer out on 33. That was pretty much where he'd grown up. Wells wasn't around much because he was always working on rigs, but he made good money and even paid for Randy's mom to go to beauty school in Stillwater, which was pretty much one of her proudest accomplishments in life. Which is no big deal to some people, but Randy understood. Randy had a few friends at school, and he joined the Cub Scouts with them, and he thought that was all right. His mom seemed so happy that he kept it quiet at first when Wells started coming into Randy's room at night. At first, he'd just talk to Randy, which seemed all right—almost nice—but later he started taking his pants off, too, and pressing himself up against Randy. He'd pull up Randy's shirt and kiss him on the stomach, and the stubble on his face would leave what looked like a red rash. When he finally told his mom, she screamed at Wells and broke a beer bottle across his face, and the two of them left without anything. They did what his mom called *starting fresh*, which meant living in a hotel-room-turned-apartment.

That's why she got so pissed. That's why, when he lay still at night and listened, he could hear her crying sometimes. When he was fourteen, she drove him to his grandparents' house at Christmas because she said she thought they'd finally be ready to meet him, especially considering the holidays, and told him to stay in the car while she went up to the door and rang the doorbell. Someone he couldn't make out answered the door, and they stood there for a while talking. When she came back to the car she was crying. "Listen honey, this year I want to get you something extra special for Christmas. Anything you want." She was crying, but she still smiled. He'd wanted earrings. So the next day she'd driven him to the Claire's in Stillwater, and he'd gotten gold studs in each ear.

Not long after that they moved to Seven Suns and things felt a little better, and they started to really get along despite the fuckwit Wyatt being around all the time. Things were all right. Not picture perfect. But all right.

And then she was gone. Now he hated those fucking earrings. But he didn't want to take them out because he was scared the holes would grow shut and he'd never be able to put them back in again.

Bones, bones. She was dead and gone, he knew it. And he had to get away from those bones. But if she wasn't? She could come back. And there was Squints. And Kitty—and, though he hated to admit it, Wyatt.

Maybe not Wyatt. What would happen to them all without him? What would happen to them all *with* him?

"Do you want it to have teeth?"

"Duh. As many as you can fit in there."

"That'll take longer."

"That's fine." He wanted to feel the burn of the needle and the cool of the washcloth and the warmth of Squints's gaze as long as he could before it was all over. He stretched his arms back and stitched his fingers together behind his head, closed his eyes. He focused on every muscle in his body and imagined they were as heavy as the world, and then he imagined they were light and then gone, and there was only Squints hovering over him, doing his work. And before long he had a hard-on. And he could tell it was pretty obvious, but Squints didn't say anything. He finished the teeth and started on the eye sockets, which were simple but took the longest because he had to fill them in.

He wiped it off one last time. "There you go, yo. You're one hard-ass motherfucker."

Randy got up and looked in the mirror and was immediately struck by the fact that the skull would be on his chest forever. It was puffed up and pink and bleeding in places. It wasn't quite symmetrical—one of the eyes was bigger than the other, and the top of the skull on one side didn't quite slope at the same angle. But he liked it. He thought he could pack all of his memories and general thoughts about Squints into that tattoo, let it sit there until he was ready to pull them out. Just like his mother's dress.

13

Now HERE is my story before I was me, when I met me for the first time. I remember it all, for both of us. Can you imagine seeing an event from two places at the same time? The human mind can't conceive of it, would be driven mad by the plasma globe of dimensions that have never been seen. This is what happened to him:

He'd had a dishonorable discharge and spent time in the brig for accidentally beating a man to death. After the man found him with his wife after returning from Busan. That's a whole story in and of itself—love, terror, hate, remorse, etc. All that matters is that it left him broken. And broken is something I can work with. He didn't know how many months he'd been drunk with his buddy in Dallas when he got the call about his daddy dying. I guess in a way he killed him, too. The guilt and the fear and the insanity made him hot and slick like a fiery worm.

He was careening into the gray, wet wall of water called Oklahoma on his way to Muskogee for the funeral—his pickup's panicked wiper blades not doing a lick of good—when he met me. I was a long, lean woman, a cattail soaked on the shoulder of the highway—a black trash bag in one hand, a thumb out on the other. A position I continually find myself in. I'll still be hitchhiking across the broken, split-open face of a god until the eons end like the shattering of some dark mirror.

I told him about the family—took him awhile to realize I was say-ing *The* Family. The Family Who'd Gone on Before Me. But that's also another story. His eyes swam over me with need and malice and love. I wore a long black dress, the hem of which rode up my legs a few inches from my army boots. My legs were covered in thick black hair. My hair was just stubble. I'd done it myself with a pair of scissors.

Goddamn I was beautiful. And he knew it.

That's when I showed him the cracks slowly splintering the highway and the orange burning below and the hate and the need and the rot and all the lives of horror ever lived.

What he'd find later when he went through my trash bag: rotting flesh—so much rotting flesh—a blue retainer case, no retainer, a book of facts about the Titanic, a teen study Bible with a *Hello My Name Is* sticker on the front. Name? Believer. The putrefied body parts and sweet watermelon lotion. He still longs for that scent.

What we saw when we crossed the Red River and came up over a hill overlooking southern Oklahoma—vinyl letters on a truck on the shoulder: Gary's Tornado Tours. We crested another hill and the storm trackers spread out in front of us like a carnival. Vans, trucks, SUVs, families wearing plastic bags and gawking through binoculars, Dopplers on wheels, wind sensors, everybody out on their knees, bowing down again and again, begging the storm to destroy them, the atmosphere heavy and electric.

The road rolled down and cut straight across a low, flat plain, disap-peared a mile, mile and a half away in the dark belly of a massive super-cell the size of a mountain, a thousand miles across and a thousand miles high—a great and mighty storm, its walls like wet, sooty cotton, the rain pouring down a black sheet, devouring the broken country. I could see why those people would crawl on their bloody knees across the asphalt to worship it.

It looked like a storm but it was me.

I climbed down from his pickup and ran through the rain to the truck behind us. Naturally he followed. He'd have followed me anywhere. A wind monitor clicked on top of the truck like a board game dial, a casting of lots.

Can I help you, missy? He had a thick gray mustache and round glasses. Rain dripped from the edge of his black Stetson.

Is that going to be a tornado?

Hope so (this was my kind of man). One drumming to the south, too. Fuses lit on both ends.

I knew about a place, I told him. A motel.

He looked all around us at the middle of nowhere, Oklahoma. He said All right. He said I'll ride that train.

From then on, we were simply driving deeper into my mind. Out of the rain and the thick dark clouds, and then there were stars.

Those stars!

I could tell he would drive on forever for me until we came to the end of the world. The trip clock said he'd gone more than two thousand miles. I drew him on. Hours and hours, but never a sign of a sun.

The motel was L-shaped. Pink, still-wet stucco that glistened beneath the glow of the neon sign. An empty parking lot guarded an empty pool. I cannot count the number of times I've been to that hotel, that temple of dead gods, where they weep and gnash their teeth. Where I sharpen mine and break my own heart, again and again and again.

If he had looked into that empty pool: The orange glow of hell rising

up from the deep end to the shallow end, spilling over the edges, sucking at his boots and his legs and his life, and he'd see even more—the
world battling against the waves of my destruction. Whirling, churn-
ing. Imprisoned in cold, burned-out suns. I scream out my name into
the vacuum.

Nobody was behind the counter but the lights were on. The back
door to the office stood open like somebody had just left. Like they'd
seen us and scrammed. But there was a film of dust over everything,
like they'd been leaving for a hundred years.

I shut myself in the corner room—he needed more time to think, to
be broken, to think about the loveliness of death—and I watched him
between the curtains. He sat in a plastic chair at the edge of the empty pool and smoked a roach and put together that he was somewhere
else, on a dusty plain with a horizon so flat you could see the curvature
of my world.

And then he looked up and found my collection. I'll never forget how
he saw it: a great fleshy planet approaching us slowly, the hands and feet
and faces of all the bright and beautiful people I had ever loved—taken,
destroyed. Jesus how they slip through my hands.

And just as I expected, he came to me.

He barreled into my room without knocking and grabbed me around
the waist and shouted I love you I love you I love you! His breath was
hot. He forced his hand between two buttons of my dress over my
breasts. I tried to speak but he covered my mouth with his own. He
lowered me to the bed and he kissed me again, wet my mouth. And
I could feel what he was feeling: He couldn't tell if he was taking me
someplace or I was taking him.

I laughed. I laughed until my face was wet with tears. He rolled off
me and buried his face in the cheap bedspread.

And every bit of loneliness the world had ever known found him there like that, contorted and crying on the bed.

I stood over the bed and unbuttoned the front of my dress. I let it fall to the floor. And just believe me when I say he saw what amounts to the most beautiful thing he'd ever seen. Surely no description of what he saw would do the diamond galaxy of my being justice. And for that I'm truly sorry.

But this is where things begin to change. Where I begin to see what he sees and think what he thinks. And this is what he saw: When he looked to my face, my eyes were flat and black as nothing. Eyes like an ocean floor, a dark desert. And somewhere out on that dark plain, a small light appeared—a point of radiance, a firefly. Yellow, then red, then blue. It came closer and closer to him, dancing, and then came out into the motel room.

He understood that it was his if he wanted it, that I was his if he wanted me. I made him understand that he simply had to accept my grace.

And he did.

And whose story is it that starts?

When I looked back to her, she was a coyote. A residual animal that turned and ran into the night.

What creature will I leave behind when the boy becomes my story? I'm out of time. We need each other tonight.

14

THE SKY had been clear all day, but two blue-bellied clouds appeared, small, a warning, and then the rain to the south became visible, a crooked black wall that pushed wide, menacing clouds in front of it. It looked like big fat drops would start to land on the car's windshield at any moment.

"So are you going to officially deputize me or anything?" Brock asked. "Make me say an oath and put a badge on me, all that?"

"It's nothing like that." They were sitting in the fogged-up car in Brock's parents' driveway. Both his parents stood at the picture window in the living room waving. Brock sank into the seat. "I could just use a hand," Esther said. "It's only for a weekend, but I'm worried things are getting—a little out of hand." She had already gone chest out against the world for a day doing something she knew nothing about; asking for help felt like defeat (mercy).

"So this Randy Strange kid—what a name, am I right?—had blood all over him?"

"It looked like blood."

"Could be a painter."

"I doubt it. Could be wax."

"Did you say *wax*?"

"Yes. I saw it on a wall in a motel once, and it looked like blood."

"And you think *that's* what it is?"

"Well, I don't know."

Brock looked deep in thought. "I've seen the kid around. He doesn't look like a painter. More like he writes broody poetry or destroys the walls in his bedroom."

"Blood aside—which doesn't necessarily mean anything—he was also the last person to see Kitty. As far as I know. He said it had something to do with rats." She pulled out her notepad and opened it. "Rats. A run-in with some rats."

"A *run-in?*"

"At the old video store. That's where he saw Kitty, too."

"I know the place," Brock said. "We used to drink beers in there."

She parked in the alley behind the Showbiz. A broken sidewalk ran behind all of the buildings in the alley, dead grass bursting from tar mouths. A rusted-out *No Parking* sign sat atop a leaning pole next to a dark spot on the brick where a dumpster had been. The place gave Esther a lonely feeling.

"Oh god," Brock said as they got out. "Do you smell that?" He held the back of his hand up to his nose and mouth and shook his head.

She did. Something rotten. Maybe the rat story would check out. She said, "Why would they be here if it smelled this bad?"

"Well, I'm sure it's gotten worse since they were here."

"What's gotten worse?"

"The smell."

"Never mind."

Esther pulled back on the door, and the stale air wafted out at her— warm in the bitter cold—and made the smell of rot even stronger. While Brock cursed and waved at the air, everything grew quiet around Esther. The smell was acrid, but she breathed it in and out, slowed her heart. She clicked her flashlight to life and scanned the steps with her beam.

Midway up the stairs: steps wet with red. She motioned Brock over. "Blood?"

"You tell me." They stood, waiting. "Go check it out."

He propped the door open with a cinder block to let fresh air in, and Esther stepped inside. What was living in that building? She shivered: spiders of all shapes and sizes, webs stretched from corner to corner, wasps—oh the wasps, she remembered the wasps—the raccoons and skunks and rats and snakes, coiled around their soft-shelled eggs, bats huddled together like rock formations on the ceiling. All of them crawled all over her body at once, and as her breathing quickened, she began to taste the dust in her mouth.

Halfway up, she squatted, trained her light six inches from the next stair. Most of whatever it was had dried and turned dark and brown, but in the grooves and shallow places in the wood it was still bright red. She hovered her hand over it for a moment and closed her eyes, centered herself with a prayer, and swiped her finger, held it to her nose. The smell was somehow both metallic and alive. She gagged. "It's blood," she said, coughing. "He said he didn't know what it was. It's blood."

"What kind of blood?"

"I don't know, Brock. I guess let's go upstairs and find out."

The blood continued up the stairs and into the main room. The beam of her flashlight washed over a spray-painted swastika and a brass doorknob. The trail continued, and the sheer amount of it, tacky under her boots, was enough to tell her that something bad had happened. Something really bad. She turned to Brock. "I think we should get out of here." She took a step back toward the stairs and a fresh breeze blew in through the open door, and for a moment, the smell of rot was gone.

"No way," Brock said. "Not now. Now we *have* to see." He stepped toward her, and she had no option but to turn around. Something cold clicked down in her bones, and she readied herself for the great

icy inpouring that was about to rush past the open nerve of her exis-
tence. But nothing came. Nothing came, and it dawned on her: she was
already swimming in it. She turned back to Brock, and the light caught
him smiling in the bright white.

Inside, the darkness was so thick and unnatural that it had a surface,
and the rot grew so strong it became a physical presence beyond simply
a smell. It filled Esther's head space, quaked the earth beneath her. The
blood stopped not far from the top of the stairs, where it spread out like
a starburst. Tiny—claw?—marks striped the spot all over, as if something had been frantically eating whatever was there. *Whatever was there.*

They both scanned the room with their flashlights. There was a
counter to one side of the room with a doorway behind it leading to a
small back room. Someone had spray-painted a penis on the front of
the counter. At the opposite end, another doorway opened into a side
room. The main room was full of red wire shelves, a few of which still
held dusty VHS jackets. An inch of dust covered everything. Brock
returned, and she motioned for him to check behind the counter. The
room dimmed around her as he disappeared with his flashlight.

A lone rat came running from the side room, and when she turned
her light to the floor there were two more. She stepped toward the
room, and her eyes watered. She had to stop and calm herself to avoid
retching. In the room were more red shelves and more dusty boxes. She
followed a wall of what looked like romantic comedies to the far end
of the room and turned down the last aisle. Her boot made a slapping
noise in something wet. In the light: tacky, drying blood.

(What Esther found at the back of the old video store was not the
culmination of a series of trips to the brink, but rather the crashing
breaker coming from above as she looked down, obsessed with falling
over the edge, measuring distances.)

And then along with the blood: a trail of phalanges, a rib cage, a whole hand, a foot. Apart from a few indiscernible organs, the muscle had been chewed to the bone, clearly the work of those rats—but many more of those rats. One still picked at a rib.

Esther went to her knees and crawled, followed the bones to the corner of the room, where she found a skull, one eye socket still a fleshy pouch, the eyeball gone. The bottom half of it still held muscle and skin. The other half of the face: muscle across the cheek but no skin, which reappeared above the eye, where there was still a brown eyebrow. A small flap of scalp remained, where frizzy, bleach-blonde hair was matted with gore.

Esther gagged and then screamed out. Scrambling backwards on all fours, she knocked over a rack on her way to another. VHS boxes tumbled everywhere. She leaned on the toppled shelf, screamed for what felt like an eternity until the bob of Brock's flashlight appeared in the room.

"Look," she cried. "Is it real? Is that real?" She couldn't stop repeating the word *real* to herself.

Brock stumbled and then stopped short. "Oh god," he said. "Oh Jesus Christ." He dropped his flashlight. "I wasn't supposed to see something like this. You said this was something small. Well that's Kitty fucking Kershaw." His voice was shrill like a boy's.

"So it's real?"

Brock pulled her up by her arm and shook her. "Esther." He shook again. "Come on, we've got to get out of this place."

When they came downstairs and stepped out into the alley, it began to rain.

15

SQUINTS GAVE RANDY a wet washcloth. "It's bleeding pretty bad, yo; you might want to wipe that off again."

Randy dabbed at what felt like an open wound and winced. He handed the now-bloody washcloth back to Squints, who thoughtlessly dropped it on the pile of laundry at his feet. They stood next to each other in silence, the rain now pounding on the roof and the windows dark with the gray of the storm, both of them examining the tattoo in the mirror.

Randy said, "Wow, man."

And before he could think about it: He turned to Squints and kissed him, and Squints kissed back. Squints's lips were chapped and sharp, and the inside of his mouth was cold, but it was Squints. They kissed and then they stepped for the bed, felt for the edge of it with their hands so they didn't have to turn their faces away from one another, and lowered themselves down. They only stopped kissing so that Randy could pull Squints's T-shirt up over his head. Randy pushed him back and kissed him again, ran his hand over Squints's smooth skin, which tightened and turned to gooseflesh under Randy's touch. He ran his hand down and circled his stomach and then put his hand on top of the crotch of his jeans, and Squints was hard. Randy tried to unbutton the jeans with his one free hand but couldn't do it. Squints reached down and did it for him, and before he could pull them down, Randy climbed off the bed and pulled his jeans and underwear around his knees.

But out in the hall: Mrs. Sherman yelled out Squints's real name—
Franklin Thomas!—and Squints said *Shit-shit-shit* and Randy thought
No no this is my chance this is my chance this is our chance and Squints
was still trying to pull his pants up when the door flew open.

"Franklin Thomas are you going"—and she saw what was happening,
and whatever she was drinking from her pink, plastic cup poured out
on the floor, and she flew into a frenzy of anger Randy had never seen
before in his life. "What the fuck are you two doing?" Randy couldn't
help it, but he wiped his mouth on the back of his hand. "I *said*, What
the fuck are you two doing? Are you?—Are those tattoos? Are you
two giving each other tattoos? And"—she looked sick. Her bottom
lip curled out like she was going to vomit. "You two little faggots." She
looked at Randy. "You little faggot. No wonder. What were you doing
to my boy?" She splashed what was left of her drink at Randy and he
could definitely tell it was vodka, and some of it went in his eye, which
burned, and some of it hit his tattoo, where it burned, and Randy
couldn't see anything for a moment. When he opened his eyes, Mrs.
Sherman was over Squints, slapping him in the face, over and over and
over again. He was crying and asking her to stop, but she only hit him
harder, and Randy wanted to do something, but he remembered how
easily she'd fallen to the ground, and he felt so many things he couldn't
sort any of it out.

"It was him," Squints shouted. He pointed past his mom's slaps at
Randy, and every last bit of glue holding what little there was left of
Randy cracked, and he imagined the pieces of himself floating out over
the room and landing on Squints's things, dissolving. Randy pulled his
pants up. Mrs. Sherman redirected her anger and came at Randy. "What
did you *do*, you fucking faggot?" She slapped him and then balled her
hands into fists and beat him on the chest, and Randy couldn't believe

that it didn't hurt at all except for when she hit his tattoo.

The sight of Squints crying on the bed with his Iron Man sheet pulled over his lap sent red hot anger coursing through Randy's body. He pushed Mrs. Sherman out of the way and stood over Squints, who cried. "This is *your* fault, faggot," and, without thought, he balled his hand into a fist and hit Squints square in the eye. It wasn't like he expected—there was just a fleshy thud, and pain shot up his arm. "Fuck you *both!*" He stormed down the hallway, huffing, his hands still balled into fists. He kicked a pot full of dripping water across the living room. He threw open the door and walked out into the freezing rain, still without a shirt, the purple skull on his chest weeping blood.

By the time he'd walked the three and a half miles between the Sherman place and the edge of Seven Suns shirtless in the freezing rain, his skin was beginning to turn blue. The shivers that had crawled all over his body while he walked had consolidated into a single involuntary convulsion that shook through his whole body like a hiccup or a heartbeat. His jeans were soaked through and heavy. His tennis shoes were soggy; the cheap vinyl had begun tearing apart at the seams. At first he stopped every few hundred feet to retie them, but eventually he gave up and just let the wet laces slap across the bottom of his legs as he walked. The rain was so heavy now it roared around him, deafening him. He had no idea what time it was, just that the earth and the trees were dark, jagged silhouettes against a charcoal sky.

So the sight and colors of town—the blue-white under the canopy of the Tote-A-Poke and the yellow rectangle of glass at the front of the Napa Auto Parts and the half-shorted-out yellow sign at Dollar General and the green glow of the Simple Simon's Pizza—felt significant, like they'd been placed there for him, like the people inside had been waiting for him all day. Exhausted, he stepped under the canopy of the Tote-A-Poke and smiled, staggered once, and collapsed. He rolled over on his back in a pool of antifreeze and focused on his breath.

And then the clerk, Tommy Thompson, was standing over him, his acne-ridden, mutton-chopped face something transcendent.

"Did it stop raining?"

"Hell no, you're just inside." Randy was sitting on a stack of boxes in the back room of the store. "You want some hot coffee or something?" Tommy asked. Randy shook his head. The walk in the freezing rain had given him an obstacle, something to overcome, to absorb his mind in, and now that he was in the stale back room of a gas station surrounded by boxes of Styrofoam cups and stacks of two-liters of sodas, Squints and his mom began to rise above the surface, and a thought materialized in his mind for the first time—a thought he hadn't been able to look at, but one that had circled around him like the penny he'd once dropped in a giant funnel at the mall in Oklahoma City, which now rattled around right at the bottom and then fell in:

He wished he were dead.

Tommy came back with a steaming cup. "Here's some cappuccino. It's not really coffee. Sort of. But it's warm. And this"—He draped a yellow Tote-A-Poke uniform over Randy's shoulders. "Get yourself dry. By the way, that tattoo isn't looking too hot." Randy looked down and the pink puffy places had turned blue, looked bruised. He pulled the shirt on, and it was scratchy and not warm. "You want me to call someone?" Randy dug into his pocket to show him that he had a phone.

He called Wyatt, but Wyatt didn't pick up.

16

THE RAIN hadn't started yet when Wyatt wrapped Roxy in his jacket and lowered her into the steel-barrel firepit in the picnic area—the closest place he could find that felt safe, like a destination. But blue-bellied clouds were passing overhead, and a darker wall of storm hung further to the south.

He debated whether he should sit tight and wait until dark as they'd planned or go looking for Del. There was that wall of storm making it their way. And the cat was still out there. He'd decided, in his sharp pain, that looking for the cat had been a fool's errand. No cougar—master at hiding—would be found unless it wanted to be found. And look what it had resulted in. He thought he might just swear off hunting altogether after today.

Before dark: He crossed the creek and went to the west.

There was no sound but the crunch of leaves and the occasional rockslide beneath his boots. The birds had even gone quiet. He watched the sandstone ridge jutting like a crooked spine on the west side of the mountain. The perfect place for a cougar or a cougar hunter.

Goddammit he'd fucked up. It took everything in him not to just give up. He considered lying. He could say the cougar was going after her, that Roxy was seconds away from being mauled, and that he'd taken the shot to save her, and did, in a way, by sparing her from the gruesome end of being eaten alive. But he'd killed the man's dog, and the truth was the least he owed Del. He'd search and he'd find him. And they'd do whatever it was that they were going to do: argue, sort out their feelings, trade punches until they were both exhausted.

He blazed switchbacks up the side of the mountain where the forest floor would allow it. Now and then he'd stop, shout Del's name through cupped hands. But only an echo returned. When he felt like he'd covered a quarter-section or more—as far as Del would probably have made it—he hoisted his rifle from his back and fired two shots in the air. As if in response to the shots, dry, noiseless lightning flashed, flashed again.

But still, nothing. Except another flickering vein of dry lightning. After a long pause, the low rumble of distant thunder sent birds in the trees all around him—birds he hadn't even noticed were watching him—off in a panic. Near to him, the chaotic songs of a tree full of sparrows reached critical mass and they rose—a momentary doubling of the tall oak's crown—and scattered. Lightning flashed again, closer, and the thunder cracked louder, sharper.

He shouted hoarsely again and went on. It began to rain sparse but fat drops. One landed beside Wyatt's ponytail, in the space between his collar and the soft hairs of his neck, icy cold. He shivered. The rain began to pour, and the surface of the fall leaves grew wet and shiny, some of them falling to the ground under the new weight. By the time he got back to the picnic area, he was soaked through. Freezing and exhausted. He was weary, afraid of the cat. And it was now dark.

The world grew dim beyond the reaches of the small flashlight he kept in his hunting vest. He'd take the ATV trail straight back to the house. He could call someone there or at least take the ATV and the spotlight back out to search. Both. The fact that he only had a couple of hours until he had to meet Gordo rose up in the back of his mind, and for some reason he wanted to throw up. He began to run, and within the tunnel of his flashlight's light, the gray and splintered buffalo grass unspooled on both sides as he made his way over the rocky, muddy ruts.

It was because of all that drab that the cherry-wood stock of a rifle, deep and bright, stood out to him. He stooped down, picked it up, and confirmed what he already knew—Del's rifle. He squatted and scanned the area with the light. Beyond the rifle there were two saplings snapped in half, standing guard over matted-down grass.

And like that, he felt the woods watching him. The visibility through the trees was next to nothing, and he began to understand that he was completely vulnerable, that he was in a dark forest with a dark cat who'd been bred by nature for millions of years to climb trees, to attack from above. His one advantage in the rain was that he wouldn't carry a scent, so he cut off another of the cat's senses and clicked off the light.

When his eyes readjusted to the dark, he stepped off the trail and followed the trampled grass and saplings, Del's rifle shouldered. Further down the trail, there was a loud crack to his left—twenty, thirty feet—high in the branches, and he shouldered his rifle and pointed it out into the darkness. A rustling, followed by a thud. A branch, heavy with rain. He scanned the canopy all around him. Not looking at the ground, he stepped right into a thicket of something, where the thorns stuck to his hands and pulled at the strap on his rifle.

He was tangled badly enough that he had to use the flashlight again. He clicked it alive, and the light washed over something unnaturally white some fifteen feet away near a fallen tree. For some reason he was prepared for what he found—a human skull. He squatted, turned it toward him, gagged. Not so much from the broken body, but because of the new reality swallowing him. Like waking from a dream and having to reorient yourself. Or waking from a dream into a nightmare.

The other half of the skull still had part of Del's face on it—the stubble on the lower jaw, the ear, his curly yellow hair. The rest of his friend was stretched out around the stripped and fallen tree. One of his legs was still mostly intact, his jeans still on, but the other had been broken from the body, snapped at the femur, and was six, seven feet away in a low spot where the water was rising up around it, the flesh stripped away to the bone. Much of his torso was still in place, but he was eviscerated, his organs picked through like the animal had been a half-interested diner at a buffet.

The blood was fresh, *fresh*, and his adrenaline overtook everything. The cat was still nearby. He understood then that it hadn't just been passing through—it had chosen this place to stalk and hunt—and every branch of every tree around him suddenly became an arrow, knocked and drawn, a thousand sharp points trembling in the canopy. He shouldered the rifle again and scanned the woods.

Back at the trail, he felt them watching him before he saw them, just twenty feet away from the road opposite of where he'd been—four deer—three doe and a buck—taking shelter beneath a bald cypress. Their coats were gray and matted in the weak light of his light. Lightning flashed and their eyes turned white. The thunder that followed—a booming crack, the lightning drawing closer—made the deer flinch in one accord.

They began to shift, to back up into one another, as if to accommodate something moving in their midst. The buck backed up, tripped, let out a throaty screech, and all of them turned their attention from Wyatt at once, which jolted him from a state of strange reverie. More screeches followed, and the deer grew frantic, trampled one another, righted themselves, fled into the woods in every direction, the pencil pound of their hooves on the wet earth playing up Wyatt's spine. When they'd all retreated, he saw what had frightened them. The shimmering black of its bulbous tail, the ripple of the spring-loaded muscle along its back, its black fur. It lowered its head to its front two paws and a pink tongue flashed, flattened a set of whiskers. It raised its haunches and flicked its tail—its whole body coiled, ready to attack.

Without thought Wyatt shouldered the rifle, and the cat lunged. His hands were shaky and numb from the cold, so he fired before his sights were lined up. A chunk of sod exploded just before the cat, flew up in its face. The dirt in its eyes was enough to disrupt the attack, and the momentum of its hindquarters carried through its abrupt stop and the cat stumbled, tumbled through the understory. Wyatt cracked the action on the rifle and fired again. A thud and a burst of blood from one of its splayed back legs. It screamed and stood, turned back toward the woods. Wyatt fired again, and a fallen log exploded. The cat shot back into the cover of the forest, moved smooth as a ghost over the shattered log. He fired again. And again. Again into the wet, dark woods, unforgiving, until he was out of rounds. Rainwater dripped from the smoking muzzle.

17

Esther was strangely composed. She was cold, inside and out, but it was no longer a tidal wave that overcame her for a moment and then disappeared with a tremble; she was beneath the surface, swimming endlessly, resigned to drowning, waiting. The whole time she was on the phone with the state police, though—and the whole time they discussed what was happening, what they were to do—Brock hugged himself in a firm embrace. His ruddy cheeks had darkened to a deep red. She wanted to reach out and console him, pat him on the leg. He said, "So they're in Muskogee?"

"Yes, but they might be able to get a highway patrolman here sooner."

"Muskogee is an hour away."

"More like an hour and a half. She said we were to sit right here and keep the crime scene secure until they get here."

"I wasn't supposed to see that, you know?"

"I know."

"I thought we were just going to find her making out with Randy Strange or smoking pot with her girlfriends. That's the kind of thing you and I figure out."

"I said I know. I'm sorry. It landed on me just the same."

He put on his hat and zipped up his jacket, pointed out the windshield. "Well, I'm going to go to the Tote-A-Poke and get some coffee.

Mini-Donuts. You want anything?"

"A lot," she said. "No."

The alley was dark, and the rain battered down on the roof. The heater fogged the windows. She felt wrapped up by the dim, yellow dome light, protected. Just like her bedroom in the rain when she was a girl. In the summers she would open the windows to heighten the sound and build tents from sheets and sit inside of them, waiting for the rain to hypnotize her. Her father had yelled at her once for getting her bed sheets wet. Later: When she went to her parents' bedroom to apologize, she found her mother sitting at the end of the bed, her father standing over her, shouting, the capillaries all over his face as red as the sun. He slapped her then. Not the brief, reactionary kind of slap that stings for only a moment and is followed by regret, but one that required him to haul back his arm, punish her.

She got out her phone and called her mother. She answered after only one ring. "Hello?"

"Hi, Mom."

"Esther?"

"Yes, Mom. Are you doing okay?"

"Yes, ma'am. Got up once to go to the bathroom. Keeping watch from my post. Oklahoma Gardening is doing a marathon today."

"Okay, Mom. Good, Mom. I'm going to be home just as soon as I can. I'll be back to make dinner. Okay, Mom?" There was silence on the line and then a click. She called back but was greeted by the blare of a busy signal. She called again, and this time it rang: on and on. She let it ring beyond reason. A knot somewhere between Esther's heart and her throat tightened.

She startled at a knock on her window, but she couldn't see or hear who it was with all the rain. She took a breath and rolled down the window. It was Brock, the rain collecting at the front of his Stetson and falling down in a stream, and—like she was inside some strange fever dream—there was Randy Strange, looking like a wet skeleton beneath a Tote-A-Poke uniform.

Brock's smile was cartoonish. "Look who I just happened upon in the back room of the Tote-A-Poke? Randy. Strange." He held a coffee in one hand and the back of the boy's neck in the other. He handed Esther the coffee and opened the back door, closed it when Randy, unexpectedly compliant, crawled in. He shivered and his skin was somewhere between blue and sheet-white. He didn't speak, only watched the floor of the car. He seemed as if he were crying or had been crying.

Esther said, "What were you doing in the gas station?"

He looked at her, and his eyes looked alive (angry) for the first time. "What does that matter? Minding my own business."

"What were you doing in the old video store yesterday?"

Randy's expression went blank, and much like that morning, she could sense him calculating something. "My friend Squints and I sometimes hang out there after school." He looked down. "Just to check out the boxes for the porn. Okay?"

"We were just in there, Randy. We know what's up there."

Brock said, "Listen, Randy, you can tell us what went on. The way I see it, there's no way you could have done something like that. But maybe there was some kind of accident, or you saw something happen?"

"What are you talking about?"

Esther shot Brock a look. *Don't say anything.* She wasn't sure why, though; part of her just wanted to spare the kid the details if he wasn't involved. But he was involved. He was there. There was the blood. Simple math. She pulled out her notebook. "Now who is this Squints character? That his real name?"

"What is it with you and your names?" Brock said. "Squints and Strange. The Adventures of Squints and Strange?" A smile spread across his face but quickly faded.

"What?" Randy asked. "What are you talking about?"—calculating—"What do you think I've done?" His anger transformed into wondrous terror. "Is this all about Kitty?"

"You tell us," Brock said.

Esther said, "Do you have Wyatt's number?"

"Why would you call him?"

"He's your dad."

"He's not my dad."

"Guardian."

"He's not my guardian." He gave her the number, but no one answered. Randy looked surprisingly disappointed.

"Well," Esther said. "I guess you'll just have to wait here with us."

Her phone rang, and she jumped with excitement at the timing of the state police (mercy). "Sheriff speaking."

"Hello, Esther. Elvis Kithawk here again." Dammit. "Got a couple scrapping in the middle of the dance floor. Gordo Ramirez again. And that preacher. Sure could use some form of the law out here."

"Elvis, I don't know how to tell you the whole story, but I'm stuck downtown and can't go anywhere until the state police get here. There's been a lot of trouble."

"Well, you got trouble bad out here, too. The whole bar is descending on them. Blood everywhere. You might need the state police out here if you wait any longer." She knew they needed to wait, but something about the prospect of the next thing down the line loosened the knot just a bit, somehow put blinders on her.

"We'll be right there." She hung up. "Let's go." She pressed on the gas. "Can't have anyone else dead. Brawl at Red Door."

"Wow, what's the hurry?"

"I've learned you've got to get to these things fast."

They sat in the parking lot and discussed what to do. Esther's lips were chapped so badly that they were cracking, but she couldn't find her Carmex anywhere. Brock said that he wouldn't involve himself without a weapon. She offered him her baton. "No, not that. A gun."

"No, sorry."

"So I'm just supposed to walk into a fight with nothing but my karate moves? At least you've got that taser."

"We don't have one anyway. Besides, I need you to stay here and watch Randy." She opened her door. "It's nothing but a barroom brawl. Even if you had a firearm, it would be rash and irresponsible—" She hated the way she sounded like a schoolteacher. "Stay with the kid. I'm just going to see what's going on, ask some questions. Then we'll go back and wait on the state police."

"Fine." He scratched his nose, crossed his arms, and looked out his window.

Rain drummed on the brim of her hat. The gravel in the parking lot was polished pink with the reflection of neon signs hanging in the high, narrow windows that ran the length of the bar. A wave of smoke overtook her as it had the night before, but she forgot it when she heard the shattering of glass and a man crying out in pain. She hadn't missed this one. She stood frozen at the end of the bar opposite the dance floor and pool tables.

She couldn't bring herself to reveal herself to everyone there; it was an act that couldn't be undone. An announcement. There was another shout and then the boom of a roomful of people shouting threats, a few hollers of joy. She took off her hat and shook it out. When she put it back on her head, she ran her fingers through her styled bangs and pushed them flat against her hat, pulled the hat down snug. To herself, with confidence: Now what's the problem here, gentlemen? She hitched up her utility belt, unsnapped the strap on her taser holster, and walked the length of the bar toward the wide backs of men, cigarette smoke curling up around their cowboy hats with tightly curled brims.

Elvis stood at the end of the bar, a towel over his shoulder, a cigarette hanging from the corner of his mouth. He spoke in a whisper, as if they were conspiring. "Gordo again but this time the preacher. But bad. The two of them have been going at it forever. Preacher came in bleeding tonight. Almost called you just at the sight of him. Weird guy, Navy man. Ought to be careful."

"He tell you he's in the Navy?"

"Gunnersmate tattoo." He rolled up his own sleeve and showed her a tattoo of a skull with two cannons crossing behind it, *Gunnersmate* on a scroll beneath it.

"My Lord."

"Never seen a tattoo, sweetheart?"

Her jaw tightened at the word *sweetheart*, and she felt the lump in her throat, the swallow turning into a yellowjacket. She was almost grateful that he shook her a little. "What are they fighting about?"

"As far as I can tell, nothing. I told him not to come back."

She left him there and came up behind one of the men watching the fight, tapped him on the elbow. He looked down at her. "Excuse me." He smiled—a crooked smile with a toothpick in the corner of it, and stepped aside, where she fell in line with the other spectators, took in the situation. The dance floor was streaked with blood—some dry and darkened, some fresh and bright.

In one undisturbed puddle, there were two chunks: teeth. Esther's stomach turned when for a moment the two teeth became Kitty's. She saw the cracked jaw and that fleshy eye socket. And she understood then that her life in just a short time had become walking amongst bones.

Gordo shifted his weight back and forth, his left foot forward, his fists up. But lazy and tired. Fresh blood poured down his chin like tea from the lip of a pitcher. He looked beat up. Beat up, sure, but worse: beat up for the second time in two days.

The preacher was short and wiry and scabbed all over. Beaten, too. His long, greasy hair was tied in a knot at the back of his head. He wore a dingy red sweater with a reindeer on it. There was what looked like a wound on a dark, stained thigh. The stubble on his sharp jaw looked like it could cut you. He laughed. Gordo's shirt was torn in half, exposing a zombie Sleeping Beauty on his chest. He twisted his hip and swung his right fist at the preacher's face, but the preacher simply stepped to the side, laughed again. Gordo stumbled forward, breathing heavily.

"Goddammit you fucking niñito!" He put his hands on his knees. "Are you going to fight or just fuck around all day?"

The preacher laughed, and there was immediately something about his laugh that went right through Esther's bones and stirred up her marrow. "This land is doomed," the preacher said. "Doomed a thousand dooms."

She knew she didn't have the luxury of remaining a spectator when Gordo reached behind his back and pulled out what looked like a utility knife. Two men in the circle whooped and the stranger stopped where he was, contorted his razorblade face and whistled like the prettiest girl he'd ever seen just walked in the bar. The lights in the whole place flickered, and thunder boomed overhead.

"Aren't going to be so smart with your guts on the floor, are you?"

Esther stepped forward. "Hey!" The sound of her own shout startled her. "Put away the knife, Gordo." The room went silent. "This is
unacceptable behavior."

The stranger whistled again. "Goddamn! We got us a bear-pig in the
house." He laughed. He wouldn't stop laughing. Everyone's eyes were
on her.

"This fight stops right this instant, you hear? Or I'll cart both of you
to lockup and you can explain all this to Judge Bean." She liked the way
that sounded, and she felt herself getting fired up, the space inside her
rib cage swelling.

The preacher laughed. "Judge Bean? Y'all got a Judge Bean here? God
has surely spit me out into the goofiest-ass town in eastern Oklahoma.
Who's his bailiff? Deputy Jelly?"

Every man in the room looked at her. She was amazed at the sympathy she felt being directed at her from behind all their smoke and
steel-thick stoicism.

"We're not big fans of strangers with big mouths around here." She
felt another wave of the same sympathy roll up under her, began to feel
a weapon not hooked to her belt. "Especially big mouths full of bad
things to say about us." She could feel the heat of the circle pressing
in some. The preacher could, too, because the smile wiped away from
his face and he began to scan the threats in the eyes of the men around
him. "Now both of you cut this out right this instant. These folks just
wanted to come and have a drink tonight."

A man somewhere in the back shouted, "We came to see a fight!" and
a few of the others laughed. She drew her taser. She wanted to point it,
to threaten them, but she knew her hand would be shaking and that it
would be over just like that. "Now I've drawn my taser, as you can see,
and I want it to be clear that I will apply my right to use of force in an

effort to protect myself and these here bystanders." Someone shouted, "Preach!" and a few of the men clapped.

Gordo said, "Ma'am—" He turned to her and lowered the knife. She felt her shoulders relax and started to holster the taser when the preacher snuck up behind Gordo and pulled the knife right from his hand. Before Gordo could turn to him, the preacher jumped on his back. Gordo stumbled backwards, righted himself. The preacher wrapped an arm around Gordo's neck and held the hand with the knife up in the air, balanced himself like he was riding a bronco. He laughed.

Esther raised the taser but couldn't find a shot. Gordo spun in a circle and faced her, drove the stranger back into the wall, where a shelf of vintage beer cans came crashing down. The stranger simply yelped. When Gordo saw that Esther had the taser trained on them both, he stepped away from the wall and turned his back to her so she had a clear shot. She hesitated and lowered the taser slightly but remembered the knife and fired. The downward-aimed prongs sank into the small of Gordo's back, just below the preacher. Gordo shouted, turned to her. He fell to his knees and then hands. He groaned and tried to stand, fell forward on his face, and then pushed himself up again.

"Drop the knife and get off of him, now."

"Or?" The preacher smiled. She dropped the taser to the ground and reached for her baton. He held the knife out to his side as if to drop it, but instead brought it around in front of Gordo, held it to his neck. Gordo's mind was returning. He looked at Esther, anger boiling up behind his eyes. Esther took a step to her side and held up the baton, terrified at its uselessness.

He smiled broadly. "Oh, please do." The preacher held out his cheek expectantly as if waiting for a kiss.

"Drop the knife."

He stared at her, and although he still smiled, the humor was gone from him. She could tell by the way he studied her that he was reading her, measuring her. That he'd seen a lifetime of things she would never even dream up. That he saw every one of them that way, a series of familiar faces he'd dealt with again and again, and whom he'd begun to slide amongst, to know their every move, to swallow them one by one.

He sat up straight and held up the knife again, stretched out both arms as if to offer himself up. But he flipped the knife over in his hand and plunged it into the side of Gordo's neck. Gordo immediately rolled onto his side, taking the preacher with him. He coughed and gagged— made a wet, choking sound. Blood poured from his mouth and pooled out onto the dance floor. The preacher tore the blade out from his throat and there was a single squirt of blood, which spattered across the preacher's face. It slowed and the blood pumped thick out of the wound, joined the blood coming from his mouth and fanned out, ran like a river around Esther's boots. The preacher pulled himself out from under Gordo's weight, and Gordo flopped to the floor, already dead.

"For the last time," Esther said, "put down that knife."

He smiled. But before he could say a word or make a move, the circle of spectators descended on him, the blunt force of their bodies swallowing him up, brave against the knife because of their numbers. Esther stood apart from them. She told them to stop, but no one heard her or even looked at her. Ernie Burkhart backtracked from the group and went to one of the pool tables. He picked up a cue stick and looked at it, bobbed it, felt the weight of it. He put it back down and instead picked up the yellow one-ball and felt the weight of it, returned to the group. The other men had the preacher pinned, and they parted a path for Ernie when he returned. He disappeared in their midst. There was a thud and a grunt, another thud, a grunt, a thud and spitting, a gurgle similar to the one Gordo made before he collapsed to the ground.

She had no idea who she hit first, but the baton made a cracking sound when it came down on their flannelled back, and a wave of anger carried the baton back again, and she hit him again. And then the back of a large man in a gray sweatshirt and suspenders, then the back of his legs. The crowd still pressed in, but the more of them she hit, the more they slowed, began to stop and look around. Finally Ernie stood and came at her, and she did what she just now realized she'd wanted to do when he'd shouted at her from the jail cell: She cracked him in the face. He went to the ground. The group turned to her.

"This is going to stop right now." She stood, heaving, catching her breath. "I'll figure out a way to arrest every son of a bitch in this room or die trying if everyone doesn't just calm themselves and swallow down whatever god-forsaken macho nonsense you've got in your hearts right now." At their feet, the preacher sat up and smiled. His bottom lip was split in two, and his mouth was empty of all his teeth save a few jagged stragglers.

He got to his feet and made a show of dusting himself off. He wiped his lip with the back of his hand, the knife still gripped tightly in it. "I thank you, ma'am. You must be a connoisseur of real justice. I can see the light of God shining all over you." He staggered toward her. She raised the baton but was exhausted; he caught it in his hand mid-swing. He fell forward onto her, and she fell back against the wall. Her baton clattered to the floor, and she slid down underneath his weight. Of all the things that could have gone through Esther's mind, all she could think about was his stench: the sweet, nauseous fetor of body odor and piss and cigarette smoke.

He crawled off of her and then squatted back down to where she sat, held the utility knife to her throat. He held his hand in front of her—his nails long and black with dirt—and felt around until he had her by the collar.

He pulled up on her. "Come on now." He pressed on the knife, and she stood. He wrapped his arm around her neck from behind, pointed the knife at the men and then put it back to her throat, pointed it again at the men. "I'm guessing you fat-gut chuckleheads understand how a situation like this plays out. Am I right?" He walked backwards down the narrow space between the bar and the wall. When the two of them passed Elvis, Elvis stepped backwards and put up his hands. Esther choked on her tears, and the edge of the blade nicked at her neck with each swallowed sob.

Just before they got to the door, she felt a draft of cold air and an icy mist on the back of her hands, and then felt a jolt travel down her body and to the ground. She fell backwards, hit her head against the stone corner where the wall met the door. She moaned on the ground and rolled on her side, dry-heaved.

Gasping for air, she got to her feet. The preacher lay crumpled on the ground.

Brock Bosco stood in the doorway, his shoulder against the glass, a broken cinder block in his hand, smiling. He lowered the bloodied rock to the stranger's head and pointed out the gash where he'd struck him. He held the rock up in front of his face. "It's not a gun," he said, "but I guess it works." He smiled.

"Cuff him, quick. The more he bleeds, the stronger he seems to get." She leaned in the doorway and breathed, listened to the rain and the low thunder, which calmed her. A part of her she would never share with anyone realized the fear that had been pumping through her, drumming behind her ears, was now indistinguishable from joy. In just a few deafening moments, the endless, grinding cycle of faith and doubt had disappeared, and no amount of prayer or higher ideals would do a thing. With her life at stake, the surface of the universe was nothing more than the pooling blood, the glint of the swinging knife, the smiling rage on the preacher's face.

18

THE INSIDE of the car was growing cold, but it was dry enough that Randy was beginning to grow comfortable again. He leaned his head against the window and watched his breath fog on the glass until he dozed off—something he wasn't sure he could do at that point—and came to, dozed off again. He woke with a click and a groan that Randy turned to see was the hatch. The dome light cast yellow light across the three of them: the deputy guy Brock, the sheriff, both holding an unconscious man by his armpits. It was the preacher, Randy could see, and the vision of his cat-like eye played icy up his spine. All three were soaking wet.

"We'll just put him back here," the sheriff said. "We can't put him in the back with Randy."

"Let's ditch the kid," Brock said. Randy burned at the word *kid* but was suddenly overcome with a feeling of futility. "He's not safe with this guy anywhere, even if it is the back."

"Absolutely not. We'll head straight back to the video store with both of them until the state police show up. They'll deal with it, I promise. Just get those bolt cutters out of there—and that first aid kit—just clear some of this out."

They heaved the cuffed preacher up into the back and he rattled against the back seat. He immediately began to snore, and Randy backed away, leaned against the door behind the driver's side. He said, "What's he done?" But they simply closed the hatch. In the front seat, they had a conspiratorial conversation in hushed tones that Randy could hear all of. The man didn't have any identification on him—surprise, surprise—he didn't have *anything* on him, except for a tied-off sandwich bag with a thimble's worth of what Brock said he was sure was tweak. He examined it with a pen light and one eye closed. "Not very high quality."

"How would you know?"

"I watch TV."

Silence except the sound of the rain on the roof and the quiet snore of the man in the back. They all trembled.

"I don't want to be here," Brock said.

"What has he done?" Randy asked.

The sheriff turned to him. "We'll put Randy in the passenger seat. I guess we can't have him back there with that lunatic."

"What has he *done?*" Randy asked again.

"That's not your concern." She looked at him in the rearview mirror. "He was in a fight."

"Where am *I* going to sit?" Brock asked.

"This is the plan"—Randy could tell by her face and the way her hands shook that she wasn't so sure about her plan—"We're going to get back in there, call Dr. Fraij—he's our medical examiner, right? And he'll know the man at the funeral home to call, and—"

"What about folks' statements, eyewitnesses, that stuff?"

"Let's just start with Dr. Fraij."

They put Randy in the passenger seat and left him there.

The man in the back stopped snoring. And the sound of the rain stopped, though it continued to fall on the windshield.

And then something unexpected: The small reflection of the dome light on the back window drained down the face of the glass and entered the man's mouth, from where it immediately reemerged, only now a small blue point, red, yellow. It hung in the air.

Every bit of Randy's body warmed. The longer he looked, the better he felt. And so he couldn't look away. He felt like he felt when he was another person in the woods. He thought of his dress and cap and boots and the warmth of the wig—

And he was in them. A wind—a hundred-degree block of heat— warmed his face. A pleasant warmth. He thought he could hear wind chimes. He sat in a rickety beach chair at the edge of an empty swimming pool. All around him was a vast desert plain and orange sky, and for some uncanny reason Randy immediately understood that it wasn't his planet. His mother's denim dress was clean, warm and soft like it was right off the line. He turned around in the chair and was surprised to find a building: a motel, squat and L-shaped. The white stucco walls blinked pink with the flashing neon sign above. The sound of wind chimes again, then, and *they* were standing in the open door of the room at the corner of the L, their shoulder propped up against the doorframe, blackness behind. Them. The bones. *Her?* The blank eye sockets and the vacant stare. He turned his back to them and willed them away.

Stars burned beyond an orange dome. What he hadn't seen before, in the mid-distance: an orb as big as the moon. Its surface pulsed with what looked like human skin. He thought he saw hands and faces pressed against it from the inside. From behind it came the same point of light (it could have been one of the stars)—which moved steadily along the plain in Randy's direction.

Wooden wind chimes behind him and the metallic scrape of another chair being pulled up next to him. The bones leaned back in the chair and made a scraping, sighing sound. When Randy turned back, the light was gone.

"It's me," the bones said.

"What?" (And like that he was talking to a skeleton, whose voice seemed to come from everywhere now. Tuned in and kind.)

"The light."

"Then who are *you?*"

"Me. And that's me snoring away in the back of that piece-of-shit hatchback. This"—he pointed out to the strange world—"This is just my mind. A place I remember fondly from many lives ago. Man is that story a trip. Maybe I'll tell you another time."

"So you're not my mom?"

They sat in warm silence, and Randy watched the pulsing orb. He thought he heard a muted scream coming from somewhere inside. The sudden realization that this *wasn't* his mother (what had he been thinking?) left him lonely and broken.

"Man am I lucky to run into you like this. So: I'm going to ask you a few questions. Here we go: a) do you want to live the rest of your life in an orderly march to hell?—b) you're sending distress signals out all over the place, buddy. That's not a question—so b) do you understand that everything that's happening is only happening to you?—c) do you understand how fucking lonely that is, man?—and d) they're all in your mind, just like you're in mine. Also not a question. So what do you think?" It turned to him. The light didn't seem to have a source, and the skeleton cast no shadows. Just bone, present. "We can get out of here, just you and me. Live *differently*, you know. Not afraid of death because we're a sort of death ourselves, right?"

"Did you do something to Kitty?" He didn't know why; he just understood. "Is that what this is all about?"

"These are some lies that the devil is going to tell you: You're not worth anything, your opinion doesn't matter, your words don't matter, you're alone, etc., etc. You've got world conditions to worry about, total self-sufficiency to master. Miracles are dead. God hates you. All of that, you know? Get you in a corner and on your knees and sucking his dick and all that, right?

"It doesn't *have* to be like that, though. That's the whole point—they're *lies*. The truth is that you *do* matter. You matter much more than you or anyone could know. That's why I picked *you*. Of all the impoverished masses: You."

"Did you do something to Kitty?"

"Yes."

"Did you do something to my mom?"

"No."

Randy said nothing.

"Oof, that one stings, doesn't it? You'd almost *rather* it be me, right? At least I could tell you something, give you some kind of news. Wait. Maybe she's *alive*. But I don't know. That's your trip, between you and God, you know?"

And then, again, those three visions:

His mother: In the yellow blinking lights at the carnival, the sounds of screams growing behind her.

His mother: Pulling him from the icy water of the Illinois River, her black hair wet, matted against the side of her face.

His mother: Digging beneath the green, bruised sky.

But also this time: Squints, pinned against the blue pole barn at school by the bigger boy with the red, angry face. Squints turned to him, and the flat bill of his hat caught the wall and tumbled to the ground.

"Where would we go?"

"I don't know, Texas? Dallas? You ever been to Dallas?"

"What would we do?"

"You know, the usual stuff: stalk cemeteries, invent nightmares, howl at the moon, enforce curses. I don't *know*, man. What do you *want* to do?"

"I don't know."

"You want to know what *I* want to do right now? I want to smash my own skull in until every winged nightmare in the universe pours forth. Maybe I will or maybe I won't; that's just what I *feel*, you know. Earlier I wanted to get piss drunk and later I wanted to cut off a head—now I want you to come along. Anyway, you know where to find me."

And the bones and the fleshy sun and the unsourced light were gone, and Randy was freezing and wet in the passenger seat of the sheriff's shitty car. The preacher groaned.

He did know where to find him.

19

THERE WERE several directions Esther needed to move in. She needed to get back to the old video store to wait for the state police—who, when she checked her phone, still hadn't called. She needed to do something with Randy, to get him away from all of this. But she needed him. She needed to get home to her mother. They'd still have to interview witnesses at the bar, take down their statements. She'd need the state cops in two places at once. Randy sat next to her, still compliant, placid. He stared outside at nothing.

Brock said, "Have you ever smelled someone stink this badly before? Like an animal." He was sitting in the back seat, watching the sleeping man.

She tilted the rearview mirror and leaned in, examined her neck. There was a dark laceration on her neck where he'd held the utility knife.

Brock said, "We could quit right now, you know."

What would echo until the end: "We're just getting on a roll."

"Are we going to just leave these people and go back to the old video store?"

"I am. You stay here with Randy. Keep calling Wyatt." She handed him her pen and notepad. "Just write down what they all say they saw. Get the gist at least, from as many of them as possible. Until we get some help. I'll drive the deadbeat back over there and wait on the state cops."

There was a groan from the back. The inert lump began to move. "What in the hell?" He sat up and slurped at a string of drool hanging from the corner of his mouth. He looked around him. "Well I'll be. Looks like I finally got bested." He had to tilt his head slightly so it didn't hit the roof of the car when he sat up. He cracked his neck and then moaned. "My god, my head. Someone really did a number on me. Goddamn. My, this pain." Esther and Brock just stared, amazed at his recovery, at the fact that his wild personality was now alive in Esther's hatchback. Even Randy's trance was broken. He turned to the preacher, who grinned back at him, winked. "We'll get to you in a minute, buddy. Friend." Esther wasn't sure if she was sickened or scared or thrilled. The preacher looked up at the roof of the car, where the rain was hammering down. "I can feel every one of those hitting the outside of my brain. My. He was a man of suffering, and familiar with pain."

Brock said, "It was me; I was the one that did that to your head." He smiled.

"You?" The preacher shook his head. "Well, you did a mighty fine job. Bang-up job."

"Well, you held up your end all right, too. If I ever win a Knocked-You-Unconscious Award, I'll make sure and add a line at the end of my acceptance speech about how I never would have got there without the help of all the little people that made it possible." His smile broadened.

Esther couldn't tell if they were becoming best friends or signing one another's death warrants. "You got a name?"

He leaned forward enough that Brock backed away. "She asked him his name." He laughed. "That's priceless. Sweetheart, I don't have a name. Sweetheart, the only time you'll ever hear my name is when I call it out to you at our meeting place, the city of corpses."

Brock said, "Man, you are just fucked out of your mind. Just fucked."

He licked his lips. "Now come on and let me out of here."

Brock laughed. "We might. But probably Esther will just take you to the state cops. Maybe they'll beat you to death. These are corrupt times, after all."

Esther said, "Go on and sit back."

Randy's voice cut straight through the rain and the arguing. "He's the one. He's the *one*. We saw him yesterday, at the old video store."

The preacher turned his head like a roaring lion—"Let me go!" He rocked back and forth like a toddler throwing a tantrum with his hands cuffed behind his back. "Let me out of here let me out of here let me out of here let me out of here let me out of here you'll be sorry you'll be sorry you'll be sorry!"

"Shut up!" Brock shouted.

The preacher leaned back and lifted up his boots as high as he could, kicked at the back window. He kicked it and kicked it, and Esther began to wonder if it might actually be possible for him to get through.

Brock continued shouting. "Will you just shut up already?"

The preacher grew quiet for a moment and then continued to kick the window, one foot at a time, stomping like he'd heard a hilarious joke and couldn't contain himself. "Let me out of here let me out of here let me out of here." He rolled over on his side and began kicking at the side window. He shouted, "I've got places to be! A thousand galaxies to swallow!" He stopped, and the four of them sat and listened to the sound of the rain on the roof and the hood. He said, "I want to show you something." They waited, but he only stared ahead.

Brock: "And?"

The stranger ignored him, seemed not to have heard. He stared ahead, not blinking, and it was unnerving to Esther—like his body was still right there, but he was gone. His head jerked up like he'd seen something, and his eyes moved around the cab like he was following whatever he'd seen. Esther looked to Brock, who shrugged. "What the fuck?" The stranger's gaze froze dead ahead, and then he gasped like he'd just come up out of the water after swimming from a great depth. He gasped again and flung himself forward, smashed his face against the back of the seat. He did it again, and again, each contact harder.

Esther said, "Now stop that right now. There's no reason to hurt yourself." After the third smash, he leaned back and his eyes were all white—not as if he'd rolled them back in his head, but as if they'd been replaced by cue balls. No blood veins, no moisture, just white. Rivulets of blood ran down from a fresh wound on his forehead, trickled across his face, right across the front of those white eyes. He smashed his head against the back of the seat, but this time there was a loud crack, and blood began to pour from his mouth and nose.

"What the fuck?" Brock said. "What do we do?"

"I don't know. Help him, I guess."

"How do you help that?"

"Restrain him?" But Esther wanted to do nothing. His blank stare and his not-there-ness had already begun to make her shake. He smashed his head forward again, and his right brow flattened out against the metal skeleton of the seat. Blood soaked the upholstery. What frightened her almost as much as the eyes was the fact that he didn't make a sound. There was nothing but the squelch of flesh and the crack of bone, which grew worse each time. The smashed brow began to droop, to slide down his face, and a tear appeared above it. He dragged his face downward across the seat rest, and the skin around the brow began to tear. His jaw popped and went upwards into his head. When he leaned back, the skin on his face was gone, and his jaw fell downwards. He turned and looked at Esther then—with his white eyes and his black maw yawning, drooping until it fell in his lap.

"Holy fuck holy fuck," Brock said.

All three of them jumped out at the same time. They stood in the rain and watched him through the hatch window. Brock reached for the handle.

"What are you doing?"

"Helping him."

"Don't. Wait."

The preacher turned and slammed his caving head against the back window. A crack appeared in the glass, and he smashed his head against it again. He struggled against the handcuffs behind him until both of his arms broke, and the cuffs came off with his hands. His radiuses and ulnas were broken, jagged spears.

And from between the skin and what little fat there was and the bleeding musculature of his arm, something poked its way out, something familiar, and Esther leaned toward the window and watched the end of that arm intently while the preacher seemed to drown in his own blood.

A flicker. Something black and spiny, and then there were two, no longer than a fingernail, feeling their way out. And then two flat black eyes on each side of a narrow head, a burst of yellow between them. Yellow, translucent wings, wet with blood, wide and sharp. And then it was out all the way, balanced at the end of the self-severed arm, and when the skin began to slide down it took flight, came toward her, slowly as if drifting, and then landed on the glass before her face: a mud dauber. And with glass between her and it, she noticed for the first time how elegant a wasp's form is, how minimalist. The abdomen twitched and twitched again, and she saw the stinger; it was mad, stinging the glass again and again.

Brock stepped in front of her and opened the hatch. Esther's fixation on the wasp snapped, and she became aware of the rain pummeling them and the thunder rolling overhead and Brock's frantic cursing.

When the hatch opened, what was left of the preacher was limp on his side. A swarm of the wasps burst forth from his belly and all the openings in his body that his violence had made. Esther cried out, but the sound was absorbed by the electric scream of the collective beating of their wings. The swarm was so fast and huge that within seconds the car had filled with them, and the preacher had disappeared within their midst. With a sickening feeling, though, she understood that he hadn't disappeared at all but had appeared for the first time. They flew in crazed circles until they found the open hatch and poured out and up in a huge, coiled arm—twenty, thirty feet high. Brock looked at her. "Oh fuck." The look on his face wasn't fear but that of a calm realization, an acceptance.

"What? What is this? What is happening?"

They gathered into a wide sphere above the car—frantic, black-and-yellow static, shimmering amongst the dark rain—and Esther's wits returned to her. "Let's get inside, now." She turned and pulled at Brock's arm, but he didn't move. "Come on." But he stayed. "Goddammit, Brock." She took him by the hand and yanked as hard as she could. He turned to her and staggered once to his left like he was drunk. The left side of his face was a swollen, blood-red cluster of golf-ball-sized stings. A dozen of them, maybe more, crawled all over his face, stinging him again and again. Right before her, his eye swelled completely shut, and the other began to swell. He staggered forward and tried to speak, but nothing came out of his mouth except the wet garble of someone gagging and a single wasp, which perched on his lip before flying back toward the storm. She backed away from him. He staggered again and fell to a knee, balanced as best as he could. And the whole swarm descended on him, swallowed him up from her sight.

She ran but they didn't follow her, and she understood that enough that she circled back and slammed the hatch of the car, got inside and slammed her own door, where she was shortly joined by Randy. For a moment they both sat in the silence of the car, breathing.

"I know where it goes," Randy said. She didn't weigh her options, calculate her fears, or consider the duties; she just kept swimming downward into the cold. She simply couldn't exist in a world where a monster like that existed; she would no longer abide it. She jammed the car into drive and tore across the parking lot. When she was out on Broadway, she rolled down all the windows to let the smell and the last remaining wasps out. The preacher was still in the back, nothing more than a spilled-over bucket of catfish parts after a cleaning.

She followed Randy's instructions, her headlights threading the dark eye of a dark needle—the thread stretched out behind her, trembling in the storm.

The rest of her life.

20

Before Wyatt came out of the woods, he stopped and closed his eyes. Even amongst everything falling down around him, he still couldn't give up on one last habit: Each time he returned home, he prepared himself for the possibility that Darlene's purple Civic would be parked out in front of the trailer.

But all he found was Esther Grundel's hatchback: the doors open, the car lit up, a tall figure on each side. The two figures—Esther and the kid—came to him at once and began to speak at the same time. He didn't understand what they were saying, and everything began to take on an underwater feel. He pushed them both out of the rain and onto the front porch. Things tilted. Then, in the rain-driven madness:

"Del's out there."

"What?" Grundel asked—he could tell she'd been crying. "Who?"

"Del Baker. His body. It's out in the woods. Totally mutilated." He tried to hold it back, but a gasping sob came out. He pointed over his shoulder toward the woods with his thumb. "I told you," he said. "That cougar is out there."

"Well, I now think there might be a bit more credibility to your story on account of—"

"This fucking thing turned into *wasps*, man," the kid said. His eyes were enormous, and his hands carried every word he spoke side to side.

"You don't understand," he said. "Like wasps came out of his *insides*. The *preacher*. From downtown?"

"Del Baker is dead," Wyatt said, unable to process any of it.

"Brock Bosco is dead," Esther said.

"Kitty Kershaw is dead," Randy said.

"They're all dead?" Wyatt asked. "Three-Point Bosco?"

"Who?"

"The cougar? Got all of them?"

Grundel and the kid looked at each other. The kid said, "Did you listen to anything we said?"

"I went into the mountains today with Del Baker looking for a black cougar that isn't supposed to exist. It killed Del. Del's dead. He's *dead*."

"We know," Esther said. "We get it. He's not the only one. You're not the only one finding dead people today. Do you understand?" He didn't. "When did he die?"

"I don't know exactly. Sometime this afternoon?" What they'd said finally cracked open like an egg. "Wasps? You're telling me a man turned into wasps?"

And Grundel and the kid told Wyatt the most outlandish story he'd ever heard. They'd both witnessed the transient who hangs around downtown transform into thousands of wasps—the kid described it as the man splitting his own head open, from whence the wasps exploded. The kid knew where to find it, they told him, though he hesitated when he told them, looked at the ground.

Esther took Wyatt by the arm, and he let her pull him abruptly to her car. She opened the hatchback and motioned with her head. And there he—it—was. Blood had soaked through the upholstery so much that it had pooled on top. Bits of bone and tendon, a handful of cracked teeth, a flap of fat and skin that still bore a belly button. All he saw was Del.

"This is some seriously fucked-up shit. This was your guy?"

"Yes."

"I guess I'll be the first to admit that things have been strange around here."

"The weirdest Saturday on record. Anyway, your boy Randy knows where it's at."

"It's up on Robbers Mountain," Wyatt said. "I've been tracking it."

"Well," Esther said. "We've got to go after it before it kills someone else. Or one of us?" He realized then how crazed she was, how manic.

"Now calm down," Wyatt said. "Now listen, Grundel. There's no reason to go and do that. What do you have there, a taser?"

"I'm out of cartridges."

"Then a baton?" He found himself laughing. She was some creature entirely different than the nervous one he'd found at his door that morning.

"The state police are on their way."

"Well, there you go. Let's just hold tight."

"But we know where it's at," the kid said.

"I just came from there," Wyatt said. "Trust me—you don't want to go back there. Listen," he said. "I need to warm up, at least. Let's go inside, sit down, and talk it over. Call someone. But I've got to warm up. I'm soaked to the bone." He looked at the kid. "And you're not going looking for it."

Look after the kid, Darlene told him.

His room was warm and yellow, and Darlene was waiting for him—on her toes in the closet, feeling for a pair of boots on the top shelf. Or under the bed, stretched out toward a long-gone sock. In the shower. At the kitchen table, reading one of the kid's books. Somewhere just out of sight.

He plugged in his phone and turned it on. Six voicemails. Fourteen text messages. Gordo, pissed. He closed the phone and put it down. For a moment he could do nothing but stand there—slack-jawed, head bowed—and watch the water drip from the edges of himself down into carpet, which bloomed dark. His boots were caked in mud. He turned to the door and spoke to no one in particular. "I made a mess."

As he was putting on dry clothes, he heard two distinct sounds: the deafening silence of the rain stopping and the growl of the ATV, which whined and disappeared. Moments later, Esther was standing in his doorway.

"It's Randy," she said. "He wouldn't listen. He's gone."

And there, with Darlene with him, he made the decision.

21

Τhe rain had stopped. Thunder continued to roll, quieter and quieter, quieter still, and silenced, moved on. The sounds of the forest,
having lain in wait, rose up around them: the chirps and honks of the
frogs that still held out in the cold, the warble of a single whippoorwill
somewhere in the distance, the ghostly cry of a barred owl. The sound
of their boots through the wet grass and bramble.

Esther had grown quiet too: Her prayers had amounted to nothing;
what she needed now was to keep acting.

They moved through the woods because Wyatt believed they'd be
too exposed on the ATV trail. She thought going through the woods
just meant more places for the thing to hide, but he convinced her that
meant that they had more places to hide too. A spotlight with a buck-
et-style handle hung from the crook of her elbow, set as low as it could
go, just enough so that they could see their feet as they moved through
the understory.

Wyatt stopped in front of her, and she froze. He'd given her his friend's
rifle. She'd been trained on how to use one, but she had no idea what
she was doing when it came to actually wielding one, alert in the woods.
Wyatt held back an open hand as if to press her backwards, a warning, and they both listened. He made a twisting motion with his hand
to indicate the light, and she clicked it off. A cracking in the trees. A

strange buzzing, as if they heard someone's bug zapper from far away in the woods.

Wyatt crept back to her and whispered: "We have to be careful—the branches are falling under their own weight." He wiped his face. "And every time one does, all I see is that cat." He was afraid too, which comforted her.

She leaned in by his ear and said, "Do you hear that buzzing?" He nodded but said nothing. She felt wasps crawling all over her, down the back of her collar and up her pant legs, and almost screamed. Quiet (madness). Another crack came from the same direction followed by the wet brush and knock of the branch falling through the canopy. Wherever it was, it landed on the ground. They moved forward cautiously, both with their rifles shouldered, pointed to the ground.

She turned the spotlight back on, and two narrow-set green eyes appeared in the trail ahead of them, ankle-high: a possum. It disappeared with a rustle into a cluster of slate and mistletoe. The buzzing stopped like someone had flipped a switch. Wyatt halted and leveled the barrel of his rifle at something in the branches of a tall oak to their right, and she flinched, expecting a shot. He looked back at her and nodded, whispered *Light*. He went to one knee and leveled the rifle again, ready to take a shot at whatever her light brought into the world.

She let go of the rifle's fore stock and straightened her arm, let the spotlight handle slide down to her hand. She pointed it into the branches, and more green eyes appeared before the blacks and browns and whites of an owl. It spread out its wings and screeched, dove down toward their heads before taking flight into the night. Eyes, everywhere. The way Wyatt shook his head, she could tell that he knew the woods better than this, more intimately, but that something had come between him and it.

The tumbledown sandstone and slate from the hill began to appear in greater size and number, the rocks silvery and green and black with lichen under her light, which she had come to despise. Just enough light to make her aware, make her feel afraid: a universe of darkness beyond. The thought made her look upwards, where the clouds had begun to tear apart from one another, stretching and thinning, revealing a rich white moon. She stopped and turned off her light, and Wyatt turned to her. She pointed upwards at the moon, and he nodded. They stopped and decided without speaking that they should sit tight for a moment, let their eyes adjust to the moonlight.

The Milky Way stretched overhead like a great, blue gash, framed by the pitch-black outline of the tall pines all around them. A whippoorwill cried out. Wyatt signaled to her, and they moved forward without the aid of the light, the ground around them fresh with silver from the drawing out of their pupils. As they neared the base of the mountain, the rush of Olim Creek and the runout coming down from the cave rose around them.

Another branch cracked, this one louder, but Wyatt moved on, both growing more confident in the noises around them. A shadow appeared on a wide, shallow boulder ahead to the left, and Esther froze. Wyatt went ahead. She whispered, "Wyatt," but it was lost in the growing crash of the creek. She broke their cover and spoke aloud: "Wyatt, Wyatt." At the same moment she reached down and clicked on the spotlight, the hulking, yellow-eyed cat let out a scream—sent Wyatt faltering backwards, just ten feet away. The scream was hideous: guttural but high-pitched, wild but human. The cat flattened its ears. Its whiskers glowed in the light, and its eyes turned into green discs when it turned to face her directly. It opened its mouth wide and let out a loud hiss, lowered its shoulders. Its incisors were grotesquely long, and the cat transformed in her mind into a saber-tooth, angry and out of time and place. She found herself drawn in as she had with the wasp, wanting to study the map of its surface. It lowered itself closer to the rock and took two small steps forward.

Wyatt's rifle cracked and spat a blaze of orange and tore the forest apart. A spot on the boulder near the cat exploded into a white burst of rock and grit, and the cat growled, slipped down from the rock into the dark beyond Esther's light, and was for a moment somewhere between the two of them. She turned the light onto the floor of the forest to their right. There was a movement in the wet leaves and Wyatt fired again: nothing. Esther leveled her rifle and did her best to keep the light trained in the same direction. She turned to where it had appeared from and Wyatt turned too, but nothing.

He turned back to her and pointed farther up the hill, where she understood the higher they went, the less cover and darkness it would have—the face of the bluff now silvery beneath the moon, every shadow sharp and clear. Esther's heart drummed heavy and fast. Another scream came, this time from above, and her light found the cat on the branch of a tree just above her, the sheen of its coat white with her light around the edges of its muscles. She turned and lifted the muzzle upwards, but the cat sprang downward, took her down to the muddy ground with a thud and a grunt, pinned her beneath its weight.

It must have weighed two hundred and fifty pounds, maybe more, and with its heavy paws pressed against her chest—its fingers spread out, claws protracted, piercing just below the surface of her skin—she could barely breathe. She cried out when the cat tightened its grip, drove its claws further in, gripping the muscles in her chest. It lowered its face down next to hers and breathed, drooled, drank her up. In all her pain and fear, Esther was still struck by the strange sight of crushed, broken wasps between its teeth—one of them still alive, a single antenna flicking slowly.

An explosion came from behind the lion, and a *thunk* and a squelch sounded in the side of the cat. A spray of blood came from between two of its ribs. The cat toppled over and off her. In her periphery, she saw Wyatt struggling with his rifle while the cat found its feet, lowered its head, and screamed at them both. She heard the action crack and the plink of the spent cartridge on rock, but the shot didn't come, and she understood that the cat had lowered itself enough to put her between it and the barrel of the rifle in Wyatt's hand.

"Move! Out of the way!"

She rolled toward him. The cat growled and swung a paw at her ribs, knocked the wind out of her again. Its claws hooked into the meat of her side and tore through her, sliced through like fire. A claw caught one of her ribs, and the snap of the exposed bone made her scream.

The rifle exploded again, and another shot went through its stomach. It screamed and pulled away with the weight of its whole body—leapt into the dark of the woods, stumbling. It moved across the ground without any of the grace or elegance of a cat, nothing more than a brutal, wounded animal. Wyatt fired again, and the outside of a nearby tree splintered. Esther rolled over on all fours and felt for her rifle in the grass, the whole right side of her body on fire. She felt woozy.

Wyatt came to her, frantic. "Are you okay?"

"Absolutely not." She gently touched her wound, and her side was wet with blood. She reached inside her jacket, winced, and groaned when her hand came down on a strip of flesh and an exposed rib. "Let's go." She stopped and turned again. "Thanks."

"Don't thank me yet."

As she stepped, she stumbled; Wyatt had to catch her. He leaned her good side against his body and wrapped her arm around his back. "Let's get you somewhere safe," he said.

"No, let's go," she said. And they did.

22

When Randy began his blaze through the woods, his intention was to go to the cave, to confront it, to put a stop to all of this. But the closer he got to the cave, the more he felt his resolve and anger dissolve. What was it, exactly, that he was putting an end to? He understood that there were only two ways for it to end—with it or with him. Did he want to stop people from disappearing, or did he just want them all to disappear?

When he understood that choice, the light appeared.

He followed the point of light up the face of the mountain through the broken bluff, ignoring the red arrows that pointed the way. He climbed upwards thoughtlessly, pulling himself up boulders, sometimes slipping on the wet rock. He was no longer afraid or angry but drawn. Some hundred feet up, he made it to the top of the broken bluff and the opening of the cave. Below him he heard the loud crack of a gun. Then more. He hadn't meant for them to follow him, didn't know what he'd put them up against. He'd assumed that they wouldn't follow. The only solution was to keep going, to get away from them all.

The cold was less biting in the small cave. It was nothing more than three collapsing sandstone walls that triangulated toward a singular point some twenty feet from the opening. A stone coffin.

The small blue light turned red and illuminated the cave for a moment before disappearing somewhere in the back. He followed until he had to squat down to move forward and then fell to his hands and knees to crawl further into the shrinking space. Cold air from fissures in the rock licked at his legs. Fissures that led to god-knows where. He pulled his lighter from his pocket and flicked on the flame. He held it out in front of him toward where the cave's three walls closed in on each other. There was an opening—maybe two feet wide, a foot tall. He moved the lighter toward the opening, and the wet, gray-brown walls of the tiny space came to life. His heart began to pound. The lighter went out and he clicked it to life again, the flame's wavering light dancing liquid across the small opening.

Keep going; get away from them all.

He lowered his head, lay down face-first, and moved his arms and head inside of the hole. The lighter went out again, and he couldn't get the flame back in the small wet space. Too dark to see. But he flattened himself out and squirmed further in, until the cold, rough rock came down to his shoulders, the back half of him still out in the cave. He wriggled further. When his body was completely inside of the airtight passage, he stopped, unable to move further. He tried to move backwards but found no way to push himself in that direction. His breath quickened and his heart hammered, and he felt the cold, quick rush of panic coming over him. He tried to relax his body—took deep, slow breaths. When the panicked moment passed, he took one last deep gulp of air and then exhaled every bit of breath in his body. Flattened, he pulled himself forward. His hands found purchase on both sides of the opening at the other end.

There was what looked like a curtain in front of the opening, but when he got there, he found that it was a bed skirt. He crawled out from under the bed, and there he was, in a dusty old motel room. It was warm.

The preacher stood in the doorway, a nuclear-orange glow behind him.

"Figured you'd come," the preacher said. He stepped outside and waved at Randy to follow him. They crossed the motel parking lot, went around the pool. They stood in silence and observed their surroundings.

The same desert plain he'd seen before, the same silence, the same warm wind. He was dry, in his dress. And above him—the same sphere, only larger, pulsing with pink light from some hellish combustion against a starry night sky. The contours of the skin—its creases and pock marks—became more detailed as the world moved closer. The hands and elbows and faces pressing out from within looked as if they were willing the seamed, fleshy planet closer.

The preacher pointed, and Randy followed his gaze to the point of light, which moved toward the orb.

He followed it.

He followed it for what felt like a hundred miles.

And where was the thing that had made all the promises? The bones and the preacher had said that they were the light—that *he* was the light—but he didn't understand what any of it meant. All he understood was that it was *all* him, really. He seemed to be everything, and everything seemed to be him. He was running away to an inevitability.

He was beginning to sweat through the thick denim dress, and as he got closer to the orb, the air grew hotter, and something began to feel as if it were pulling him. He felt lighter, moved more quickly, felt stretched out. He understood that the two worlds were getting so close that the other world's gravity was pulling at him.

He stopped. The pull was strong, and he knew if he took one more step that his foot wouldn't touch back down—that he'd be falling upward then, tumbling miles and miles and miles and miles through the boiling atmosphere of the seamed, fleshy planet. And into its world. Into *his* world.

Gravity pulled at him, stretched at his cells. He tried to imagine his mother—saw the bones, which blinked away to her, standing in the front door one Saturday morning, holding the screen door with one hand and waving him on with the other—and understood that he would never see her again. Not even her bones. It would always be a mystery. He was running from her, from that mystery.

But he loved his mother, and he also understood that his love for her would outlast anything, withstand any mystery. Things would pass, but not his love for his mother. And there were other things that would never pass, like the hole he would leave in the people in his life, no matter how few. Like their care for him, no matter how wobbly and thin.

That last step became remorse and a great sadness with no resolve and the end of all possibility. Behind him was mystery and grief and love.

He turned and ran.

23

THE RUSH coming down from the mountain had slowed—almost stopped—but Olim Creek still roared. Wyatt carried the semi-automatic strapped across his back, held Del's rifle in the crook of his left arm, and supported Esther with his right as they waded through the cold, white-capped rush of the creek. She'd insisted she was fine but quickly faltered. With the wound on her side, he couldn't wrap his arm around her, and with all of that weight on him, he could barely stand in the water, where at the base of the ravine, the creek broke hard over the same rocks and boulders that tumbled down from the cave. Esther had her jacket wrapped tightly around her, but Wyatt couldn't keep the image of water splashing through her ribs and into her body out of his mind.

The current swept his left foot out from under him, and he went to his knees. Esther went face down into the water, and he lost the rifle in his arm, watched it ride the waters and sink. He helped her stand back up again and she coughed, water and blood dripping down the edges of her mouth. When they got to still, shallow water, he helped her sit down at the base of a lichen-covered rock. She tried to stand but collapsed with a groan. The bleeding had slowed, but he was certain it hadn't on the inside. She groaned again and put a hand flat against the rock as if to brace herself against some coming force and cried out. When the hand fell, it landed in the shallow water, motionless in a small whirlpool that washed away the blood.

"It's up there," he told her. But her face was motionless now, too, her blank gaze fixed on some unseen spot in the woods. For a moment he stood in amazement at the woman's crazed sense of duty, but terror and reality set back in when he heard a scream—*that* scream—up above him.

And then a wash of relief when a shadow came bounding down the rocks. The kid—the kid! "My God, kid. Thank God. You're here."

But then, in the rocks above him: the cougar—panting, wounded, struggling from rock to rock in much the same way that Esther had. He yelled at the kid and groped for the stock of the rifle on his back. The cat dropped itself down onto a boulder ten feet above the kid. Wyatt pulled the rifle from his back and shouldered it. When Randy saw him struggling with the rifle, he turned to find the cat. His feet scrambled beneath him. The cat lowered its shoulders and ears, and as the kid struggled to find his footing, it lunged toward him. Wyatt leveled the barrel, and the kid fell backwards.

He fired.

The cat contorted in midair and landed next to the kid, tumbled down an incline of small rocks, which carried it in a roll and spilled it out on a boulder not far from Wyatt.

Randy hopped down and stood next to Wyatt. "Are you all right?" Wyatt asked. But he knew that he wasn't. Knew he might never be. They both stood over the cat. It was alive. Its chest rose and fell with quick, shallow breaths. Its lids hung heavy. Fresh blood pumped thick from a hole in its throat. It lifted its head and looked at them, dropped it back down. They stood there and watched it until its chest stopped rising and falling. The trouble was over, Wyatt figured.

But there would always be more to come.

LATER

1

M<small>Y BODY GONE</small>! And now my soul is lost amongst the voiceless gargoyles. A flopping hoard of flesh and demon dancers at the heart of a universe of chaos.

Somehow I'll make my way back.

But I should probably end the story with the end of *his* story. The end of his story before he met *me*.

He'd made it out of Dallas and through Gainesville. He wasn't a mile from the Red River and Oklahoma beyond when a Texas state patrolman appeared. His blue lights beamed like jellyfish in a pale blue sea. He pulled his pickup over onto the shoulder and looked at his red-rimmed eyes in the mirror. There was a roach in the ashtray.

It wasn't until the patrolman was standing outside his door that he remembered the window crank was in the glove box. The patrolman rapped on the window with a single knuckle.

Roll it down, son. His voice sounded underwater through the glass.

It doesn't roll down.

What?

The crank's in the glove box. He reached for it, and the patrolman reached for his sidearm, pulled it from the holster, pointed it at him. He opened the door and yanked him by the foot, spilled him out onto the hot highway shoulder, his right elbow in the glitter of a shattered Corona bottle. He groaned and reached for the elbow, already wet with blood.

I said the window crank's in the glove box!

Good god, the patrolman said. Do you know what you could have done, son? He holstered his weapon and pulled him to his feet.

The patrolman had a mustache and wore aviators and this fierce-looking cowboy hat. He asked him if he knew why he pulled him over and he said he did, that he was speeding, and the patrolman wanted to know if he knew how bad he was speeding.

Sure, six over. He smiled.

The patrolman looked behind him into the cab of the pickup, and while he stole a look, a mangy coyote ducked and weaved through the barbed-wire fence on the other side of the highway.

Where you headed, son?

Muskogee.

Is that where you live?

Yes.

He looked toward Oklahoma. Storms before you get to Ardmore, what I hear. Pretty dangerous.

Maybe I'll turn back.

Storms there, too. Tornado, maybe.

Radio says it's just a watch.

The patrolman leaned on the open door and looked south, somewhere deep in Texas. He leaned his cheek against his shoulder and spoke into his radio. Barbara Lynn? Over. There was static and a click and silence, and thunder rumbled somewhere out in the distance, slow and quiet. Barbara Lynn? Over.

Another click. Who's this? Over.

ST 91, Barbara Lynn. What's the news on that storm up by Gainesville?

Still a tornado watch? Over.

It's a warning now. Over.

He put his aviators back on. Not a watch, son. It's a warning.

Those days! Those people! I want it all back so badly it breaks my heart.

How long have I wept in this life? How long have I gnashed my teeth and torn my clothes and wet myself and moaned and begged and spit and died? Too long. Too many times. Enough time to fuel the stars for eons.

But I also lived a short and shameful life, and for that I am truly sorry.

2

BERTIE GRUNDEL didn't understand the funeral. She remembered her sister's funeral, and felt, to a degree, like *that's* where she was, but that didn't seem right. Simple blank confusion. It was probably her sister's. She was just having one of what Esther called her *daytime dreams*.

People she'd never met came to the house and took her. She'd fought them at first, cried out and pounded at the man who tried to escort her out the door and to a truck. They told her they were from the church, and for a moment she recognized a short, round woman's face. It surfaced but quickly sank back into the ocean of her mind. While she sat in the truck, crying, two men took her things—her and *Esther's* things—and put them in the back of the truck. They took her to her new home. It was an asterisk-shaped building with a blue roof called West Haven.

It wasn't her home, but it was some *version* of home—her orange recliner, their TV, their TV trays, her pictures and Precious Moments in the windowsill. Sometimes, with one of the figurines in her hand— their big dopey eyes pleading with her—she was at home again or in the Christian bookstore weighing the price against the compulsion to collect. The place smelled like feces and antiseptic.

It had been a long time since Esther had visited her. She wasn't sure how long, wasn't sure exactly how long she'd been at the home. A few times she'd been there, always at night. Checking in on her before she went to bed. Helping her with a shower. She tried to speak to her, but it was as if Esther couldn't hear her. She simply completed her tasks flat-faced.

Other times she knew that Esther was there, somewhere in the hallways—looking for her mother, just out of reach. She wished in those moments that she could will her to come to her. She sometimes cried out her name, hoping that she would hear where she was, but the nurses would come and stop her, put her in her bed.

She watched the winter from the window at the end of her hallway. Sheets of rain, snow, brutal winds. But on some days striking light washes over her, warms her skin.

She knows that when Esther comes, she will take her away.

3

July. Wyatt couldn't believe how tall his crop had gotten—shoulder height. It wasn't the thick garden he was used to but a *canopy*, each greenhouse an ecosystem unto itself. They were humid and quiet except for the crunch of gravel beneath his boots and the oscillating fans. The green-and-purple bushes crowded the walkways.

Greenhouse growing hadn't been what he'd expected. He'd had an aphid infestation early on that had been a nightmare to beat. He had supplemental lighting but still couldn't get a hold of the ever-changing nature of an actual sun. Still, he already had some interested dispensaries lined up—small places in small towns around eastern Oklahoma. Being above board felt like breathing fresh air, too. He wished every day that Del could see what he'd done.

Experts—at least that's what they were calling the professors from a few of the nearby colleges—determined that the animal attacks had been the result of freak weather. Flooding had taken place elsewhere. There were tornados outside of Tulsa, one of which destroyed a school in Broken Arrow. It was the dramatic change in air pressure, they said, that drove these animals to behave in strange and unexpected ways. That was their theory, at least, though Wyatt and the kid knew otherwise.

Seven Suns made the news again just a few weeks later when Del's

fluke red heifer finally gave birth. The calf was stillborn but had two
heads. Judy took Meg and moved to Texas to be near Del's family. She
leased out the back half-section to the farmer living across the road
and sold him their cattle. He planted alfalfa. The front half-section,
which included the house, she leased to Wyatt at a fair price. He sold
the trailer and as many of his trophy mounts as possible, donated all of
Darlene's things to Goodwill, and he and the kid moved into the squat
brick house on 96th so Wyatt could continue work on the grow-op.

He made the kid help him maintain the property. He kept the back
half brush hogged, the front mowed. He'd cleaned out everything the
Bakers had left in the garage, something Wyatt couldn't bring himself
to do. He'd helped Wyatt finish the greenhouses, which took some six
weeks. There were plenty of hours of work to be done. That's all Wyatt
knew to do—keep him busy with hard work and get him through
school. He was making the kid complete his freshman year through
an online program the state offered. If he passed, he'd be let back in
at the high school. Hard work and school. Those would amount to
something, he figured.

The farmer across the street paid Randy to haul hay a few times in
the early summer. Wyatt helped—he hated the work, but the farmer paid the kid ten cents a bale, which he needed. The farmer would
drive slowly, up and down the rows. Randy would pick up one of the
rectangles, hoist it to his knee, and then toss it up on the back of the
flatbed truck, where Wyatt would retrieve it and add to the growing
stack. The pasture all around was yellow, the stubble yellow, the neat
grid of rectangles sun colored.

They still fought a lot. But there were other moments now, too, like
the two of them sitting on the back of that truck, their backs against
the cab, the air rich and heavy with humidity and alfalfa, sharing a milk

jug of water that the farmer had brought out for them, their chests rising and falling.

He still sings to the buds as he tends them. He plunges his hands deep into the foliage, leans in, searches for damage, signs of insects. He inspects the texture and color of the fan leaves, measures the success of his blend of nutrients.

The kid had become his company, the last part of Darlene he had left. And something intangible, something like possibility that hovered all around him. That made him want to keep the kid near.

He would be with Wyatt a little while longer, but Wyatt already missed him.

4

The next November, Randy made the basketball team. He didn't start, but the coach told him he had the height and strength—he just needed to learn the game. He learned fast enough that by the end of the year he was getting to play a fair amount. He even scored eight points against Eufaula, who beat them by forty.

Tommy Thompson had talked him into trying out; otherwise he would have never thought about a sport. But basketball wouldn't be so bad—it wasn't one of the sports that Wyatt went on and on about, so there was that. It wasn't just the games that he loved—the way everything beyond the sweat and the yellow floorboards and the squeak of sneakers just disappeared—he loved the practices, too. He loved all the running and running and running, the lifting they did after practice. They had so many weights he stopped lifting at home.

Despite Randy's protests, Wyatt was at every game. He'd sit at the top of the wooden bleachers in his Wranglers and a red Seven Suns Robbers sweatshirt. He'd bought the shirt at a booster event in the school cafeteria. There was a raffle, and Wyatt won a red foam finger, which he also brought to every game. When Randy was in, he stood and shouted, waved the finger in the air. It embarrassed Randy something fierce. They'd fought about it more than once.

But still.

It turned out that the whole time Randy knew Wyatt, Wyatt was growing pot in the Quonset hut out back. He told Randy all about it. He
didn't say anything to Wyatt, but it turned out to be the same pot that
he had been smoking. The good stuff that he and Squints kept getting
off Gordo. When he found out, he felt amazed and betrayed at the same
time. He ultimately determined that he never would have guessed how
much of a badass Wyatt was.

They moved to the country, then—well, *farmer* country—and Wyatt
made him help set up the greenhouses for his legit grow. Most of what
Randy did was the framing, something he found he loved to do. Wyatt
helped him once, but he took it on himself from there on out, moving
efficiently alongside Wyatt. He was fascinated with the whole process,
loved the idea of laboring and laboring and being able to see the fruits
of your labor. The whole thing, in totality. And the measure of success
was simply if the thing stayed up, served its purpose, persevered. He
told Wyatt then that he might think about going into construction
someday. Wyatt told him that he should think about college—be the
boss of people doing construction, but Randy didn't know how he felt
about that. Not yet, anyway.

Squints's mom had packed them up and moved them to California,
where they were going to be with his dad again. The house was still for
sale. Randy had talked to him a few times on the phone. They always
talked about getting together to hang out but never did. Randy felt
weird, but he didn't have that much time anyway. Between basketball and
school and Wyatt working him to death, he could barely fit anything in.

And when he could fit something in, it would be Tommy. He had
Tommy in both Spanish and Physics, and Tommy had quickly learned
that he could get rides from Randy, who had Wyatt's old truck. Tommy

had tried to get Randy to hang out with some of the players on the basketball team. He'd done it once and it had been all right, but he mostly
just liked being around Tommy—liked the way he treated Randy like
he was normal, didn't have some weird, fucked-up past. He liked that
he was nice to Wyatt. He liked that he was always telling Randy what
he should do, always telling him what he needed to do to *get to the top*.
He liked that he sometimes asked him questions about his mom.

What Randy still liked most, though, was being alone. Any chance he
could get—at night or the weekends—he'd go driving on the country
roads. He drove the open grid, burned all of the right angles into his
heart, could drive with his headlights off and the road signs gone and
with no moon or stars if he had to. Everything was either right or left.

He was beginning to love the openness of the prairie, the way the
sky gave you an opened-up feeling. You could breathe, and the plains
breathed through you. The unbroken horizon to the west. A sky so big
and blue it would break your heart.

As fall fell, though, the days grew shorter and the scenery grew bleaker.
He spent more time in his room reading—he'd moved on from King,
was into sci-fi now—maybe smoking a pinch. And when Wyatt came
to his door, he let him come in, talked about whatever Wyatt wanted
to talk about. He was, after all, almost all he had left of his mom.

And sometimes, when the air is warm enough and the moon just right,
he crawls out of his window into the night and becomes something else.